By the time she hit her teens, Susie Bower had lived in 8 houses and attended 7 schools. This theme continued in her working life: she's been a teacher, a tour-guide, a typist, a workshop facilitator, a PA and a painter. She formerly wrote and directed TV programmes for children at the BBC and Channel 4, for which she won a BAFTA Award, and she currently writes audio scripts. *School for Nobodies*, *The Three Impossibles* and *Shoo!* are also available from Pushkin Children's. Susie lives in Devon.

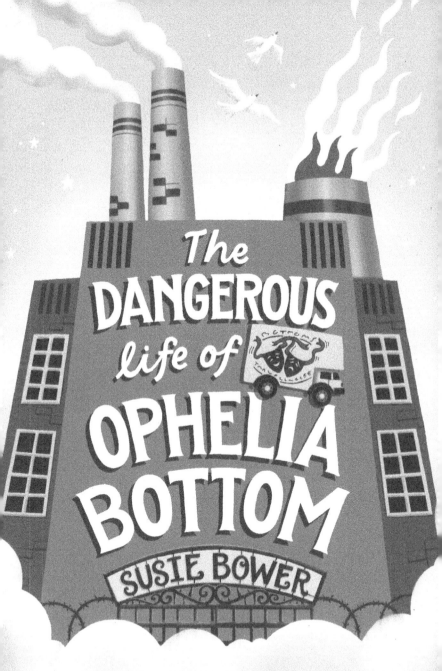

The DANGEROUS life of OPHELIA BOTTOM

SUSIE BOWER

PUSHKIN CHILDREN'S

Pushkin Press
65-69 Shelton Street
London WC2H 9HE

The Dangerous Life of Ophelia Bottom was first
published by Pushkin Press in 2022

1 3 5 7 9 8 6 4 2

ISBN 13: 978-1-78269-360-4

Designed and typeset by Tetragon, London
Printed and bound by Clays Ltd, Elcograf S.p.A.

www.pushkinpress.com

for Satya Robyn,
who fights for the Earth
and for Hazel and Leo,
who are part of its future

'There is too much sameness.
The world seems only to have a
desire for more of this sameness.
To be different is to be alone.'

—LUISA CASATI

PANTECHNICON:

a large van for transporting furniture

'**W**e are APPROACHING our DESTINATION!!!'

Ar's voice boomed and echoed round the cab of the Pantechnicon. I blinked awake, rubbed my eyes and sat up in my sleeping bag in the tiny bunk bed behind the driver's seat. Through the grimy windscreen the sky grew paler. It must be almost morning.

'*Hush*, Arthur Bottom!' hissed Ma from the passenger seat. She always called Ar by his full name when she was annoyed at him, which was most of the time, lately. 'You're not *onstage* now! And Ophelia's *asleep!*'

Ar glanced back at me over his shoulder, and the Pantechnicon swerved on the narrow country lane.

'WRONG, Marina! She is FULLY CONSCIOUS—are you not, Ophelia?'

Ar was my father, only he wouldn't let me call him 'Dad'. He was big as a mountain with a deep, booming voice, and a wild black beard exploding from his chin. He always talked—or rather shouted—in capital letters and he

9

never used a short word if he could use a long, complicated one instead. Ma was my mother. Like me, she was tall and skinny with tangled corkscrew curls of fiery red hair. She always spoke in italics, which meant she made every word sound *very important*. They talked this way because they were actors. But it was no fun being squashed up close with them in a van, even a van as large as the Pantechnicon.

'It's alright, Ma,' I yawned, unzipping my sleeping bag. 'I'm awake.'

Ma ignored me. 'Ophelia needs her *sleep*, Arthur Bottom. And she needs *stability*. Life on the road is *no life for a child*.'

'NONSENSE, MARINA!' roared Ar. 'Theatre is in our BLOOD. And a THESPIAN'S home is ONSTAGE!'

The Pantechnicon swerved again.

'Look *out*, Arthur Bottom! Keep your eyes *on the road*!'

And they were off again.

'Stop arguing!' I muttered.

'Don't MUMBLE, Ophelia!' yelled Ar. 'ENUNCIATE!'

'Anyhow, we're not *arguing*,' snapped Ma. 'We're *discussing*.'

I stuck my fingers in my ears and stared out of the windscreen. Life with Ar and Ma was never quiet: it was all earthquakes and blizzards and hurricanes and thunderstorms. I wished, wished, *wished* I had normal parents...

Parents who had ordinary jobs, instead of being actors.

Parents who dressed sensibly, instead of in tatty old costumes from Shakespearean plays.

Parents who lived in a proper house, which stayed *still*.

Parents who were called Jones or Smith, rather than Bottom.

It was *so* embarrassing having Bottom as a surname. Ar said it was a lucky coincidence, as Bottom was the name of an actor in *A Midsummer Night's Dream.* But to most people, Bottom just meant... well, *you know.*

A clean white sign loomed up out of the shadows:

STOPFORD

and the sun peeped out above the heavy clouds, sparkling over Stopford's clean red roofs, lighting it up like a magic town. The sky streaked red and pink.

'Red sky in the morning,' muttered Ma, *'Shepherd's warning.'*

Why did Ma always moan and groan about everything? We were only here for three nights, so I was going to make the most of every single second.

We drove along Stopford High Street. My eyes ate up everything in the shiny shop windows: the computers, the huge televisions, the soft, billowy duvets and the pretty flowery curtains. All the things we couldn't afford. The Pantechnicon lumbered past Stopford School, and past little roads, each with a different name: *Chestnut Street; Magnolia Drive; Elm Close.* Of all the towns we visited, Stopford was a million times the prettiest. The houses stood in tidy rows, all just the same size. Each garden had a perfect square of green lawn, flowerbeds waving with bright flowers, a white wooden gate and a neat gravel path leading up to the front door. Each door was painted a different colour: pink, blue, yellow, red or green. I stared through the windows. What must it be like to live in a proper house, with different rooms for washing and cooking and sleeping and watching television?

All too quickly, we headed out of town. Just ahead was Stopford Bridge, where the river wound down towards the sea. Suddenly, Ar slammed on the brakes and I only just avoided knocking my teeth out on the driver's seat. A huge lorry blocked the bridge. On its side was painted:

PRATT'S PLASTIC PELLETS

The driver, wearing overalls, leant on the bridge, sipping coffee from a takeaway plastic cup.

'ROAD HOG!' Ar stabbed the horn, his beard quivering with annoyance.

The man stared up at Ar, and smirked. I was used to this. People always stared at Ar and Ma. They always stared at the Pantechnicon too, with its rusty patches and flaking paintwork, and at the words painted on its side:

BOTTOM'S TRAVELLING THEATRE

The man made a rude gesture, dropped the empty plastic cup into the river, and slowly climbed into his cab.

The river looked different to the way it had last year, when we came to Stopford for the first time: it was all choked up with junk. The lorry pulled away in a cloud of exhaust.

'LITTERBUG!' roared Ar.

I ducked down behind the driver's seat, my face burning. Ar crashed the gears of the Pantechnicon and accelerated after the lorry, but it soon veered off up the hill, where a huge, windowless concrete building stood on its own beside the river, surrounded by high walls.

The Pantechnicon rattled and bumped down an uneven lane towards Stopford Common, the trees bent in one direction by the wind. Ar gave an earth-shattering cough and my eyes began to sting. Wiping them, I peered up at the building on the hill, where the lorry had gone. A fat chimney belched out black smoke—even now, at six in the morning. The smoke followed the same direction as the bent trees: down over the Common and out towards the sea. It seemed to crawl in through the windows of the Pantechnicon. Ma wound up her window and snapped at Ar to do the same. Then she drummed her fingers on the dashboard and said:

'Why, why, *why* do we have to come *here* again?'

'Because they pay GOOD MONEY in Stopford,' said Ar. 'And we need all the REMUNERATION we can get.'

Ma's face looked like someone had slapped it with a wet fish. 'The air is even *worse than last year.* And the audiences here always *laugh at us.*'

'You're far too SENSITIVE, Marina!' boomed Ar. 'They're laughing at the COMEDY.'

'They laughed through *Hamlet*,' muttered Ma.

'That's true,' I said. 'They laughed through *Macbeth* too—'

Ma gave a sharp intake of breath and I realized what I'd done. I shoved my fist over my mouth, but it was too late—I'd said it.

'She spoke *the name of the Scottish play*,' groaned Ma. 'And we're performing it *tonight*.'

'That's mere SUPERSTITION!' rumbled Ar.

'*It. Is. Not.*' Ma crossed her fingers on both hands. 'Actors should *never* say that name. It brings *bad luck. Disaster.*'

'NONSENSE, Marina!' rumbled Ar.

'Anyhow, I'm not an actor,' I said, adding *thank goodness* under my breath. 'So it doesn't count.'

The Pantechnicon bumped over the Common and ground to a halt in the middle of it, beside a solitary tap. A large notice said:

STOPFORD COMMON
PARKING STRICTLY BY PERMIT ONLY

This would be our home for three precious days. Ar threw open his door and leapt out on to the scrubby grass. He took a gigantic breath.

'Wake up, STOPFORD, and prepare to be ENTERTAINED!' he roared, in between coughing from the fumes. 'BOTTOM'S TRAVELLING THEATRE IS BACK!'

SUPERSTITION:

*a belief in fate or magic, leading
to good or bad luck*

Ar was all for unpacking the Pantechnicon straight away, but Ma wasn't having it.

'Washing and breakfast *first*, Arthur Bottom,' she insisted.

Ar gave a gusty sigh, but he got back into the Pantechnicon and they both climbed over the seats to join me.

Ar called our van the Pantechnicon because pantechnicons were old-style furniture vans—ours used to be a removals van before he converted it into our home. A flimsy hardboard wall divided it into two parts: our living quarters at the front; and a large storage area at the back. My little bunk bed turned into a seat in the daytime, and Ar and Ma's bunk became a table.

I squeezed past Ar to the tiny sink to clean my teeth. We used the sink for washing ourselves as well as washing the dishes. Ma squeezed past me to get bread from the 'larder'—a box under my bunk bed—and milk from a tiny fridge. Then she elbowed me out of the way to fill the kettle from a bucket of water under the sink. Ar squeezed past *her* to visit the toilet. The toilet was the only sort-of private place in the Pantechnicon, but because it was just behind a makeshift curtain, people could hear—and smell—*everything* you did inside it.

'WITH A HEY, AND A HO, AND A HEY NONINO...'

Ar's voice boomed out from behind the curtain. We had to sing loudly when we were in the toilet—not only to stop people hearing what we were doing, but to stop them bursting in on us. No wonder I was an only child. Ar and Ma had no privacy to make a baby—not that there'd be room for one if they did.

Ar returned from the toilet and squeezed past me to fill a glass of water. He glugged it down and then stood and gargled for ages like he did every morning.

'Out of the *way*, Arthur, and make yourself *useful*!' growled Ma.

Ar spat out the water into the sink. 'An actor must preserve his VOICE.'

Soon the Pantechnicon was full of the sounds of the whistling kettle, and Ar's vocal warm-up.

'MEEE, MAAAAY, MAAAAH, MOW, MOOO!'

'Here, Ophelia.' Ma handed me a slice of bread and butter and a mug of tea. 'Now get out from *under my feet*.'

Carrying them, I climbed over the driver's seat into the cab of the Pantechnicon and jumped down into the grass and the lovely quiet.

The sun had disappeared. Heavy black clouds hung over the concrete building on the hill. Ma was right about one

16

thing: it *was* going to rain. Ar leapt from the Pantechnicon, still chewing and waving a mug of tea, and hurried round to the back.

'I'm off to TOWN!' he yelled, coming out with a large cardboard box, 'to put up the POSTERS!'

I quickly swallowed the last of my bread and butter and gulped down the dregs of my tea.

'Can I come too, Ar? I can help you put them up quicker.' This might be my only chance to explore Stopford.

Ma stuck her head out of the window.

'*No*, Ophelia! Mornings are for home-schooling, not *gadding about*!'

I kicked the grass. If I went to a *proper* school, I wouldn't have home-schooling on a Saturday morning. But Ma insisted we home-school every day.

'She needs a *proper education*,' she told Ar. 'And she doesn't get enough learning time, what with all the travelling and performing.'

Because Ma home-schooled me, I knew everything there was to know about plays and literature and poetry. But Ma wasn't interested in subjects like maths and history and geography and science. If I lived in a *normal* house, I'd have a bedroom with shelves for books, and I'd belong to a library. And I'd go to a proper school where there were lessons about *everything* and maybe then my mind would stop being so hungry.

'ACTION STATIONS, EVERYONE!'

Ar was back from Stopford.

Ma sighed and closed the book of poetry we'd been reading. I jumped over the seats of the Pantechnicon and followed Ar, with Ma drifting behind, grumbling.

'It's going to *pour*,' she said, staring up at the darkening sky.

'What's a little PRECIPITATION?' roared Ar. 'We'll simply put up the TENT!'

He threw open the huge doors to the storage area at the back. We each grabbed a corner of the tent and hauled it out on to the grass.

The wind shifted round and the smoke from the chimney on the hill blew the fumes in our direction again. Ma groaned and we coughed and spluttered. Huge drops of rain fell, wrapped in a gusty wind, as we struggled with sopping canvas and steel tent pegs and mallets. The wind never seemed to blow bad air over the town, only over the Common. If I lived in a proper house in Stopford I'd be warm and dry now, instead of soaked to the skin and struggling to breathe.

The next thing to put up was the rickety wooden stage. It came in sections, so Ma and I carried one, while Ar took another. We hefted them inside the tent and slotted them together. Suddenly, Ma pointed at the roof of the tent.

'*Arthur Bottom!*'

My heart sank into my trainers. Water dripped through a jagged gash in the canvas and pooled on the wooden stage. Ma had been nagging Ar for days to mend it. Ar jumped down from the stage and disappeared, returning with a huge, black-painted witches' cauldron which was one of

18

the props for *Macbeth*. He plonked it in the middle of the stage and the water plopped steadily into it.

'Problem SOLVED!' he announced.

'And what happens *after* the witches' scene?' demanded Ma. 'Why would there be a witches' cauldron in the middle of a *Scottish castle?*'

'Never mind the DETAILS,' Ar said. 'We have a MATINEE to prepare for.'

That was the trouble with Saturdays. If it was any other day, we could've waited for the rain to stop before putting up the tent. But today we had to do two performances—one at two, and another at eight.

At least it was a bit dryer inside the tent. Except, there was still all the other stuff to get out of the Pantechnicon: the rusty folding seats for the audience; the heavy velvet curtain; the lights; and the scenery (a couple of painted trees and a section of castle wall). The costumes and masks, thank goodness, stayed in the back of the Pantechnicon. Ar and Ma used this as their 'green room'—the area where they got dressed up.

At last, the theatre was ready. Ar and Ma squabbled off to sort out their costumes, leaving me to set out the props (a painted crown, a battery-operated candle and various swords and daggers) and check I had the right music for *Macbeth* on the ancient CD player. I put the Book—the script of the play—at the side of the stage, though I never needed it. I knew the whole play off by heart, just like I knew all the other Shakespeare plays that Bottom's Travelling Theatre performed. Ar said I had a *sticky memory*: I only ever had to read through something once, and it sort of stuck to my mind, like a photograph.

There was just time for lunch—sausages, which Ma fried in a pan on the one-ring gas stove, and cold baked beans from a tin—before we had to get ready for the afternoon performance. Ma and Ar climbed into the back of the Pantechnicon and got into their witches' costumes and wigs.

The first scene of *Macbeth* was where three witches sat around a cauldron and prophesied trouble. Except, of course, we only had two witches. The problem with Bottom's having just two actors was that Ar and Ma had to play all the characters. This meant they had to change very quickly from one costume to another, so there were long pauses between scenes—and that's why they wore masks rather than wearing make-up: there simply wasn't time to wipe off the make-up and apply more.

'This is *ridiculous*,' moaned Ma, like she always did. 'How can *we two* be expected to perform a play with a cast of *thirty*...'

'It's an OPPORTUNITY to demonstrate the BREADTH OF OUR TALENT as ACTORS.' Ar fixed a long grey wig over his curly black hair and pulled a shawl up around his beard to hide it. Then he turned to me and opened his mouth to speak.

'*No*, Arthur Bottom!' Ma snapped. 'Ophelia *cannot* be an actor. She has enough to do as it is.'

Thank goodness, even Ar couldn't force me to get up onstage. If I didn't keep the show going backstage, there'd be no play at all. It was my job to sell the tickets before the show, to open and close the curtain, operate the lighting, hand out the props, play the music and be the prompt. In between performances, I sewed the costumes and helped Ar paint the scenery. I also had to try and cheer Ar and Ma up when the audience booed them. Sometimes it seemed like *I* was the parent and they were the children.

The rain and wind buffeted the tent, and clouds of dark smog from the building on the hill swirled around the Common. Ma grumbled on about me saying *that word*.

'I've got a *bad feeling* about being in this place again,' she muttered. '*A very bad feeling indeed.*'

I was so used to Ma grumping about stuff, I took no notice.

But as it turned out, I should have paid more attention...

BREAK A LEG:

theatrical slang, meaning 'good luck!'

At one forty-five, a grumbling queue stood in the rain outside the tent.

The Stopford folk all wore neat plastic macs and shiny welly boots. The gusty wind kept blowing their umbrellas inside out.

Everything was always a scramble before curtain-up. I checked the scenery—two painted windblown trees, rather like the ones out on the Common—and made sure the red velvet curtain was drawn to hide the stage, where rain dripped steadily into the cauldron. The canvas of the tent billowed in the gale, as if it was taking deep breaths. I only hoped the tent pegs would hold. I hurried to my little table just inside the entrance, adjusting my mask. When we performed a comedy, I wore a sort of jester's outfit with bells, and a white, smiley mask. Today, because *Macbeth* was a tragedy, I wore a black-hooded cloak and a black mask with a turned-down mouth.

As I took off the lid of the old teapot we used for the takings and checked the tickets, people muttered in the queue.

'...soaked to the skin...'

'...coming all the way out here...'

'...stuck waiting in this deluge...'

I began taking money and handing out tickets.

'Excuse me, young lady!' The woman I'd just sold a ticket to waved it at me.

'Yes, madam?'

'Why does this ticket say *Macbeth*?'

'Um... because that's the play we're doing today.'

The woman turned to the queue behind her. 'She says the play's *Macbeth*! I came to see *A Midsummer Night's Dream*!'

A chorus of voices shouted: 'And me! And me!'

The woman turned back to me, hands on hips. 'This simply isn't good enough!'

A plump man in the queue, carrying a bulging plastic shopping bag, said: 'It's fraud! Duplicity!'

'I-I don't understand...' I said. 'The posters—'

'We haven't paid good money for this!' The voices rose.

'Just—just a moment.' I stood up, grabbing the teapot. 'I—I'll go and ask—'

'Get a move on, then! We're getting soaked!'

In the Pantechnicon, Ar and Ma were doing their pre-performance breathing exercises.

'Ar—which posters did you put up in the town?' I gasped, wiping rain off my face.

'POSTERS?' Ar looked puzzled.

'The audience think we're doing *A Midsummer Night's Dream*!'

There was a long silence.

'Arthur Bottom, you *didn't*, did you...?' Ma turned to the cardboard box where we kept all the posters and picked up the top one. Her face changed.

'You *did*! You put up the *wrong posters*!'

Ar went pale. 'It was... it was an OVERSIGHT.'

'I *knew* something like this would happen if we came to this *wretched place again*!'

'Never mind all that!' I interrupted. 'What do I tell them?'

'Tell them... tell them we're APOLOGETIC,' said Ar, the bit of his face not covered by his beard flushed pink. 'Tell them we're CONTRITE. REGRETFUL.'

'I don't think that'll make them stay.' I glanced over my shoulder. People in the queue were already stomping off.

'Tell them we'll let them in *half-price*,' hissed Ma, looking daggers at Ar.

I dashed back to the tent. People were leaving the queue with thundercloud faces.

'Wait!' I shouted. They stopped and glared at me. 'There's been a—an Administrative Error...'

'You're telling us!' smirked the plump man.

'And—and we're very sorry. And if you'd like to come anyway, the tickets will be half-price!'

The people muttered to one another, and I held my breath. Then, they slowly formed into a queue again.

The wind howled, sending the canvas billowing. The audience were still muttering about the mix-up between *Macbeth* and *A Midsummer Night's Dream*.

'Ready?' I whispered to Ar and Ma, who were sitting on stage behind the curtain in their witches' costumes and masks. There was a steady *drip drip drip* as the rain splashed into the cauldron from the tear in the roof.

Ar nodded.

'BREAK A LEG!' he whispered. He and Ma always said this before they performed—it was an old theatre tradition which was supposed to help the performance go well.

I drew back the red velvet curtain, making sure no one in the audience could see me, and crouched behind it. Then I slowly brought up the lights and played the opening, eerie music on the CD player. Ar and Ma stirred the cauldron, and Ar spoke the opening lines in a witchy voice:

'When shall we three... er, TWO... meet again?
In thunder, lightning, or in RAIN?'

A rumble of thunder almost drowned him out, and the muttering from the audience got louder.

'Call this entertainment? We might as well go and sit outside in the rain!' shouted the plump man, and the others laughed loudly. Ar and Ma ploughed on.

'Where the PLACE?' Ar said.

'Upon the heath,' Ma replied.

A swirl of fumes blew into the tent, sending the audience spluttering. Ma, her eyes streaming behind her mask, was overtaken by a coughing fit.

'Health and Safety!' shouted the plump man, to raucous laughter.

Ma swallowed, cleared her throat, and she and Ar struggled through the final lines of the scene:

'Fair is FOUL, and foul is fair:
Hover through the FOG and filthy air.'

'What FOUL acting!' shouted a voice from the audience.

By the time we got to the last act, the audience had begun a low chanting.

'Diversus periculosus est... diversus periculosus est... diversus periculosus est...'

'What's going on?' hissed Ma in a pause between the final scenes. 'They keep *heckling* us!'

'It sounds like a foreign language—like Latin,' I said.

'They're probably getting CARRIED AWAY by the TRAGEDY...' said Ar.

Ma rolled her eyes. 'We should *refuse to go on* unless they shut up!'

'You can't stop now!' I whispered, handing Ar his staff and double-checking he was wearing the right costume for his role of Lord Macbeth. 'There're only seven more scenes to go.'

Ar nodded. 'The SHOW MUST GO ON!'

He stepped out on to the stage, narrowly avoiding the cauldron which was still onstage to catch the drips.

'BOOOO!' chorused the audience.

This was meant to be one of the saddest scenes of the whole play, when Lady Macbeth died. Surely they wouldn't laugh through this? I lowered the lights, and played the sound of slow, mournful drumbeats. Ar stood alone onstage, as Ma, dressed as his servant, entered.

'The queen, my lord, is dead,' announced Ma.

'GERROFFF!!!!' shouted the audience. 'Make us LAUGH!!!'

Ar's face was red with fury behind his Lord Macbeth mask. But he lifted his bushy chin and yelled out his lines:

'OUT, OUT, *brief candle!*

Life's but a walking shadow, a poor player,

That struts and frets his hour upon the stage,

And then is heard no MORE. It is... it is...'

There was a long silence. Ar had forgotten his lines. Quickly, I hissed:

'*...a tale told by an idiot...*'

But the audience was chanting again, drowning out my voice. Ar cupped his hand to his ear towards me. But it was hopeless.

Then, something red and squashy landed with a splosh on the stage. I glanced up at the roof of the tent, but there was only the rain dripping down into the cauldron. Another red, squashy thing hit Ma on the shoulder. She gasped and wheeled towards the audience, her face white. I pulled the curtain back a teeny bit and peered out. The audience was still chanting. The plump man pulled the red squashy things from his plastic shopping bag and lobbed them at the stage. Tomatoes. And judging by the way they splatted and stank, rotten ones. Soon, the whole stage was a blood-red mush.

'HOW DARE YOU!!!'

Throwing his mask aside, Ar glared at the audience. Even in the dim light, he was a fearsome sight with his huge beard and furious eyes. Another grumble of thunder boomed over the tent.

27

Then a large tomato hit Ar full in the face. It splattered down his cheek and ran into his beard. He stumbled across the stage towards the plump man.

'You'll be SORRY for that, you RABBLE-ROUSER!'

'*No, Ar!*' I shouted, but it was too late.

Ar cannoned into the cauldron in the dim light. It overturned, sending rainwater cascading over the wooden stage among the slimy tomatoes. Ar's boots slid over the slippery wood, skidded on a tomato skin and he landed on stage with a terrible crack. At the same moment a massive gust of wind bellowed through the tent, lifting the tent pegs from the ground and bringing the sopping canvas tumbling down over the stage and on to the heads of the audience.

The silence was broken by Ar's voice.

'Call an AMBULANCE, OPHELIA!' he roared. 'I think I've BROKEN MY LEG!!!'

SILVER LINING:

*something positive that comes out of
a sad or unpleasant situation*

'**A** HORSE—A HORSE—My kingdom for a HORSE!' Ar roared, struggling to get out of bed, and failing.

'He's had a very nasty break,' said the nice woman doctor, who'd been extremely patient with Ar so far.

Ar lay in bed in Stopford Hospital still wearing his Macbeth costume, his bushy beard streaked with tomato. His leg was in a plaster cast. I was busy drawing the masks of Comedy and Tragedy on the plaster cast with a felt-tip pen, to cheer him up. Ma sat by the bed with a face like thunder.

Everything that happened earlier that afternoon was a bit of a blur. I'd managed to burrow my way out of the capsized tent to the Pantechnicon, found Ar's ancient mobile phone and dialled 999 for an ambulance. By the time I got back to the tent, people were crawling out from under the sopping canvas, furious. The plump man shouted, '*Health and Safety!*' and the woman who'd complained about the tickets was threatening to call the police. But no one yelled as loudly as Ar. Luckily the ambulance arrived, lights flashing, in just a few minutes and two kindly ambulance men helped me to lift the tent. Ar lay on stage, his leg bent at a strange angle, with Ma at his side. The ambulance men lifted Ar on to a stretcher and took him away, leaving Ma and me to follow on foot.

'TO BE, OR NOT TO BE—THAT IS THE QUESTION!'

Ar must be confused, because of the strong painkillers the doctor gave him. The other patients in the ward stared at him. I hunched my shoulders and concentrated on my drawing.

'*Hush*, Arthur Bottom,' hissed Ma. 'If you hadn't insisted we came to *this place again*—and if you hadn't muddled up the posters—and if you'd mended the tear in the roof of the tent—and if you hadn't lost your temper, *none of this* would have happened.'

'Don't be mean to him, Ma,' I whispered. 'He's hurting.'

'Try not to worry.' The doctor bent down to me, lowering her voice. 'Your mum's cross because she's had a bit of a scare. But your dad's going to be fine—just fine.'

'The SHOW must GO ON!' roared Ar.

Ma took a deep breath. 'Listen to the doctor, Arthur, and *calm down*. The sooner you behave yourself, the sooner you can get out of here.'

'We'll keep him in for a few nights,' said the doctor. 'He's in a bit of shock.'

'How—how long will it take for him to recover?' I asked.

'About six weeks,' said the doctor. 'And he'll need to use crutches to walk.'

Ma went pale. 'You mean—he can't perform?'

'Strictly no performing.' The doctor turned to leave. Ma grabbed her arm.

'What—what about driving?'

'Not for at least six weeks,' said the doctor.

Ma went even paler. She stared at the doctor's white coat, disappearing into the corridor. I knew what she was thinking. How would we survive for six whole weeks if Ar couldn't act? There was no way Ma and me could put up the tent and run the whole show by ourselves. And if there were no performances, there'd be no money.

'Stay here with your father,' Ma said suddenly, pulling her phone from her pocket and heading for the corridor.

I finished my drawing and sat on the plastic chair beside Ar. His eyes were closing. The painkillers must be working.

This was the first time I'd ever been in a real hospital. Each patient lay in a clean, white bed with a little table on wheels for their books and their bowls of grapes and their jugs of water. Ar's bed was messy from all his thrashing about, and streaked with mud and tomato, which looked like bloodstains. It felt all wrong, somehow, for him to be this quiet. Very carefully, so as not to disturb him, I pulled the white cover up over his chest and slipped my hand into his big, warm one.

It was a long walk back to Stopford Common in the drizzle, especially as Ma moaned non-stop about not having enough money for a taxi. In the fading evening light, we gazed at the mess that used to be our theatre. The red-and-white stripy canvas lay spread out on the grass where the ambulance men had left it, pools of rainwater puddling its surface. The wooden stage, red with squashed tomatoes, was still standing, but the velvet curtain was crumpled on the grass and smeared with mud, the lights toppled over and all the seats upended. I waded through the debris and picked up the teapot, which was luckily still in one piece.

Ma gave a heavy sigh. 'We'd better have supper.'

'Shouldn't we sort all this out first?'

Ma glanced at the dark sky. 'What's the *point*? Everything's soaked. Even if we get it into the Pantechnicon, it'll only go *mouldy*.'

'The sun will shine tomorrow,' I tried to sound optimistic, like Ar. 'Then it'll all dry out.'

Ma didn't answer. She turned slowly towards the Pantechnicon, swung open the door and hoisted herself over the seat.

After a silent supper—tinned soup and bread and butter, followed by an apple each—I rinsed our dishes in the tiny sink while Ma removed the lid of the teapot and emptied the money out on the table.

'We—we'll be OK, won't we, Ma? Ar will be out of hospital soon and—'

'And *what*?' snapped Ma. She separated out the notes from the coins. 'He'll be good for nothing for six weeks.'

'What'll we do till he's better?'

Ma pursed her lips. 'We'll make the best of a *very bad situation*.'

'What do you mean?'

'If we're going to be stuck in this... this *place* for six whole weeks, we'll do what I've been meaning to for years.'

'Wh-what's that?'

Ma turned to face me. 'Your father and I have always disagreed about your *education*. He thinks this travelling life is the best education a child can have, but I've always maintained that you need *proper schooling*. And so...'

I stared at her, holding my breath.

'...I'm enrolling you at Stopford School,' said Ma.

I gasped. 'I'm going to school?'

Ma nodded. 'We've just enough money to buy your uniform, with a little left over.'

'But—what will Ar say?'

'Your father will just have to *put up with it*,' said Ma, her eyes flashing. 'If it wasn't for his *thoughtlessness*, we wouldn't be in this situation.'

I gazed out of the windscreen of the Pantechnicon, my heart fluttering around in my chest like a butterfly, my mind tick-tocking from one thing to the next.

We're staying in Stopford for six whole weeks!

I'm going to go to a normal school!

And I'm going to wear a proper uniform!

Outside, the rain had stopped and a streak of sun peeked through the clouds, lighting up their edges with silver. Ar always said that every cloud had a silver lining. Maybe he was right—maybe good things *could* come out of bad ones. It was horrible that Ar was stuck in the hospital and that he wouldn't be able to act. But maybe, just *maybe* he'd get used to staying in one place. Maybe he and Ma would decide

33

to stay here, in Stopford. Maybe they'd give up travelling and buy a pretty little house and... I shook my head. That wasn't going to happen.

Then I saw it.

A dazzling rainbow, beginning right above the Pantechnicon and sending an arch of sparkling colours across the sky like a magic bridge, its tail landing right in Stopford.

Maybe... just *maybe*, miracles could happen, after all.

QUOTIDIAN:

ordinary

Two days later, I stood in the back of the Pantechnicon, staring at my reflection in the greasepaint-speckled mirror that Ar and Ma used to check their costumes. I ran my fingers over the Stopford School uniform, with its red blazer and gold trimmings. The tie was red too, with gold stripes. Under the blazer was a crisp white shirt and a grey pleated skirt.

It had been thrilling going to the department store on Stopford High Street. Everything would have been perfect if only Ma could have looked like all the other mothers. But she wore an ankle-length dress made of crimson velvet with dozens of tiny mirrors stitched into it. And over this, the long blue cloak from her costume in *Othello*. Her mess of tangled red curls tumbled to her waist. The other shoppers, with their neat haircuts and trendy clothes, had stared.

I turned back to the mirror and grabbed a handful of my own messy red curls. They looked all *wrong* somehow, like I was just pretending to be a normal schoolgirl. I divided my hair into two sections, braided each section into tight plaits secured with rubber bands, and breathed a long sigh of relief. Now I looked *real*.

'Ophelia!' Ma's voice broke into my thoughts.

I jumped down from the back of the Pantechnicon. The wind had died down and the sun had been shining non-stop. All our stuff must be dry by now.

'Are you *still* wearing that uniform?'

'I love it, Ma. It's so cool!'

'*Cool*? I hope that attending school isn't going to ruin your *vocabulary*.'

'It won't! I promise!' It was like ants were scurrying over every inch of my skin, I was so excited. Tomorrow I'd be there. At a real school. I fingered the soft material of my blazer.

'Ma...'

'Yes?'

'What's this writing on the pocket? Is it Latin?'

Embroidered in gold on the top pocket of the blazer were six words:

PLASTICUS STUPENDUS EST
DIVERSUS PERICULOSUS EST

Ma glanced at it. 'Looks like it.'

'What does it mean?'

Ma shrugged. 'No idea.' She tossed a broom at me. 'Now take those clothes off and get into your jeans. There's *work* to do.'

I really, really didn't want to take the uniform off. Then again, I'd hate for it to get mud—or rotten tomatoes—on it. I was heading back to the Pantechnicon to change when a sound made me turn.

A taxi jolted over the Common towards us and pulled up beside the Pantechnicon.

The door swung open and Ma's eyes went all glassy.

'I. Do. Not. Believe. It,' she whispered.

A white-plastered leg heaved out of the taxi, followed by the rest of Ar. He grabbed two crutches from the seat, fitted them under his arms, and staggered to his feet.

Ma's face was chalk-white with fury. 'What are you doing here, Arthur Bottom?'

'DISCHARGED meself,' roared Ar. 'Place was full of RULES and REGULATIONS!'

'But the doctor said you should stay in for—'

'PIFFLE!' said Ar. 'I'm right as RAIN!' He turned to the taxi driver. 'I am INDEBTED to you, sir.' He began to hobble over the grass towards us.

'Never mind indebted, mate!' shouted the taxi driver. 'You owe me a tenner!'

'TO THE TEAPOT, Marina!' said Ar. 'And I'll REIMBURSE this fellow for his trouble.'

If looks could kill, Ar would be a pile of dust. Ma stomped to the Pantechnicon. Ar seemed to notice me for the first time. He narrowed his eyes.

'Ophelia... why are you dressed in that REGALIA?'

I twirled round proudly. 'D'you like it? Ma and I got it in Stopford.'

'What, pray, is its PURPOSE?'

'I'm going to school, Ar! Real, proper school!'

'WHAAAAAAAT????' Ar's roar was louder than any lion's.

Ma returned, frozen-faced and tight-lipped. Ignoring Ar, she shoved a ten-pound note through the window of the taxi. It turned and jolted off over the Common, back to town.

Ar glared at my uniform. He opened his mouth to shout again, but Ma got in first.

'*That ten pounds*,' she hissed, 'was the last of our money, apart from a few coins.'

'How SO?' yelled Ar, gesturing at my blazer. 'Could it perchance be because you spent the rest on that RIDICULOUS OUTFIT!'

'Ophelia needs a *proper education*.' Ma's cheeks flushed pink. 'And she's going to have one, since you've *forced* us to stay here.'

'And how did the school react when you told them it'd just be for SIX WEEKS?'

Ma looked flustered and said nothing.

'AHA!' roared Ar. 'You didn't INFORM them, did you?'

'That's not the *point*,' Ma said, flushing. 'The point is that Ophelia should be getting an *education.*'

'So you want our CHILD to associate with the offspring of the IMBECILES who BOMBARDED us with tomatoes?'

Ma stamped her foot. 'That would never have *happened* if you'd put up the right posters!'

And off they went again, neither listening to the other. It was like being caught in a world war, with words being shot back and forth over my head.

'—no better education than life on the ROAD—'

'—how are we supposed to *eat* when we can't perform—'

'—she doesn't RESEMBLE Ophelia Bottom in that get-up—'

'—and if you hadn't *got above yourself* and come out of role—'

'—no child of mine will be QUOTIDIAN—'

'—I *knew* this would happen if we came here again—'

I couldn't stand it any longer. I ran to the Pantechnicon, grabbed my swimming costume and towel and—still wearing my uniform—pelted across the Common. Ar and Ma didn't even notice me go, they were so busy yelling.

I kept running, down the rough road at the end of the Common and past the woods. My cheeks felt all wet, and I wiped them with the towel. Ar and Ma's quarrels seemed to get worse and worse. At least when I was at school all day, I wouldn't have to listen. Hot from running, I pulled off my blazer and tucked it carefully over one arm.

The road wound down towards Stopford Cove. The cove was another reason why I was so happy to be here: for three whole days, I could wash *all* of me in fresh seawater, instead of struggling to use a flannel in the tiny sink of the Pantechnicon.

I smelt the sea before I saw it—fresh and clean, with a tinge of saltiness. My trainers sank into the soft sand of the dunes. Then it was in front of me: a perfect, horseshoe-shaped beach. There were no kiosks or cafes—which was strange, since it was so close to Stopford. Stranger still, there'd been no one else here last year: just pale, gritty sand with tiny pink and white shells and odd-shaped pieces of driftwood and glass, softened by the sea. Close by, at this end of the cove, was the cave I'd discovered, half hidden by jagged rocks. At the far end of the cove, the river ran down into the sea. The only sounds were the lapping of the waves and the mewing gulls. It was *my* secret beach.

The sea was glassy and turquoise and seemed to beckon me in. I threw my towel on to the sand and carefully placed my precious blazer on it. But before I could take off the rest of my uniform, a white puppy with a black patch over one eye lolloped towards me, yapping fit to bust.

I dropped on to my knees in the sand and the puppy bounced around me, licking my face. It had no collar or tag, and it hadn't learnt how to bark properly yet—it just sort of squeaked—but its stumpy tail wagged crazily. I buried my hands in its soft fur. If I lived in a proper house, I could have a puppy of my own. No way could I keep a puppy in the Pantechnicon.

A piercing whistle echoed over the beach. At the far end of the cove, near the river, a boy stood. He was thin and wiry, with black skin and a cloud of dark hair. A white plastic sack was slung over his back, like Santa Claus. He dropped the sack, raised his fingers to his lips and whistled again. The puppy hesitated, gave my nose a final lick, and pelted over the sand towards the boy. When he reached him, he jumped right up into the boy's arms. The boy stood still as a rock, staring at me, the dog wriggling against his chest. No way was I going to get undressed while he was here.

I picked up my blazer and towel and headed for the cave. When I looked back, the boy and his dog had disappeared.

REGALIA:

special dress, finery

It was dank and echoey and dripping inside the cave. Long strands of green seaweed made the floor slippery. Right at the back, where it was darkest, there was a ledge, too high for the tide to reach. I took off my uniform, folded it carefully and stood on tiptoes to put it safely on the ledge, then, shivering, I pulled on my swimming costume. I kicked off my trainers, wrapped my towel around myself and hurried down the beach to the sea.

There was no sign of the boy or his puppy. Something gleamed white in the sand. Last year, I'd collected delicate shells and speckled pebbles and pieces of driftwood and kept them in a little box beside my pillow. I ran over to pick it up—then dropped it in disgust. It wasn't a shell; it was a plastic bottle-top. And there was other junk: a flip-flop, its sole torn; a squashed coffee carton; an empty plastic bottle, strands of polythene wrapping. I wrinkled up my nose. They must have drifted in with the tide.

A cool wind gusted around the beach, giving me

goosebumps. I gritted my teeth and dropped my towel on to a rock. Then I shut my eyes tight and ran as fast as I could into the sea.

The first minute was always the coldest. I gasped and splashed about to keep warm. A white plastic sack swirled around my legs, clammy and cold. There was writing on it:

PRATT'S PLASTIC PELLETS

—and I kicked free of it. Maybe if I swam out a bit further, the water would be clearer.

It wasn't. There was *loads* of junk out here, clumping together: more white sacks, bits of plastic netting, polystyrene balls, even a yellow plastic washing-up bowl. What was it all doing here? At this rate, I'd be dirtier *after* swimming than before. I turned over on to my back so I didn't have to look at it, and floated for a while. The sky was the softest blue: baby clouds puffed, and seagulls glided and soared. But it was too chilly to do this for long, and I turned on to my front again.

The big clump of junk seemed to have washed closer. And from the middle of it, the top of a round, dark head surfaced. Was it a seal? In a moment, it disappeared. I scanned the water. I'd never seen a seal here before, far less shared the water with one. Were seals dangerous? Did they attack humans?

I kept staring at the mass of plastic junk, and the head surfaced again. I turned and kicked towards the shore. When I was almost there, I trod water and glanced back.

42

The water seemed empty again, but there was a scary feeling in my tummy. What if the seal—or whatever it was—was swimming towards me under the surface?

Suddenly, there was a churning in the water beside me. Something grabbed my leg and pulled me under. My mouth filled with salt, my arms and legs thrashed to get free, but whatever-it-was held on tight. Just as my lungs felt like they were about to burst, it let me go. My head broke the surface and my frantic feet found the sand. No sooner was I upright than the water churned again and a *thing* reared up out of the sea right in front of me: it had plastic goggles for eyes, sharp white teeth and a long mass of tangled plastic-and-seaweedy hair. I screamed and scrambled out of the water, choking and gasping for air. Then I crawled up the sand, my eyes and throat stinging, my legs shaking out of control.

Where's it gone? I scanned the sea, but the water looked just the way it always did, calm and turquoise and still, the beach a sweep of emptiness.

It took a few minutes for my legs to work properly. I stumbled over to the rock, grabbed my towel and wrapped myself in it, my teeth chattering. No way would I ever swim here again. My special place was spoilt. Sniffing back tears, I hurried to the cave for my uniform.

My trainers, which I'd kicked off on to the seaweed-covered sand under the ledge, were missing. I dropped to my knees in the semi-darkness and felt around. *Nothing.* That same scary feeling crawled like a beetle in my tummy. I stood on tiptoes to reach up to the ledge for my uniform. But the ledge was empty.

Maybe I forgot exactly where I left it. I felt all along the ledge, my fingers scraping on barnacles. Then I ran to the cave's entrance. A muddle of footprints tracked over the wet sand, from the sea to the cave. Were they all mine, or were there someone else's footprints among them? I swallowed and stared from one end of the cove to the other.

But it was empty, and my precious uniform was gone.

When I squelched, barefoot and wrapped in my wet towel, on to the Common, Ar was sitting with his leg propped on a chair and Ma was trying, single-handedly, to drag the tent to the Pantechnicon. When she saw me, she growled.

'So you went *swimming*, Ophelia! When there was *work* to do! I've been *sick with worry!*'

'S-sorry,' I muttered.

'Let the child BE!' yelled Ar. 'At least she's got out of that BENIGHTED REGALIA.'

Ma looked me up and down. 'Where are your trainers? And what have you done with your school uniform?'

I hung my head. This was going to cause the biggest row *ever*.

'They—they got stolen.'

'*Stolen?*'

I opened my mouth to explain, but Ma was already yelling.

'...only bought it *yesterday*... cost almost every *penny* we have... *careless... selfish...*'

And then Ar joined in, yelling at Ma:

'...RIDICULOUS UNIFORM... just so she'll BLEND INTO THE BACKGROUND...!'

When they finally stopped, I said: 'What—what about school tomorrow?'

'You'll have to go without a uniform,' snapped Ma. 'There's no money left for another.'

'I—c-can't do that,' I whispered. Everyone'll stare at me. I'll be different.'

Ma shrugged angrily. 'You should have thought of that before you left it on the beach for *someone to steal!*'

PRODIGIOUS:

exceptional, causing amazement or wonder

It was eight in the morning. The wind was back again, and the fumes from the building on the hill seemed to sneak through every crack in the Pantechnicon, setting us all off coughing. What with Ar's leg being in plaster, there was even less space than usual. He was still asleep, and snoring like a warthog, his leg taking up all the room in the bunk. I'd already tripped over his crutches twice. Ma had to sleep draped across the seats in the driver's cab. Miserably, I pulled on my jeans, sweatshirt and old trainers, which should have been thrown away months ago—they'd got more holes than a sieve. I reached up to plait my hair, which was even wilder after yesterday's swim, then gave up. No amount of plaiting was going to stop me sticking out like a sore thumb on my first ever day at school.

Ma, frowning, handed me bread and peanut butter and a glass of milk.

'I—I'm not hungry.'

'*Eat,*' Ma said, looking daggers at Ar's snoring form. 'Soon we won't be able to *afford* breakfast.'

Time to put Escape Plan A into action. I crossed my fingers behind my back.

'Actually, Ma, I've got a tummy ache. Quite a bad one. I don't think I'd better go to school today.'

Ma glared at me with narrowed eyes. 'You can *uncross* those fingers, Ophelia,' she said. 'And you're *going*, like it or not!'

I took a few half-hearted bites of my bread and drank my milk. There was nothing for it but Escape Plan B, which was to set off towards school, then double back to the cove and search for my uniform.

'Well, goodbye.' I pushed open the door of the Pantechnicon and jumped down on to the grass. 'See you after school.'

'*Oh no you don't*, Ophelia.' Ma climbed over into the driver's cab, dragging her cloak with her. Today she was wearing a long, white, wispy costume I knew all too well. 'I'm coming with you.'

'There's no need! I'll find the way—'

'You have to be *registered* on your first day,' Ma leapt down from the cab, her dress—which was practically see-through—swirling round her knees.

Oh, great. Not only would I be turning up for my first day at school without a uniform and in holey shoes. Ma would be with me, dressed as Desdemona from Shakespeare's *Othello*.

I dragged my feet as we walked over the Common and crossed Stopford Bridge. Soon we passed the neat little roads, with their lovely names: *Chestnut Street; Oak Avenue; Elm*

47

Close; *Magnolia Drive*. Any other day, I'd be thrilled about being here. But we kept seeing groups of children dressed in Stopford School blazers and ties, and each time my heart sank a bit further.

'Get a *move on*, Ophelia!' Ma said.

Why couldn't she be like normal mothers, and talk quietly? The children turned to stare at Ma, nudging each other and smirking. I hunched my shoulders and lagged behind, to pretend I wasn't with her.

Stopford School was shiny and new, just like the shops in the High Street. My heart beat faster as we approached it—whether because I was scared or excited, I wasn't sure. Most of my life I'd dreamt of going to a proper school, of being like normal kids. But this was the worst possible beginning. Carved in stone over the entrance were the same words that had been embroidered on my blazer:

PLASTICUS STUPENDUS EST

DIVERSUS PERICULOSUS EST

—and thinking about my blazer set the worry going again. Who took it? How could I get it back? But there was no time to think any more. Ma's cloak swept ahead of me up a long, light-filled corridor with neat noticeboards towards a door marked:

MISS SERAPHINA SMITH
HEAD TEACHER
KNOCK BEFORE ENTERING!

Ma knocked loudly on the door, and after a few moments a voice called: 'Come!'

A thin woman with a long face, her hair in a neat bun, sat at a desk in front of a shiny computer. The walls were all shelves, with rows of files and folders arranged on them. The woman looked up. Her eyes widened at the sight of Ma's outfit.

'How may ay help you?' she asked, in a posh voice.

'My name is Marina Bottom,' announced Ma. 'I rang the other day to arrange for my daughter to *attend school*.' She pushed me forward. 'This is my daughter, Ophelia.'

Miss Smith glanced at me, then turned to Ma. 'Mrs Bottom, ay believe we did discuss the subject of uniform.'

'We purchased the uniform, but it was unfortunately *stolen*.'

'Stolen?' Miss Smith stared at Ma as if she didn't believe her.

'*Stolen*,' Ma said firmly.

'So you're intending to purchase a replacement?'

Ma flushed. 'When... when funds allow.'

'Hmmm.' Miss Smith turned to the shelves, pulled out a file and took out an official-looking form. 'Have a seat, Mrs... er, Bottom, and ay'll take some details.'

Ma sat in the one plastic seats, her cloak flowing over the floor, and I stood awkwardly beside her.

'Full name?' said Miss Smith.

'Marina Rosalind Bottom.'

Miss Smith sighed. 'No. Ophelia's name.' She pronounced it O-*failure*.

I wanted to stick my fingers in my ears—or better still, race out of this room, down the corridor, out of Stopford School and over the hills. Because I knew what was coming.

Ma drew herself up proudly.

'Ophelia... Cleopatra...'

Miss Smith scribbled busily.

'...Cressida... Cordelia... Goneril... Hippolyta...'

'How do you spell those?'

Ma spelt them out, while I cringed and Miss Smith scribbled.

'... Portia... Perdita... Juliet Bottom,' Ma finished triumphantly.

Why, why, *why* did Ar and Ma give me a name so long that people tripped over it? Why couldn't they have called me Sophie, or Emma? Ar believed he was a direct descendent of Shakespeare—or THE BARD, as he called him—so all my names were the names of Shakespearean heroines. Ophelia was the beautiful and tragic heroine of *Hamlet*—only I was thin as a pin, with sticky-out elbows and bony knuckles and knees, not to mention red hair and freckles. Whenever I moaned about my name, Ar always boomed:

'Consider yourself FORTUNATE, Ophelia. We almost called you TITANIA BOTTOM!'

Miss Smith passed a weary hand over her forehead.

'Age?'

'Forty-two.'

'No, O-*failure's* age.'

'Ten,' I said quickly. 'I'll be eleven on June the fifteenth.'

Miss Smith wrote this down.

'Address?'

I stared out of the window, pretending to be interested in a pigeon strutting across the playground.

Ma hesitated. Then she lifted her chin and said: 'The Pantechnicon, Stopford Common.'

'Ay'm sorry? Can you spell that?'

'P... A... N...'

I bit my thumbnail. Would this torture *ever* end? But at last the questions were over and Ma stood up to go.

'I'll collect you at three-thirty.'

'*No!*' The word jerked out before I could stop it. 'I mean, it's OK, Ma. I—I remember *exactly* how to get back.'

Ma smiled. 'Ophelia has the most *prodigious* memory.'

'Railly?' Miss Smith smirked. 'Ay suppose that must come in handy, given the length of her name.'

Ma pursed her lips together and drew her cloak around herself. Then she bent and dropped a kiss on my forehead.

'Farewell, Ophelia, and make the *very most* of this opportunity. And don't forget—' She gazed upwards, and I just *knew* she was going to quote from Shakespeare.

She did.

'*This above all: to thine own self be true.*' Then she swept from the office, leaving Miss Smith gawping after her. At the door she turned and whispered:

'*O, this learning, what a thing it is!*'

My cheeks burned so hard I wouldn't have been surprised if they'd set off the school fire alarm.

PREFECTS:

*senior pupils who are authorized
to enforce discipline*

As soon as Ma had gone, Miss Smith got up and walked out into the corridor.

'Merry Jones!' she shouted.

A girl—about my age with tousled conker-coloured hair escaping from a ponytail—stopped skipping down the corridor and turned.

'Yes, miss?'

'Ay'd like to remind you that we do *not* skip in the corridor. Nor do we wear our tie undone.'

The girl slowly fixed her tie.

'Particularly when we are approaching eleven, and shortly to become a Prefect.'

Miss Smith turned back to me. Merry, her green eyes sparkling, stuck her tongue out and gave me a wink. I grinned back.

'This is O-*failure*,' said Miss Smith, 'who is starting school today. Kindly take her to class.'

'OK, miss.' Merry grabbed my arm and led me down the corridor. As soon as we'd turned the corner, she stopped and jerked her head back towards the office. She wrinkled her nose and put on a posh accent.

'Ay'd like to remind you that we do *not* skip in the corridor.' She sounded *exactly* like Miss Smith. 'Smith's *vile.*' Suddenly, I felt more hopeful again about being at school.

Merry stared at me with interest. 'That's a funny name you've got—O-*failure.*'

'It's actually Ophelia,' I said. 'Only—could you call me Fee?'

If I was going to be a new girl, I'd call myself a new name too.

'OK.' A dimple appeared in Merry's cheek. 'Fee it is!' *Her* name was just right. She looked like she was always laughing and having fun.

'How old are you?' she asked.

'Ten—almost eleven.'

'When's your birthday?'

'June the fifteenth.'

Merry grinned. 'We're almost the same age, then, only I'm two weeks older! Mine's coming up soon—June the first!'

A bell rang, and Merry grabbed my arm again and hurried me down another spotless corridor to where a line of children stood outside a classroom. Merry pulled me to join the end of the queue and the other children turned to stare at me. They were all dressed in uniform, not a hair out of place. Their faces were pale, as if they didn't go outside much. I felt even more the odd-one-out beside them: my crazy red hair seemed to curl and tangle worse than ever, and my old trainers seemed more full of holes. I stared down at my grubby hands, brown from the sun, and at the paint under my nails from painting the scenery.

'Who's *that*?' whispered a boy with plump, pasty cheeks.

'She's called Fee,' said Merry.

'Stop talking in the line, Merry Jones!' snapped a tall girl with neat blonde plaits and silver braces on her teeth. Her eyes were cold and grey and she wore a shiny badge saying PREFECT.

Merry made a face, and when the girl turned her back, she rolled her eyes until they were crossed. I covered my mouth with my hand to stop a giggle bursting out. Then another girl jerked her head at the classroom.

'Right—you can all go in now. *Quietly.*'

I couldn't help staring. Was I seeing double? This girl looked exactly the same as the other one—tall, with blonde plaits, silver braces and a Prefect badge. They must be identical twins.

The line moved forward into the classroom. I wanted to take it all in, it was so thrilling to be in a real classroom at last. Neat rows of plastic desks and chairs were set out in front of a whiteboard. Down the sides of the room were tables with laptops on them. This was exciting-and-scary mixed. I'd never used a laptop. Ar called them MODERN ATTENTION-SUCKING CARBUNCLES.

Merry took my arm, pulled me over to an empty desk towards the back and plumped down in the one beside it. The Prefect twins took the front desks, their backs straight as rods. Then, Miss Smith marched through the desks to the front of the room and stood by the whiteboard.

'We've got her all day,' whispered Merry. 'Worst luck.' One of the Prefects swivelled round, put her finger to her lips and fixed Merry with a glare.

'Good morning, children,' Miss Smith looked around the room. Her eyes rested on me for a moment, then passed on.

'Good morning, Miss Smith,' chanted the class.

'Registration.' Miss Smith picked up a book and a pen and began calling out names.

'Chloe Adams?'

'Yes, miss,' replied one of the Prefect girls.

'Zoe Adams?'

'Yes, miss,' said the other.

Miss Smith called out the names of the class in alphabetical order.

'Jack Andrews...'

My face began to burn as we got closer and closer to the 'Bs'. I dug my nails into the palms of my hands.

'O-*failure* Bottom?'

A snigger echoed round the room.

'Yes, miss,' I whispered, keeping my head down.

'Speak up, O-*failure*!' Miss Smith glared round the room and the sniggering died away. 'Harry Clark... Merry Jones...'

'Yes,' said Merry, looking bored.

'Ay beg your pardon, Merry?' said Miss Smith.

'Yes, miss,' muttered Merry.

'Kevin Miller... Emma Murray... Sophie Scott... Alice Stewart... Justin Taylor...'

At the end of registration, Miss Smith closed the book.

'So today, we welcome a new class member,' she said. 'O-*failure* Bottom. Stand up, please, O-*failure*.'

I slowly stood up. It was like I was seventy feet tall with green hair, the way the whole class stared at me.

'Perhaps we'd like to explain to the class why we aren't wearing uniform?'

'I—I had one... only I lost it.'

'*Lost* it?'

'It got, um, stolen.'

'Hmmm,' Miss Smith said, her eyebrows raised high. 'You may sit down.'

I slipped down on to my chair and wiped my sweaty hands on my jeans. If *this* was what proper school was like, maybe Ar had a point. Merry winked at me again, and I felt a bit better.

'English literature,' announced Miss Smith. 'Get out your copies of *Hamlet*.'

A groan echoed round the room.

'Divide into two teams. Team A, chosen by Chloe Adams, will choose five people as actors to rehearse the opening scene of *Hamlet* and perform it to the class.'

A little quiver of happiness ran through me. *I can do that.*

'Team B,' continued Miss Smith, 'chosen by Zoe Adams, will use the laptops to research what they believe to be the most well-known speech from the play, print it out and read it aloud to the class.'

The quiver of happiness turned to a shiver of fear. I didn't even know how to turn a laptop on, let alone how to use one. I gazed desperately at Chloe Adams, willing her to choose me for her team.

Zoe marched over to stand by the laptops and Chloe took her place by the desks. One by one, they called out names, and the children got up and stood with them. Each time Zoe's grey eyes slid past me, I breathed a sigh of relief. Each time Chloe called another name to join her team, my heart plummeted.

In the end, there was just Merry and me left. I dug my nails into my palms. *Please, Chloe Adams... please choose me.*

'Merry Jones,' said Chloe.

Zoe rolled her eyes and jerked her head at me. I stood up and crossed the room towards the last laptop in the row, every step feeling like it was weighed down with lead.

HAMLET:

Shakespeare's longest play

'Right,' Zoe said in her cool voice. 'Start researching. And no talking.'

She sat at the only free laptop—next to mine—and began tapping at the keys. All along the line, the others did the same. I stared at the laptop screen. What did I have to do? I turned to watch Zoe. Maybe if I did what she was doing, I'd be OK. Zoe pounded the keys and the script of *Hamlet* rolled down the screen.

I was so busy staring at it that I didn't notice that she'd seen me looking. She took a sharp breath and waved her arm in the air.

'Miss Smith—?'

'Yes?' Looking annoyed at being interrupted, Miss Smith came over. 'What is it, Zoe?'

'It's *her*,' hissed Zoe. 'She's *copying*.'

'I—I wasn't! It's just that I—'

'Quiet!' snapped Miss Smith. 'Ay don't know what you got up to at your last school, O-*failure*, but we don't *copy* in this one!'

'But I—'

Miss Smith grabbed my desk and pulled it, with much squeaking, a metre away from Zoe's desk. 'There. Now keep your eyes on your own work.' And she marched back to the whiteboard.

The screen in front of me was all blurry. I rubbed the tears from my eyes and tried to concentrate. If I didn't produce *something*, I'd be in even more trouble. To buy time, I began to click on the keys of the laptop, carefully spelling out *Hamlet*. Miraculously, the letters appeared in a box on screen. *Maybe I can do it after all.* Except... nothing happened after that. I stared and stared at the word, willing the script to appear, but it didn't. I glanced at the others. They were all clicking away and reading from the screen, their lips moving.

'Three more minutes, teams,' said Miss Smith. 'Team B, you should be printing out your chosen scene, now.'

My palms were wet with fear. I had no scene to print, and no idea how to print anything, even if I *did*. All the way down the line of laptops, square machines under the desks hummed and buzzed, and sheets of paper slid out into the trays.

I looked under my own desk. There was the printer, but it was silent. Sitting on top of it was a pile of fresh clean paper. With trembling fingers, I picked up a sheet and, making sure that no one was watching, slipped it into the printer tray and pretended to pull it out.

'Time's up,' announced Miss Smith. 'Come back, and stay in your teams.'

Zoe was still glaring thunderbolts at me. She made a great show of hiding her paper against her chest, as if she was terrified I'd read it. I carefully folded my blank paper in four, so no one could see there was nothing printed on it.

'Right, Team A,' said Miss Smith. 'Come to the front and perform your scene.'

Five people, including Merry, got to their feet, holding their books, and began to read. It was the opening scene from *Hamlet*, where Horatio and Marcellus see the ghost of Hamlet's father. If only Chloe had chosen me for this—I could do it standing on my head. I'd watched Ar and Ma perform it loads of times and my sticky memory remembered every line.

Justin, Chloe, Harry and Emma all read in a monotone, very seriously, stumbling over the long words. Just for once, I missed Ar's booming voice, and Ma's dramatic gestures. The only good bit was when Merry—as the Ghost—appeared. The Ghost had no lines to speak, so the actor had to show everything through mime. Merry was a really scary Ghost. When she raised her finger to her lips, she almost seemed to shimmer and go see-through, and a chill ran across the back of my neck. At the end of the performance, everyone clapped politely. I couldn't help clapping extra hard, Merry was so good, and Zoe frowned.

'Now,' said Miss Smith. 'Swap around, please. Team A, come to the front of the class.'

Clutching my sheet of blank paper, I moved with the others to stand beside Miss Smith. Zoe turned to glare at me again. Could she hear my heart thudding fit to bust? I swallowed, hard. Then a bell rang.

Miss Smith checked her watch. 'Ay see that time has caught up with us. We'll do Team A's performance after break.'

Saved by the bell.

Some of the children made a beeline for the laptops and started clicking away, but Merry grabbed my arm.

'Let's go outside—it's the only chance we get.'

I hesitated. No way was I leaving my sheet of blank paper on my desk. What if Zoe picked it up? Carefully, I tucked it into my jeans pocket.

'How did you get on with finding your scene?' Merry asked when we got to the playground.

'Oh... OK,' I mumbled.

It'd be too embarrassing to admit to Merry that I didn't know how to use a laptop, especially as we were just starting to be friends. She might think I was weird and drop me. Quickly, I changed the subject.

'You were brilliant as the Ghost!'

Merry grinned. 'I was, wasn't I? I wish we had more chance to act at school.'

Chloe and Zoe Adams marched towards us, their silver braces gleaming.

'I'd be careful hanging round with *her*, Merry Jones.' Chloe's blue eyes were alight with spite.

Merry frowned. 'What's that s'posed to mean?'

'She's a *cheat*,' chimed in Zoe.

'I'm *not*!' I whispered.

'You are *so*. I *saw* you.'

Merry stepped forward. 'Leave her alone, Zoe!'

'Ooh, Merry Jones to the rescue!' Chloe sneered. 'Showing off, as usual!'

Zoe put her arms out in front of her, squeezed her eyes tight shut and began to moan.

'I'm Merry Joooooones, the ghaaaastly Ghoooooost!'

Chloe laughed like a hyena.

'Why don't you run off to join that travelling theatre on the Common, Merry Jones?' said Zoe.

'Our mum said they were *awful* actors, like you!' said Chloe. 'And they even got the play wrong!'

'Our dad said they must've been *drunk*,' grinned Zoe. 'The leading man couldn't even stay upright—fell flat on his face on the stage!'

My insides boiled and bubbled like a volcano about to explode. How *dare* they make fun of Ar, when it was *their* parents, chanting and chucking tomatoes, that made him slip and break his leg? I opened my mouth to say so, but before I could speak a hand landed on my shoulder.

'What's going on here?' It was Miss Smith.

'It's the new girl and Merry Jones, causing trouble, miss!' said Chloe. She turned to her twin. 'Isn't that right?' Zoe nodded like a puppet.

'We weren't—' I began, but Miss Smith interrupted, her cold eyes boring into me.

'You again, O-*failure*? *Not* exactly the best start.' She turned to Merry. 'And as for *you*, Merry Jones—you

62

should know better. You'll never make a Prefect, at this rate.'

'Fee didn't do a thing!' Merry said, then muttered under her breath: 'And the very last thing *I* want is to be a... *Perfect*.'

'Back inside, both of you!' Miss Smith's voice was icicle cold. 'Merry Jones, you will write *Prefect*—spelt correctly—one hundred times on the whiteboard.'

She turned to me.

'As for *you*, O-*failure*—you'd better practise reading out that scene you've so *carefully* researched. Ay'm sure everyone's looking forward to hearing it.'

Chloe and Zoe's mocking eyes bored into the back of my head. I swallowed, hard, and followed Merry indoors.

MOTTO:

*a short sentence to express the belief
of an organization or group*

Perfect
Perfect
Perfect

'Um, Merry...' I glanced at the classroom door. Any
minute now, the bell would go for the end of break, and
Miss Smith would see.

'OK, OK!' Merry grinned and wiped at the rows of 'er's'
with the elbow of her blazer, then switched them round. I
fingered the sheet of blank paper in my pocket.

'Anyhow,' Merry busily swapped letters, '*Perfects* is a much
better word for those two. They're so *creepy*! Perfect uniforms...
perfect hair... butter-wouldn't-melt-in-their-mouths...'

'Why do they act so important? They can't be much
older than us.'

'Dunno.' Merry added the last 're' just as the bell rang.
'Just shows what happens if you give some people a badge

64

to wear. All I *do* know is that Chloe and Zoe used to be just like the rest of us, until their Ceremonies.'

'What's a Ceremony?'

'It's a new thing. You have to go to the—'

Merry broke off as Miss Smith walked in, marched up to the whiteboard, grabbed the eraser and wiped all Merry's efforts off.

'Right,' she said. 'Team B, it's your turn to perform.'

Zoe elbowed her way through the group to stand right at the front. I wriggled to the back, behind her. She was even taller than me. With any luck, no one'd notice me.

One by one, Miss Smith called people to stand in front of the class and read their scene. Jack Andrews performed *Alas, poor Yorick!*, where Hamlet spoke to a skull, in a high, squeaky voice. I couldn't help thinking of Ar, how he stood so still in that scene, and how his deep voice dropped to a whisper with the sadness of it all.

Finally, it was Zoe's turn.

'Which scene did you choose, Zoe?' said Miss Smith.

Zoe smirked across the room at Chloe and waved her sheet of paper. 'Why, the scene with *Ophelia*, miss,' she said, staring at me. 'You know, the one where she goes *mad*.'

My face burned and I stared at the floor, while the others sniggered. Zoe's reading seemed to go on forever. She hammed the scene up just as if it was a comedy rather than a tragedy, Chloe staring and grinning at me. Finally, it was over, and Zoe sauntered back, giggling and high-fiving her twin.

Miss Smith turned to the class.

'Thank you, Zoe. A most *interesting* interpretation. And now, we'll—what is it, Choe?'

Chloe waved her arm.

'Please, Miss Smith—Ophelia hasn't read hers!'

Miss Smith scanned our group. 'O-*failure*? Where are you?'

Zoe shoved me to the front. 'Here she is, Miss Smith.'

My tummy felt like a big ball of clay was stuck inside it.

'Which scene did you choose, O-*failure*?' said Miss Smith.

A whisper of an idea wafted into my mind. Slowly, with trembling fingers, I pulled out my sheet of blank paper and unfolded it. I glanced down at it, as if to remind myself.

'Act Three, Scene One.' I tried to keep my voice steady.

'Ah yes,' said Miss Smith. 'A most important scene in the play.'

Zoe frowned. I tried to imagine that I was crouching at the side of the stage at Bottom's, ready to prompt, the whole scene printed out like a photograph in my memory. Ar's words rang in my ears: *Don't MUMBLE, Ophelia. ENUNCIATE!*

I took a deep breath and raised my chin. Slowly, I began to recite, staring at the blank sheet of paper.

'To be, or not to be: that is the question:
Whether 'tis nobler in the mind to suffer
The slings and arrows of outrageous fortune,
Or to take arms against a sea of troubles,
And by opposing end them?'

I knew the words by heart, and I said them the way Ar did, very simply. By the time I got to the end, the class had gone silent. I carefully folded my empty sheet of paper, tucked it into my pocket and walked back to join the others, my knees shaking like jelly.

The silence was broken by the sound of clapping. Were Chloe and Zoe mocking me again? But it was Merry. She gave a huge whoop and a thumbs-up.

Miss Smith glared at her. 'We don't expect such a hullabaloo, Merry Jones!'

'Sorry, miss—but she was *brilliant*, wasn't she, miss?'

Miss Smith wrinkled up her lips, but I felt all warm and glowy. This was what it must be like to have a proper friend, someone who was on your side. I was so happy in that moment that I ignored Zoe Adams' furious face, and the way she was whispering to her twin sister.

Lunch was *great*. What with the relief of getting through the reading, I was starving. The canteen was spotless, just like the rest of the school, and the food was the sort I always wished Ar and Ma would buy, only they never did. We queued up with our trays and picked up plastic knives, forks and spoons from containers on the side. Soon, rows and rows of burgers appeared, all exactly the same. Merry picked up a burger and I did. Then, we got dishes of ice cream, and bottles of fizzy drinks. We carried our full trays to one of the long tables. The not-so-good thing was that Zoe and Chloe plumped down in the seats opposite Merry and me. I picked up my plastic knife and fork.

'Wait, Fee!' Merry grabbed my arm.

'What?'

'*Duh!*' Chloe rolled her eyes at Zoe. 'Where's her manners?'

Zoe giggled. 'Some people are brought up in *pigsties*.'

'Shut *up*, Zoe!' Merry jerked her head towards the end of the room, where Miss Smith and the other teachers sat. Miss Smith stood up, and the room fell silent. She clasped her hands together as if she was saying a prayer, raised her eyes to the ceiling, and the whole room chanted along with her.

'Plasticus stupendus est,
Diversus periculosus est.'

The words sounded familiar. Of course—I glanced at Merry's blazer. There they were, embroidered over the pocket. Only there was some other memory... what was it? Before I could think about it any more, Miss Smith sat down and everyone began to eat. The burgers were delicious—they were the sort that, as soon as you finished one, you wanted another, and another.

'What were those words?' I asked Merry.

'Stopford motto,' mumbled Merry, her mouth full.

'What do they mean?'

Chloe stared over at me. 'You mean, you don't *know*?'

'She wouldn't ask, if she knew.' Merry turned to me. 'It's Latin. The first bit—*plasticus stupendus est*— means *plastic is fantastic—*'

'Why's that the Stopford motto?'

'Because of the factory, of course!' said Zoe.

'What factory?'

Zoe looked surprised. 'The factory up on the hill. You must've seen it.'

'The building with the chimney? But what's that got to do with the Stopford motto?'

'The factory makes things out of plastic,' explained Merry.

'What sort of things?'

'Oh—everything. Carrier bags, drinks bottles, all the stuff for our houses...'

'Don't your parents work there, O-*failure*?' Chloe said innocently. 'All *our* parents do, even Merry Jones's. Anyone who's *anyone* works at the factory.'

'Ignore her,' said Merry. 'She's such a snob.'

Chloe glowered. 'If it wasn't for the factory, this town would be *nothing*. And it's all thanks to Professor Potkettle.'

I must have looked blank, because Merry explained. 'Professor Potkettle's the owner of the factory.'

'He's a world-famous scientist,' said Zoe. 'A genius.'

'And he's *ever* so generous,' said Chloe.

'He didn't just build the factory,' said Zoe. 'He built Stopford too. That's why we live in such nice houses and have all the latest stuff.'

'He founded this school,' added Chloe. 'It's thanks to Professor Potkettle we've got the laptops, and the latest gym equipment, and the swimming pool...'

'Anyhow,' Merry muttered, dropping her plastic knife and fork with a clatter, 'you'll find out all about it tomorrow—'

'Tomorrow?'

Before Merry could reply, Chloe hissed: '*Shhhhh!*' and Miss Smith stood up again.

This time I knew what to do. I copied everyone else as they put their hands together and chanted the Latin words once more:

'*Plasticus stupendus est,*
Diversus periculosus est.'

—and then I remembered where I'd heard the chant before. The last words of it—*diversus perculosus est*— were the ones the audience chanted during the disastrous performance of *Macbeth*: the words that rang in my ears as Ar slipped on the rotten tomatoes and got taken off to the hospital.

Merry skipped ahead as we returned to class, so I asked Chloe.

'What does the second bit mean? "*Diversus periculosus est*"?'

'I should've thought *you* would know.' Chloe looked at me in a funny way.

'What d'you mean?'

'Look in the mirror,' Zoe said.

'I don't under—'

Zoe smirked and nudged Chloe.

'Let's see,' she counted off on her fingers. 'Wrong clothes...'

'Tatty shoes...' giggled Chloe.

'Scary hair...'

'Weird name...'

Suddenly, Zoe bent towards me and pulled the sheet of paper from my pocket. I tried to grab it back, but Chloe grabbed *me*. Her fingernails stabbed into my wrists.

'What do we have here?' Zoe slowly unfolded the paper. Then her eyes narrowed.

'What is it?' said Chloe, tightening her fingers till my wrists burned.

Zoe waved the empty paper.

'There's nothing on it! Where's your print-out?'

I said nothing.

'I reckon,' grinned Chloe, 'She doesn't know how to use a laptop.'

'That's why she was copying me!' Zoe's eyes lit up in triumph. 'Now we know why she's called O-*failure*!'

'O-*failure Bottom*—*bottom* of the class!' Chloe twisted my arms sharply. 'She doesn't belong in Stopford. She's seriously *weird*!'

She jerked me round so I was facing them both. Their pale faces were cold and cruel.

'So, O-*failure*,' Chloe whispered. 'You want us to tell you what *diversus periculosus est* means, do you?'

'Well, listen up,' whispered Zoe. 'It means...'

Then, in chorus, they chanted:

'*Diversus perculosus est...*

Different is DANGEROUS!'

DANGEROUS:

unsafe; likely to cause problems, harm, or injury

Afternoon lessons seemed to go on forever. My wrists still burned from Chloe's grip, and Zoe and Chloe's words thudded round and round in my head like a horrible drumbeat:

Different is Dangerous. Different is Dangerous. Different is Dangerous.

Why couldn't I be like everyone else? And *was* I somehow... dangerous? I sat all scrunched up in my chair, to make myself as small as possible. The more invisible I was, the less likely everyone would notice how different I was. Merry kept glancing over at me. Maybe *she* thought I was dangerous, too. Maybe she wished she didn't have to sit by me. I kept my head down and squeezed my eyes tight to stop the tears coming out. If Zoe and Chloe saw me crying, they'd never stop mocking me.

At last, the bell rang and Miss Smith told us to put away our work.

'Don't forget—tomorrow we meet inside the Potkettle Institute at nine o'clock sharp. We will have the honour of meeting our generous benefactor and owner of the factory, the renowned scientist, Professor Potkettle. And ay can tell you, the Professor will have some *surprises* for you.'

A murmur of excitement swept round the classroom.

'Ay hope ay don't need to remind you,' added Miss Smith with a sniff, 'that you will be representing Stopford School. So ay expect only the best behaviour from each and every one of you.'

She looked round the room, her cold eyes resting on me. 'Ay expect you all, of course, to wear Stopford School uniform. Anyone turning up otherwise will be sent straight home!'

Out of the corner of my eye, I saw Zoe nudging Chloe, staring in my direction and whispering *those words*. No way would I be allowed on the school visit, dressed the way I was.

As everyone picked up their bags, whispering excitedly about the visit, I miserably hauled my rucksack on to my shoulder and headed for the door. I'd tell Ma how unhappy I was at school, and if she wouldn't let me stay at home, I'd tell Ar what Zoe and Chloe said about me being different and dangerous, and he'd talk Ma round.

As I walked out of the school entrance, someone grabbed my arm, and I shook it off. If Zoe and Chloe had followed me, if they said just *one more* horrible thing about me, I'd...

'Fee! Wait!' It was Merry.

'I—I've got to get home,' I muttered. 'My parents will be expecting me.'

Merry's green eyes were full of puzzlement. 'What's the matter, Fee? You've been acting really strange all afternoon...'

'*Strange*, am I?' The words burst out of my mouth before I could stop them. 'Don't you mean *different*?'

Merry shook her head. 'What are you talking about?'

'Don't pretend!' I hissed.

'What're you on about? What's wrong?'

I pointed up at the words carved above the school entrance.

'*Diversus periculosus est.* Different is dangerous! Only I can't *help* being different.'

'Of course you're different!' Merry suddenly grinned, and it was like the sun came out all over her face. 'That's why I like you!'

'Wh-what?'

'Different is *interesting*! Look at you—you're covered in freckles, like you're allowed outside all the time. And your hair's the colour of strawberries, and wild, like it's got a mind of its own. And even better, you can *act*. D'you want to be like the *Perfects*—?'

Merry waved an arm at Zoe and Chloe, who brushed past us with their noses stuck in the air as if we smelt of something disgusting.

'No,' I muttered. 'But I don't want to be weird either. I want to fit in. I want to go on the school visit, just like the rest of you!'

Merry stopped and frowned. Then, the dimple appeared in her cheek and her green eyes sparkled.

'Come with me!' And she turned and headed off down the road. I stayed where I was.

'Come *on*, Fee!'

'Come on where?'

'Back to my place!' Merry said. 'I'll explain when we get there!'

'I can't,' I said. 'Ar and... I mean, my parents—will be waiting for me.'

'Ring them on your phone, then. Tell them I've invited you to tea.'

I felt all muddled up—or DISCOMBOBULATED, as Ar would call it. A bit of me was thrilled that Merry had asked me home for tea, just as if she was my friend. But another bit knew that Ma would be waiting for me back at the Pantechnicon. And yet another bit still felt scared about being different and not having a phone of my own.

'I—I don't have my phone with me,' I said.

Merry burrowed in her rucksack. 'Borrow mine, then.'

She pulled out a tiny, slim phone in a sparkly pink case, and handed it to me. I stared down at it. It was so pretty and light—so different from Ar and Ma's heavy old phones.

'Hurry *up*!' Merry skipped about.

I didn't know Ar's or Ma's numbers. I'd never had to call them before. I turned my back to Merry, pretend to stab numbers into the phone, and raised it to my ear.

'Hello... Mum,' I said. 'I've been asked to tea with someone from school. Is that OK?'

I paused for a moment, as if listening to the reply. 'No, I won't be long. Promise! Bye...'

I turned back to Merry and handed her the phone.

'All OK?'

'Yeah. Thanks. Only they said I mustn't stay for more than half an hour.'

If I didn't get back quickly, Ma might come looking for me. But if I raced back really fast, I'd only be a bit late.

Merry set off at a run. I followed her along Sycamore Road. I couldn't help staring at the rows of pretty houses, all just the same.

'Where do *you* live, Fee?'

I hesitated. Merry might think different was interesting, but if she found out I lived in a beaten-up van on the Common, she might change her mind. I remembered the streets Ma and I passed as we walked to school. Which would be the furthest from where we were now?

'Um... Magnolia Drive,' I said.

'Oh—that's where the Perfects live. Which number?'

Just my luck. What if the number I said was Zoe and Chloe's house?

'I—I don't remember,' I muttered.

Merry stared at me. 'How can you not know which number you live at?'

'We... we've only just moved there,' I swallowed. I *hated* lying. But right now I couldn't bear the thought of losing my new friend.

Merry pushed open a white gate with the number twenty-two on it and ran up to the yellow front door. I stared at the neat white fence, the gravel path, the perfectly green lawn with its borders of roses. The house was just as pretty, painted the softest blue. It was like a child's picture of a house, with its front door in the middle and its square windows on either side. Looking up at its neatly tiled roof, I almost expected to see my rainbow, ending right above it.

Merry pulled a key out of her pocket, fitted it in the lock and turned it.

'Hurry *up*, Fee!' she said.

I hurried down the gravel path and in at Merry's front door.

ANYONE WHO'S ANYONE:

all the most important people

We were in a porch, with hooks for hanging things, and a row of shoes and boots lined up on the floor underneath them. Merry hung her blazer on one of the hooks and kicked off her shoes. I pulled off my trainers. They looked so scruffy compared with the neat line of polished shoes and shiny plastic boots. I pushed them into a corner, behind the umbrella stand, and followed Merry as she set off along an immaculate hall.

The house was so *quiet*.

'Aren't your parents home?' I whispered.

'Nope.' Merry headed towards a door at the end of the hall. 'They're up at the factory. They start work early in the morning and they won't be back until after midnight.'

I breathed a sigh of relief. I wouldn't have to pretend to them, too. Lucky, *lucky* Merry. What must it be like to have a whole house to yourself, with no one else there, and your very own key to the door?

'Why do they work so late?' I asked.

'To earn money, of course!' Merry pushed open the door.

I followed her, then stopped. We were in a big, light space filled with white cupboards from floor to ceiling. Sunshine flooded in from a skylight. There was a long white table, a huge double sink and a cooker with *six* gas rings for cooking on. A massive white fridge hummed in the corner. What would Merry think if she saw our kitchen in the Pantechnicon—the one greasy gas ring, the sink we all had to wash in? My face burned at the thought.

'So will *your* parents work at the factory?' Merry pulled open the fridge door and took out a cardboard pizza box.

Chloe's words flashed into my mind. *Anyone who's anyone works at the factory.*

'Y-yes. I expect they will. Once they've sorted everything out at... at home.'

Merry opened a drawer and pulled out some scissors. Taking the pizza out of the box, she cut the plastic wrapping off it and tapped the top of a white bin. A lid sprang open and she tossed the wrapping inside and pushed it shut. Ma kept all *our* rubbish in a bag hanging from a hook below the sink.

Merry tipped the pizza on to a dish and opened the door of a microwave oven. She placed the pizza inside on a round glass shelf, slammed the door and pressed some buttons. Immediately, a light came on and the pizza began to spin round. I stared at it, hypnotized. I'd never actually seen a microwave working before.

'While that's cooking, shall I show you around?' Merry said.

'Yes please!'

There were rooms for *everything*. A huge room just for sitting in, with massive sofas and soft, thick carpets and a TV, its screen as big as the Pantechnicon's whole windscreen. A glass door led out to a back garden surrounded by a high fence, its flowerbeds waving with perfect roses. Behind another door in the hall was a smaller room with desks and laptops, and yet another room was full of machines, with screens mounted on them.

'Our gym.' Merry switched on one of the machines and it began to move, like the escalators in the department store. 'Go on, have a go!'

Clutching the bar above, I stepped on. It felt so strange, like the ground was moving under my feet, making me go the way *it* wanted to go. Only it wasn't like real ground. More like a conveyor belt, smoother-than-smooth.

'But what's it *for*?' I asked.

'Exercise, of course,' laughed Merry.

'Why don't you exercise outside?'

'I dunno.' Merry shrugged. 'It's just a rule. Professor Potkettle says we can go to school, and go to the shops, but that's about it.'

No wonder everyone's faces were so pale, if they didn't spend time outside.

'What—what about the Common? People came to the—'

I'd nearly given myself away. Luckily, Merry didn't seem to notice.

'Professor Potkettle says people can only go to the Common once a year, for the Entertainment. And only our parents, not us. He says the air on the Common's bad to breathe.'

'So you never go down to the woods, or the cove?' That must be why the beach was always empty.

'The cove?' Merry's smile faded and her green eyes opened wide. 'You mean, you've *been* down there?'

'Er... yes.'

'*Wow.*' Merry stared at me as I was from another planet. 'Professor Potkettle says it's dirty and dangerous. You didn't... didn't see the Ghost from the Sea?'

'The... what?'

'Professor Potkettle says there's a ghost that lives in the sea,' Merry whispered. 'And it haunts the beach.'

I remembered the *thing* I saw in the water. Was that what she was talking about?

'What's—what's it like, this Ghost from the Sea?'

'I dunno exactly, cos I've never seen it, thank goodness! But Professor Potkettle says that if you *do*—see it, I mean— you're *doomed.*'

'W-what?'

'If you see the Ghost from the Sea, bad things happen to you, and to your family!'

UNIFORM:

the same: not different in any way

I went cold. Bad things *had* started to happen after I saw the thing in the sea. My uniform was stolen. Ar and Ma had that huge argument. And Zoe and Chloe had picked on me. I gave myself a shake. *Don't be daft, Fee.* After all, plenty of bad things had happened *before* I saw it too—the horrible performance of *Macbeth*, for a start—and Ar breaking his leg. And good things had happened too—Ma sending me to school, and meeting Merry. Maybe this Professor Potkettle was wrong.

'Why do you all have to do what Professor Potkettle says?' I asked.

Merry shrugged again. 'It's always been that way since we came to Stopford. If we obey the rules, we get all the good stuff.'

Before I could ask any more, a loud *ping* came from the kitchen, and Merry switched the exercise machine off.

'C'mon, pizza's ready!'

I jumped down and followed her back to the kitchen. The pizza had stopped spinning. Merry opened the door and took it out. Wafts of cheesy loveliness drifted around the kitchen. Merry cut the pizza into slices and handed me a plate. I glanced at the clock on the wall.

'I can't stay much longer, Merry. My parents said—'

'OK, OK! We can eat it really quick, up in my room. I want to show you something!'

Merry set off up the stairs, which led to a big, light landing. She opened a door and I followed her into a room. For a few moments, I forgot everything—Ma and Ar waiting for me, the Ghost from the Sea, even the plate of pizza in my hands. Because Merry's room was *beautiful*. The walls were the palest apricot colour and there was a proper bed, with fairylights twinkling over the buttoned headboard and a soft, billowing apricot-coloured duvet. A huge white rug—so soft that my feet almost disappeared in it—covered the floor. There was a dressing table with a mirror and drawers, and an enormous wardrobe. The window had long, soft curtains, the same colour as the duvet, and out of it you could see all the other Stopford houses in their neat rows. What would Merry say if she ever saw *my* 'bedroom'—a tatty bunk bed that turned into a bench during the day?

'This is—this is *cool*,' I whispered.

Merry shrugged. 'It's OK. It'll be changed soon.'

'Changed?'

'Don't you know? We can swap all our stuff as often as we want to. We just buy new stuff from the factory, ever so cheap!'

'But...' I gazed around the beautiful room. 'This is all good as new. What happens to it?'

'Professor Potkettle arranges everything. We just take it back to the factory.'

Merry shoved the last of her pizza into her mouth so she looked like a chipmunk. I took a bite of mine, the warm, salty cheese stretching in yellow strands. Merry pulled a tissue from a box, wiped her hands, and headed to the wardrobe. I gazed at the racks and racks of clothes inside it.

'Are they... all yours?'

Merry laughed. 'Of course!' She rummaged through the hangers. I swallowed the last of my pizza and wiped my sticky fingers on my jeans.

'Thanks, Merry, that was *great*,' I said. 'But I've got to go, now.'

'Just a second!' Merry was still rummaging.

'No, really, I—'

Merry pulled out a blazer. 'Found it!'

She took it from its hanger and tossed it over to me. I tried not to touch it with the tips of my cheesy fingers.

'What d'you reckon?' Merry looked at me expectantly.

'It's... very nice.' What was I supposed to say?

'It might be a bit tight on you,' Merry appraised me. 'I grew out of it before Christmas.'

Slowly, it dawned on me. 'You mean—?'

Merry grinned, the dimple appearing in her cheek. 'Yup! If you can fit into it, it's yours!'

Suddenly my eyes were full of tears and Merry shimmered and blurred. I tried to speak, to say thank you, only my voice had gone all funny. Merry didn't notice. She rummaged in the wardrobe again. I cleared my throat and

wiped my eyes on my sleeve as she pulled out a white shirt
and a grey skirt.

'These are too small for me too. And you can borrow
my spare tie.'

'Th-thanks...' I muttered.

'You'd better try them on.'

Automatically, because I was still trying not to cry, I
unzipped my jeans.

'Bathroom's across the hall,' Merry said.

'Oh. Yes.'

I was so used to dressing and undressing in front of Ar and
Ma because there wasn't anywhere else to do it. My face hot,
I grabbed the clothes and left the room. The bathroom was
huge, with grey tiles over all the walls. There was a shower
cubicle and a massive white bath on four clawed feet. The
towels were thick and fluffy and white, and one wall was
all mirror, so I couldn't help looking at myself.

No wonder Chloe and Zoe had laughed at me. My hair
looked like it hadn't been brushed in weeks, and my sweatshirt and jeans had little patches of paint—and mud—on
them. I carefully shut the bathroom door, pulled my clothes
off and dropped them on the floor. Then I got into Merry's
uniform. I could only just do up the buttons on the shirt,
but the tie would hide the gaps. The skirt wouldn't fasten,
even if I breathed in, so I twizzled the fastening round my
waist to the back, so no one could see it was open. I shrugged
on the blazer. It was a bit too small as well, but if I left it
unbuttoned, it'd be fine. My bony wrists stuck out from
the sleeves, but if I hunched up my shoulders...

I stared at my reflection in the mirror, and a rather scruffy, freckled schoolgirl stared back. Tomorrow, I'd plait my hair neatly and scrub my fingernails.

Tomorrow, I'd fit in.

CHAMELEON:

a lizard whose skin changes colour to
match the colour of its surroundings

When I opened my eyes next morning, the first thing
I heard was Ar and Ma arguing. It began yesterday, when I
arrived home late, and the arguing exploded when Ar saw
me in Merry's uniform.

'My daughter will not take CHARITY from strangers!'
he roared. But Ma took my side, probably as an excuse to
go on disagreeing.

'She *should* wear a uniform. And if you hadn't used up
the last of our money on *that taxi*, I'd have been able to buy
her another. She ought to *fit in* at school.'

'FIT IN?' yelled Ar. 'Why should she FIT IN?'

'Because that's what uniforms are *for*,' snapped Ma.

'Bottoms don't FIT IN,' boomed Ar. 'We STAND OUT.
We are INDIVIDUALS, not CHAMELEONS!'

Right now, I would have *loved* to be a chameleon: to blend
in so no one noticed me. Much better than strutting around
like a peacock, the way Ar did—or used to, before he broke

his leg—or wearing weird, wafty costumes that everyone stared at, like Ma. If people noticed you too much, it was dangerous. Look what had happened during *Macbeth*.

Suddenly, I saw the clock. It was almost eight-thirty! Ma had *promised* to wake me at eight. I scrambled out of my sleeping bag in a panic and hurried over to the sink in my pyjamas, clambering over Ar's plaster.

'More haste, less SPEED, Ophelia!'

'I'm late!' I scrubbed at my face with my flannel.

'You don't have to be there until *nine*.' Ma looked flustered. She must've been so busy arguing with Ar that she forgot.

'I *told* you, I've got to leave early, cos I'm meeting my friend.'

I'd never said *my friend* before because I'd never had one. And Merry *was* my friend: not only was she lending me her uniform, but she'd said I was to meet her outside her house, so we could walk to the Potkettle Institute together.

'Anyhow,' Ar growled on, 'what does it matter if she's a little TARDY?'

'It's a school visit, Ar,' I mumbled, through a mouthful of toothpaste. 'We're going to the Potkettle Institute.'

'POTKETTLE?' rumbled Ar. 'And what, pray, is THAT?'

'Professor Potkettle's a scientist. He owns the factory on the hill.'

I clambered back over Ar's plaster to my bunk, grabbed Merry's uniform from where I'd folded it over the front seat of the Pantechnicon, and wriggled into it, making sure the skirt fastening was at the back, under my blazer, and that the tie covered the bulging front buttons. Then, I scraped a brush through my curls and, my fingers stumbling, braided them into two neat plaits.

'Got to go,' I muttered. 'Bye, Ar. Bye, Ma.'

Ma forced a couple of biscuits and a glass of milk on me. I gulped down the milk, shoved the biscuits into my rucksack, climbed over the front seat and jumped down into the grass. Ar was still bellowing, but soon I couldn't hear it any more as I ran, my eyes stinging from the fumes, over the Common towards Stopford.

The Potkettle Institute was a modern, square building just past the High Street. There were two great pillars on either side of the grand entrance, each carved with the Stopford motto: on the left-hand pillar, *PLASTICUS STUPENDUS EST*; and on the right-hand one: *DIVERSUS PERICULOSUS EST*. I glanced down at my blazer and tie. Today, for once, I wouldn't be different.

'This is going to be an *adventure*!'

Beside me, Merry fizzed with excitement. She didn't seem bothered that I'd made us late. 'We hardly ever get to go to on visits. And Professor Potkettle's got a surprise, Miss Smith says, about plastic!'

I wondered what was so surprising about plastic, but I couldn't help feeling a bit excited too.

As Merry and I hurried up to the entrance, a pair of enormous glass doors hissed open, then we were in a room with nothing in it except a long white reception desk. A large security guard, with a bristly ginger moustache, and wearing a blue boiler suit and heavy boots, sat at the desk.

'Visit?' he grunted.

We nodded. Blue Boiler Suit tapped his watch. 'Late.'

'Sorry,' I muttered.

Blue Boiler Suit jerked his head at us. 'Rucksacks.'

Merry and I took off our rucksacks and pushed them over the desk towards him. He opened Merry's first, rifling around inside for ages as if he expected to find a bomb. Soon all the stuff from Merry's rucksack was spread over the desk: a pretty blue plastic pencil case, a brand-new notebook, a packet of tissues, her phone in its pink case, and a plastic bottle of water. Blue Boiler Suit picked up the phone and dropped it into a drawer.

'Hey—' Merry began.

'Rules.' Blue Boiler Suit bundled Merry's belongings back into her rucksack and pushed it over the desk towards her.

Then he opened mine. Out came a scruffy exercise book, a couple of leaking pens and Ma's broken biscuits. His face puckered in disgust as he pulled his hand out, stained with ink and covered in crumbs. Then he picked up my rucksack between two fingers, as if it was too dirty to handle further, and dropped it on to the desk in front of me. I zipped it up and wriggled into the straps, my cheeks burning.

Blue Boiler Suit unhooked a walkie-talkie from his belt and spoke into it.

'Latecomers,' he said, and someone at the other end answered, with a lot of hissing and crackling. A door at the far end of the room opened, and a plump woman security guard appeared, wearing a green boiler suit, and beckoned us through the door.

We were in a theatre—a theatre Ar would give anything to have. The rest of the class sat on rows of white plastic chairs lined up in front of a massive stage. Long curtains hung in front of the stage and a pair of white plastic speakers stood on either side, facing the audience.

Zoe and Chloe sat upright on either side of Miss Smith, their Prefects' badges gleaming, not a hair out of place. As Merry and me took our seats, Zoe swivelled to look at us, nudging Chloe.

'Who's *that* with Merry Jones?' she whispered loudly.

'Shhhhh!' Miss Smith hissed, her finger to her lips. 'Eyes to the front!'

The twins reluctantly turned back to face the stage.

Merry winked at me and I couldn't help grinning. *They didn't recognize me.* I must look like a proper schoolgirl, just like everyone else. But Miss Smith was glaring at us.

'Merry Jones and O-*failure* Bottom! May ay ask why you two are so late?'

'It—it was my fault,' I mumbled.

'Another minute, and the doors would have been locked,' Miss Smith snapped.

We pulled off our rucksacks. My skirt felt even tighter, sitting down. No sooner had we done so, than the speakers on either side of the stage crackled into life. A fanfare echoed around the room, and the long curtains swept open, revealing the stage, which was empty apart from a plastic podium with three steps up to it. Then, a voice over the loudspeaker announced:

'Professor Petrus Potkettle!'

PLASTICUS STUPENDUS EST:

plastic is fantastic

We all craned our necks as the two Boiler Suits strode on to the stage, side by side. As they stomped across to the podium and turned to face us, I nudged Merry.

A third figure walked between them—someone so small that the Boiler Suits' bulky bodies almost blotted him out. It was a little man with a shock of curly grey hair and huge red plastic spectacles. He wore a long white coat which flapped around his ankles, making him look more like a schoolboy than a grown-up. As he approached the steps to the podium, the security guards grabbed his arms and hoisted him up on to it. Beside me, Merry spluttered with laughter.

The notes of the fanfare died away, and the little man tapped the microphone on the podium. He was only just tall enough to use it.

Silence fell. He cleared his throat, clasped his hands together and looked up at the ceiling. Miss Smith nodded at us, and we all did the same. In a high voice, the little man chanted:

'*Plasticus stupendus est,*
Diversus periculosus est.'

Then he gripped the sides of the podium and peered over the top of it.

'Welcome, children, to the Potkettle Institute,' he beamed, two rows of dazzling white teeth gleaming. 'I am Professor Petrus, em...'

He tailed off. Blue Boiler Suit stepped forward.

'Potkettle,' he whispered loudly, and Merry spluttered again. Miss Smith swivelled in her chair and glared at us.

'Today, I will tell you about plastic, its manufacture and its... em... uses.'

Merry and I looked at one another. So much for exciting surprises.

'Without the wonders of plastic,' Professor Potkettle said, 'the town of Stopford wouldn't... em...'

'Exist,' said Blue Boiler Suit.

Professor Potkettle nodded at Green Boiler Suit, who hurried offstage. A vast screen came down, as wide as the stage itself. The lights in the room dimmed.

A video began to run on the screen. It showed wild, open countryside with wide areas of grass and woodland. High on a hill, a river ran down through fields to a horseshoe-shaped beach. I stared at the beach. It was Stopford Cove.

'This, children, was Stopford just three years ago,' said Professor Potkettle. 'Before I embarked upon my... em...'

'Mission,' said Blue Boiler Suit.

Now the video showed bulldozers and cement mixers at work, and the square concrete building taking shape on the hill beside the river.

'The factory!' a whisper travelled round the room.

'Yes, indeedy!' In the darkness, Professor Potkettle's white teeth gleamed. 'Designed by a genius—me!'

Next, the video showed a speeded-up version of more building work.

'That's our town!' said Chloe.

'And there's our school!' said Zoe.

The video showed a lorry—with PRATT'S PLASTIC PELLETS on its side—driving into a loading bay inside the factory. The Boiler Suits unloaded dozens of white plastic sacks. The camera zoomed in for a close-up of a handful of white pellets.

'Using these plastic pellets, my factory makes every kind of thing, yes indeedy! You name it—we make it!' Professor Potkettle gave a high-pitched giggle and turned back to the screen.

Now the video showed the factory: a hundred times bigger than the theatre, lit by fluorescent lighting and filled with machinery. Huge conveyor belts ran back and forth, loaded with plastic goods. A woman dressed in a white boiler suit, her conker-coloured hair escaping from a cap, walked up and down, inspecting the belts. Merry gave a little gasp and whispered in my ear.

'That's my mum!'

Zoe pointed at the screen. 'There's our dad!'

The camera panned to a tall, thin woman with blonde hair.

'And our mum!' Chloe pointed too.

'And mine!'

'And mine!'

An excited hubbub echoed round the theatre. The video turned off, and Green Boiler Suit returned. Professor Potkettle beamed.

'How many of your parents work in my factory? Raise your, em...'

'Hands,' said Blue Boiler Suit.

Every hand, except mine, waved. The Professor's cold blue eyes rested on me for a moment, then swept on.

'When you grow up, I hope to see all of *you* in my factory, working to make the world a better, em...'

'Place,' said Green Boiler Suit.

Zoe and Chloe nodded like puppets and Professor Potkettle smiled at them benevolently. Then he turned back to the rest of us.

'But what is the em... *point* of plastic? What do we use plastic for?'

Chloe's hand shot up.

'The Prefect with the... em...'

'Braces,' hissed Green Boiler Suit.

Chloe stood up. 'It's used to make shopping bags, sir! And—'

'—and food packaging and furniture—' interrupted Zoe.

'—and televisions and laptops,' added Chloe.

The Professor nodded. 'Yes indeed! And it can also be found in... em...'

'Cars,' whispered Blue Boiler Suit.

'...and medical equipment... and vacuum... em...'

'Cleaners,' said Green Boiler Suit.

'In our carpets and even in our... em...' he glanced down at his coat.

'Clothes,' said Blue Boiler Suit.

'Yes, indeedy! Plastic can be found, in fact, everywhere. In our houses, in our workplaces, in our... em... schools. Why do you think this is?'

Chloe waved her hand again.

'Yes, young lady?'

'Because it's easy to make, sir!'

Professor Potkettle nodded hard. 'Yes, indeedy! And not only easy, but cheap. Cheap as... em...'

'Chips,' said Green Boiler Suit.

'All we have to do is make a mould and pour in the plastic. And every single item will come out looking exactly the... em...'

'Same,' said Blue Boiler Suit.

Professor Potkettle pushed his red plastic spectacles up his nose and beamed. 'Which is jolly useful, because, as we always say in Stopford... *diversus periculosus est*. In other... em... words...?'

'Different is dangerous!' chorused everyone.

I tried to stop the enormous yawn which made my eyes tingle. Merry yawned too. This was *boring*. Much, much worse than home-schooling with Ma. At least with books and poems and plays there were exciting stories and interesting characters.

Merry nudged me in the ribs. 'We should make up a new motto,' she whispered. '*Sameness is stupid.*' I giggled.

Chloe's hand shot up.

'Miss Smith! Merry Jones is *whispering*!'

Miss Smith turned to stare at us, her long face pale under the fluorescent lights.

'Ay beg your pardon, Merry Jones? Ay assume you have something important to say?'

'N-no, miss.'

'If ay have to warn you once more, you will be *out*. Understand?'

'Yes, miss.' Merry hung her head, but I could see she was still giggling.

Professor Potkettle glanced down at Merry and me, then carried on as if nothing had happened.

'Plastic,' he said, 'is the future. And d'you know why that is?'

We all looked at one another. Professor Potkettle nodded his head, and his shock of grey curls bounced.

'I'll... em... show you.'

The lights went out.

'There must be a power cut!' shouted Zoe. 'Miss—!'

Miss Smith's voice shouted above the muddle of complaints.

'Sit *still*, all of you! There is no power cut.'

Suddenly, a single spotlight picked out Professor Potkettle in his white coat, the light glinting on his red spectacles.

'Plastic is the future,' he said, in his high voice. 'Because plastic is even better than... em... *people*!'

We all stared at him. Words jumped out of my mouth before I could stop them.

'What d'you mean, sir?' I called out. 'How can plastic be better than people?'

Professor Potkettle looked down at me.

'I'll ask *you* a... em... question in return, young lady,' he said. 'How long do people live for?'

I thought. 'Eighty years, maybe?'

'Yes indeedy. And do you know how long plastic lasts for?'

I shook my head.

'Up to one thousand years!' The Professor's blue eyes shone in triumph. 'Now, where was I, before... em...?'

'People!' hissed Blue Boiler Suit.

'Ah yes. Yes, indeedy! So, plastic can outlast people. It is virtually... em...'

'Indestructible,' whispered Green Boiler Suit.

'Just imagine, young lady, if we humans could live that long!' The Professor's eyes bored into me. 'Imagine if people never wore out or broke down. Imagine if they could stay just the same for a thousand years, without getting old or ill or... em...'

'Dying,' said Blue Boiler Suit.

The Professor shivered and adjusted his spectacles. He jerked his head at Blue Boiler Suit, who left the stage.

'Anyhow, let's move on to the *fun* bit: it's time to unveil my *stupendous*... em...'

'Surprise,' said Green Boiler Suit.

Blue Boiler Suit walked on to the stage with a small bundle in his arms. It was too dark to see what it was. He carried the bundle up to Professor Potkettle and handed it to him. The spotlight shone down on something wrapped in a white blanket. Gently, the Professor lifted the bundle into the light.

'It's—it's a baby!' gasped Chloe.

The baby was tiny, maybe just born. Its eyes were closed, its hair the softest down, and it sucked its tiny thumb. Then, woken by Chloe's voice, it opened its eyes, removed its thumb from its mouth and began to cry. Professor Potkettle rocked the baby to and fro, murmuring to it.

'Hush, little baby...'

The baby went on crying.

'I'm having no... em... luck in soothing him.' Professor Potkettle turned and called down to me. 'Why don't *you* have a go, young lady?'

I hesitated. I'd never held a baby in my whole life. What if I dropped it? I stood up. But before I could move towards the stage, Professor Potkettle suddenly tossed the baby high up into the air.

Everyone gasped. I ran to where the baby was falling, falling...

...and just managed to catch it in my arms. It was warm and heavy and a bit damp. It stared up at me with its soft blue eyes.

Professor Potkettle rocked with laughter, like a squeaky toy.

'What d'you think of my baby, young lady? He giggled. 'My sweet little... em... *plastic* baby!'

PROTOTYPE:

the first version of a product

I stared down at the baby. It stared back at me, its little forehead crinkling. It *couldn't* be made of plastic. I could even feel its little heart beating.

'Unwrap the blanket,' said Professor Potkettle.

I pulled the soft blanket away, and nearly dropped the baby in shock. It had a plastic window in its tummy, and inside it, machinery whirred silently. I stared at it in horror.

'A very early... em...'

'Prototype,' said Green Boiler Suit.

'But *ever* so clever, don't you think?' Professor Potkettle nodded at Blue Boiler Suit, who jumped down, took the baby out of my arms and carried it offstage. Everyone was silent. Professor Potkettle smiled, just as if nothing out of the ordinary had happened.

'And *that* is why plastic is so fantastic,' he said, 'and why we need to make *lots* and *lots* of it.' He looked round the room. 'Any more questions?'

I waved my hand.

'You again, young lady?'

'What happens to all the plastic nobody wants? The plastic people throw away. How do you get rid of it?'

'Oh... there are plenty of ways,' the Professor waved his hand vaguely. 'It can be... em...'

'Burnt,' said Green Boiler Suit.

'Yes, indeedy! We have a simply *brilliant* incinerator in the factory...'

'What's an incinerator?' I asked.

'A sort of... em...'

'Furnace,' said Green Boiler Suit.

So *that* must be what the chimney on the hill was doing, belching out smoke and fumes. But the Professor was still speaking.

'And if there's too much plastic for our incinerator to deal with, then it can be...'

'Buried.' Blue Boiler Suit returned to the stage, without the baby.

'Or... em...'

'Dumped,' said Green Boiler Suit.

'Dumped where?' I asked. 'In the sea?

There was a long silence, then Professor Potkettle asked:

'Exactly how... em... old are you, young lady?'

'Ten,' I said. 'Nearly eleven.'

'Eleven. Yes, indeedy.' The Professor nodded a few times. 'And when would your birthday be?'

'June the fifteenth.' Why was he so interested in my age? I glanced over at Merry, who looked as puzzled as me.

'Not long now, then, until your... em...'

'Ceremony,' said Blue Boiler Suit.

'When you will see things differently. You are too young, at present, to... em...'

'Understand,' said Green Boiler Suit.

'What is your... em... name, young lady?'

'Ophelia,' I muttered. 'Ophelia Bottom.'

Professor Potkettle glanced at Green Boiler Suit, who whipped out a notebook and pen and scribbled in it.

'Bottom?' The Professor looked thoughtful. 'Where have I...?'

He turned to Blue Boiler Suit and whispered to him. Blue Boiler Suit whispered back. Green Boiler Suit went on scribbling. Professor Potkettle suddenly turned back to us and glanced at a yellow plastic watch on his wrist.

'Sadly, we have reached the end of the visit,' he said. 'But we have one last... em... surprise for you.' He turned to the Boiler Suits and nodded. They marched offstage and returned with two large plastic sacks.

'Who wants a... em...'

'Treat!' chorused the Boiler Suits.

Hands shot up around me. The Boiler Suits carried the sacks round, and there were shrieks and squeals as each person pulled out a plastic goody-bag.

'Oooh—a sweatshirt!' said Zoe, opening hers.

'A cool rucksack!' said Chloe.

Green Boiler Suit held out her sack to me. Slowly, I pulled out a goody-bag. All around me, the others were shouting about what they'd got. If it was yesterday, I'd have been just as excited. Only now, somehow, I wasn't.

'What've you got?' Merry asked.

'A T-shirt.' Across the front of it were stamped the words: *Plasticus stupendus est*, and on the back: *Diversus periculosus est*. I pulled Merry aside.

'That was all seriously weird!

Merry nodded. 'The baby!'

'And all that stuff about getting rid of the plastic.' I shivered. 'And why was he so interested in my birthday? What *is* this Ceremony thing?'

'It's only just started this year,' said Merry. 'We'll be the first to do it—apart from Chloe and Zoe.'

'Do what, exactly?'

'On your eleventh birthday, you go up to the factory in a posh limousine. And you come back next day all sort of grown up.' Merry glanced at Zoe and Chloe and grimaced. 'A *Perfect*.'

'How?' I asked. 'What happens to you?'

'Nobody knows, apart from the Perfects. But they won't tell.' Merry shook her head. 'It'll be my turn soon. I wish I didn't have to...' She brightened. 'But then again, it might be a *brilliant* adventure! And at least you'll be doing it soon after me, so we can compare notes.'

I opened my mouth to say that Ar and Ma would never let me, and that anyway, we'd be moving on as soon as Ar's leg was mended. Then, just in time, I remembered I was supposed to live at Magnolia Drive and that Merry didn't know that I was only at school for six weeks.

Miss Smith led us back to the reception area. At the desk, Blue Boiler Suit handed back Merry's phone and we all lined

103

up at the main entrance. Professor Potkettle, a Boiler Suit on either side, waved and beamed.

'What a... em... pleasure! Yes, indeedy!'

But as the glass doors swished closed, I glanced back. Professor Potkettle wasn't waving or beaming any more.

He was staring very hard at me, and his blue eyes were like chips of ice.

JOBSWORTH:

someone who always obeys all the rules of their job, even when the rules are silly

When I got back to the Pantechnicon, it was as chaotic as ever. Ma buttered bread and heated up baked beans, while Ar lumbered around on his crutches, getting in her way.

'*Sit down*, Arthur Bottom,' Ma hissed as I climbed over the seats to join them.

'I'm doing my RECUPERATION EXERCISES,' roared Ar, swinging his plaster cast. It hit the teapot, which smashed on the floor, scattering pound coins everywhere.

'That *does* it!' growled Ma. 'Go *outside*. And, Ophelia, pick up that money. Not that there's much of it.'

Ar swung his leg over the drivers' seat, grumbling.

I bent to pick up the scattered coins. Ma was right—there were hardly any left. How were we going to manage for the next five weeks?

'Did you enjoy your school visit?' Ma shovelled slices of bread on to three plates and upended the saucepan, pouring steaming beans over each one.

'It was OK.'

Ma handed me a couple of plates. 'You'd better take this out to your father.'

It seemed a hundred years since I raced off that morning without breakfast, and I never did get to eat my biscuits. Balancing our plates, I climbed over the seats and put the plates down on the passenger seat while I opened the door. Loud voices—not only Ar's—came from outside. I pushed open the door and jumped down on to the grass.

Ar stood on his crutches beside a truck with a blue flashing light on its roof. Across the side of the truck was the word SECURITY.

An argument seemed to be going on. I ran over to join Ar. Inside the truck were the two Boiler Suits, their walkie-talkies crackling.

'What's the matter, Ar?' I asked.

Ar's beard quivered with fury.

'STICKLERS! NITPICKERS! Petty JOBSWORTHS!'

The Boiler Suits opened the doors of the truck and got out. They didn't seem one bit afraid of Ar, probably because they were as big—if not bigger—than him.

Blue Boiler Suit stared at Ar. 'Leave,' he said.

'What RIGHT have you—'

'Law.' Green Boiler Suit jerked her head at the sign saying:

STOPFORD COMMON
PARKING STRICTLY BY PERMIT ONLY

'THEN THE LAW IS AN ASS!' yelled Ar.

Ma stuck her head out of the Pantechnicon. '*Now* what's going on, Arthur?'

'These—these NINCOMPOOPS are ordering us off the Common!'

Ma jumped down and hurried over to join us.

'What's the matter, officers?'

Green Boiler Suit pulled a sheet of paper from her pocket and handed it to Ma. Ma read it, frowning.

'What is it, Ma?' I asked.

Ma looked up. 'We had a permit to park on the Common for three days. It seems that it has...'

'Expired,' said Green Boiler Suit.

'EXPIRED?' roared Ar. 'I'll give you EXPIRED!'

'*Quiet*, Arthur Bottom!' Ma's face was pale. 'Let me explain, officers.'

Blue Boiler Suit shook his head. He pointed back up at the road.

'Move,' he said.

'But—but we can't leave the Common!' Ma said, gesturing at Ar's crutches. 'My husband has had an accident. He can't drive.'

Green Boiler Suit shrugged. Then they both climbed back into the truck.

I stepped forward. 'We can't leave! Ma can't drive, either.'

Ma's face turned from white to pink.

'Can't?' said Blue Boiler Suit.

'Well, she'd be breaking the law...'

Ma looked daggers at me. She'd lost her licence last

year, for driving the Pantechnicon the wrong way up a motorway.

'Tough.' Green Boiler Suit started the engine.

Ma went on reading the piece of paper. 'They'll be back in two hours,' she said. 'And if we're still here, they'll arrest us.'

'ARREST US, THEN!' boomed Ar. But the truck was already bumping away over the Common, the blue light flashing on its roof.

I turned to Ma. 'What'll we do?'

'Let them try and APPREHEND me!' roared Ar. 'Any fool who arrests a Bottom will live to REGRET it!'

'Shut *up*, Arthur!' Ma bit her thumbnail. 'We can't go to jail.'

'Will they really arrest us?' I asked.

'Probably,' muttered Ma. 'I *knew* we should never have come here.'

I shivered, thinking of what Merry had said, about how terrible things happened to you and your family if you saw the Ghost from the Sea. Maybe this was all my fault. I couldn't help wanting to cry. For the first time in my life, I'd made a real friend, and now we had to leave. But how *could* we? Ar couldn't drive, with his leg in plaster. And Ma had lost her licence...

Then I had an idea.

'We've got two hours before they come back,' I said. 'That'll give us long enough to pack up.'

Ar and Ma turned to look at me.

'And THEN WHAT?' said Ar.

'Ma can drive the Pantechnicon—'

'Don't be *silly*, Ophelia,' snapped Ma. 'I'm not allowed on the roads for another six months!'

'Not on the road!' I said. 'Just down the lane! You can park the Pantechnicon near the woods, and no one'll know where we've gone.'

Ar and Ma looked at one another for a few seconds. Then Ma grimaced.

'I suppose I'll just *have* to do it.'

'BRAVO, MARINA!' shouted Ar. 'ACTION STATIONS!'

He waved one of his crutches at the wooden stage and all the seats, which still lay out on the grass.

With Ar bellowing instructions, Ma and me hefted them, piece by heavy piece, into the back of the Pantechnicon. It took an age without Ar to help, and I kept looking over my shoulder towards Stopford, half expecting to see the truck with its flashing blue light coming back. But at last it was all done, and the three of us squished into the driver's cab, with Ma at the wheel. Ma turned the key in the ignition, crashed the gears, and the Pantechnicon lurched backwards.

'That's REVERSE GEAR!' yelled Ar.

Ma muttered under her breath and crashed the gears again. The Pantechnicon leapt forward this time, rattling and shaking over the grass at great speed.

'DECELERATE, MARINA!!!'

'Shut *up*, Arthur!' growled Ma. 'The *last* thing I need is a back-seat driver.'

The Pantechnicon shot off the Common and bumped down the lane. I peeped between my fingers. We lumbered towards the woods.

'TO THE SEASHORE!' Ar yelled.

'N-no!' I shouted. 'The security guards might come looking for us there.' No *way* were we going to park on the beach—not with the Ghost from the Sea lurking in the water.

'WHERE, THEN?'

'There!' I spotted a turning among the trees. 'Drive down there, Ma!'

Ma swung the Pantechnicon towards the turning so violently that it almost overturned. I squeezed my eyes shut. We bumped forward. It sounded like branches were scraping the windows of the Pantechnicon.

'BRAKE, MARINA!' yelled Ar.

The Pantechnicon shuddered to a standstill and I slowly opened my eyes.

ADAM'S ALE:

an old-fashioned term for water

We were in a small clearing. It was gloomy and damp-looking, but at least no one would ever guess we were here. I jumped out of the Pantechnicon—the ground was muddy from all the rain—and looked around. We were surrounded by trees, ancient and moss-covered, with huge ferns growing among their roots. Their branches and leaves made a green tent around us. The light was dim and a bit eerie.

Ma jumped down to join me, followed by Ar on his crutches.

'The perfect HIDEAWAY!' Ar's voice set off a flapping in the leaves above us. Ma didn't look so sure.

'It's too *quiet*,' she shivered.

She was right. The air did seem strangely still. No birds sang.

'It's PEACEFUL, Marina!' said Ar, stomping around and splashing mud over his plaster cast.

'And what will we do for *water*?' said Ma.

Ar waved a crutch towards the beach. 'The OCEAN is close by.'

'Not *salt* water, Arthur! Water to drink!' Ma said. 'At least on that wretched Common there was a *tap*.'

'What about the RIVER?' Ar said. 'It runs down to the SEA.'

Ma frowned. 'Have you *seen* the river, Arthur Bottom?'

'NATURALLY,' said Ar. 'We crossed over the BRIDGE where that ROADHOG—'

'Well, you obviously didn't *notice* the fact that the river is *polluted.* Full of *rubbish.*'

Thinking about rubbish in the water made me remember the Ghost from the Sea. A shivery tingle whispered down my back. There was nothing but trees around us, but I had a strange feeling, as if an invisible someone—or something—was watching us. I gave myself a shake. No one was allowed in the woods, Merry said so. And the Boiler Suits didn't know we were here.

Then, a haunting sound wound through the trees.

'What's *that?*' Ma whispered, staring into the wood.

'Is anybody THERE?' shouted Ar. 'If so, REVEAL YOURSELF!'

'Get back in the van, Ophelia!' hissed Ma.

'It's all right, Ma.' I stayed where I was. 'It's just an owl hooting.'

'An owl calling in the day is a *very bad omen.*' Ma shivered again.

'NONSENSE, Marina!' roared Ar. 'It's only a BIRD.'

'Shhhh!' I said. There was another sound, so soft I could hardly hear it. And certainly not when Ar was shouting.

'*What?*' Ma jumped. 'What did you hear?'

I moved towards the trees and began to push through the low-hanging branches.

'Come *back here*, Ophelia!' Ma's voice sounded panicky.

But I carried on. Branches whipped around my face and my trainers kept getting stuck in the mud. My hands were soon green from the moss and slime on the tree trunks.

And then I saw it. A tiny stream, tinkling and murmuring through the trees.

'Ma! Ar!' I shouted. There was a lot of roaring and crashing behind me, but at last Ma and Ar arrived.

'A RIVULET!' said Ar. 'ADAM'S ALE!'

'It won't be *clean*,' muttered Ma.

I dropped to my knees, scooped up a handful of water and took a sip. It tasted fresh and clear.

'It is! Try it, Ma!'

Her nose wrinkling, Ma took a tiny sip, then another.

'She's *right*, Arthur! It's fresh water.'

'Then we are CATERED FOR!' said Ar. 'We have all we REQUIRE!'

'Apart from money...' muttered Ma balefully, '...and *food*.'

'To the PANTECHNICON, Ophelia!' said Ar, ignoring her. 'Bring the witches' cauldron and we will fill it TO THE BRIM!'

After Ma and I had filled up the cauldron with water and lugged it back to the Pantechnicon, Ma opened a can of spaghetti, and we ate it with the last of the bread. Every time the owl called, Ma squeezed her eyes tight shut and clenched her fists. When it was time for bed, she refused to sleep across the driver's seat like she'd done since Ar's accident.

'I wouldn't *sleep a wink*,' she said.

'I'll sleep there,' I said. 'I'm not scared of owls.'

I grabbed my sleeping bag and hopped over on to the driver's seat, while Ma took my bunk, still grumbling.

At first, I was wide awake. I sat up in my sleeping bag and stared out of the windscreen at the trees. Sleeping in a wood—or trying to—was very different to sleeping on the Common. The darkness here was different, too—as if a secret world came alive at night: a darkness full of skitterings and shufflings and whisperings and flappings. Even though owls didn't scare me, I wasn't so sure about all the other invisible creatures out there. And I still had that funny feeling that we were being watched.

There was just enough moonlight coming through the windscreen of the Pantechnicon to make out the dim, sleeping shapes of Ar and Ma. It was comforting to see the hump of Ma's body in my bunk, and to hear Ar's gigantic snores. I wriggled down in my sleeping bag, and fell into a restless sleep...

I woke with a start.

Something was howling outside—a wild, unearthly sound.

The howling came again. Whatever it was must be very close. A fox?

I tried very hard not to think about the ghost, but I couldn't help sitting up again and peering through the windscreen. In the pale moonlight, the trees seemed made of silver, almost magic. Everything was still and silent. I was just about to lie down again when a dark, hunched shape slipped across the clearing and disappeared into the wood.

I wriggled out of my sleeping bag, pulled on my trainers and scrabbled in the compartment by the steering wheel. My fingers found the shape of the torch. As quietly as I could, I opened the door of the Pantechnicon and jumped to the ground, my heart pounding.

I switched on the torch and shone it into the trees. Its beam flashed over tree trunks, branches, leaves. The figure had melted away, just like a...

No. Ghosts don't exist. And even if they do, the one I saw was in the sea.

I tiptoed towards the trees, but there was no sign of anyone. My trainer caught on something on the ground. I swerved the torch beam down. Lying in the mud was a single plastic flip-flop.

And there was more. A plastic bottle. Coffee cartons. None of these were there when we went to bed. How did they get here? A cold feeling stole into my heart. *The Ghost from the Sea looked like it was made out of plastic...*

The torch beam swept over a white plastic sack, twisted into a circle. There was writing on it. I bent down to look at it.

PRATT'S PLASTIC PELLETS

What was this doing here?

On the ground next to the sack were plastic knives and forks, end to end. Almost as if they were making some kind of a pattern. I backed away until I was standing beside the Pantechnicon. Then the pattern made sense.

The plastic things were twisted into the shapes of letters. And the letters made two words, lying on the ground beside the Pantechnicon:

GO
AWAY

FOOTPRINT:

the impression left by a foot or shoe on the ground

My hands shook so much that the torchlight shivered too, wavering over the message on the ground. Who had done this? And even more scary—where were they now? I swung the beam around the trees, almost expecting it to light up a pair of ghostly, staring eyes. But there was nothing.

Should I get back into the Pantechnicon, wake up Ar and Ma?

No. Ma was already frightened and upset, and she'd have a fit if she knew someone was spying on us and warning us away. And if she thought that that someone was a ghost, she'd want us out of here—*now*—and there was nowhere else for us to go...

Think, Fee. I shivered in my pyjamas, making myself think logically, the way a detective would.

Someone—or something— was trying to scare us away. And the only way to stop them was to find out exactly who they were and where they came from. I stared down at the words on the muddy ground.

The mud!

Whoever left this message had to walk across the clearing. I crouched down and shone the torch on the ground around the plastic letters.

Yes. There *were* footprints, quite clear ones, with a zigzag pattern on the sole. I peered down at the prints. If I memorized them, I'd recognize them when I saw them again.

Then I had a horrible thought. I stood up and lifted one leg, shining the torchlight on to the sole of my trainer. Exactly the same zigzag pattern. The footprints were my own.

My next thought was even *more* horrible.

If all these footprints were mine, then whoever wrote the message *didn't leave any.* And the only thing that didn't leave footprints was...

...*a ghost.*

My mind whirled. Maybe—maybe I was imagining all this. Maybe I was actually still asleep and dreaming in my sleeping bag in the Pantechnicon. Any minute, I'd wake up and it'd be morning and time for school...

A sharp crack echoed among the trees like a gunshot. As if someone had accidentally stood on a twig and broken it. I stopped breathing.

No ghost would crack a twig.

Whoever left the message was still here, hiding among the trees, watching me.

'Wh-who's there?' I hissed. I took a deep breath and tried to sound brave, like Ar. 'Come out and show yourself!'

There was no reply. The whole wood held its breath, like me. My heart banged in my chest and my knees felt wobbly.

But I *wouldn't* go running back to the Pantechnicon. If I did, the ghost—or whatever was out there—would've won.

'Right—' I shone the torch into the trees. 'If you won't come out here, I'll come in there and find you!'

I marched across the clearing and into the wood.

It was even darker here, and the air smelt of damp and mushrooms. In the dim light it was hard to tell if the dark shadows were tree trunks or hiding figures. I swept my torch beam back and forth. Nothing moved. I tiptoed forward, shining the torch on the ground ahead of me in case there were tree roots to trip over or muddy pools to slip up in. Then I gasped.

There were footprints in the mud in front of me.

I shone the torch down on to them. The pattern was just the same as the ones in the clearing—zigzags, like the pattern on the bottom of my own trainers. Then I remembered: of course, I came this way earlier, when I found the stream.

I was just about to turn back when an eerie howling weaved among the branches: the sound I'd heard before. Except this time it stopped very suddenly, as if someone had gagged it. A dark shadow slipped behind a tree trunk and my ears caught the shuffle of running feet. I jerked the torch beam up to the trees ahead.

'Stop!' I shouted, but whoever it was had disappeared.

I pushed through the low-hanging branches. Leaves whipped my face and my trainers squelched in the mud. The whisper of the stream grew louder and then I burst out of the trees beside it.

There was no one there.

Just moonlight, which dappled the moving water with silver and touched the edges of the ferns like a fairy den.

My shoulders slumped. It was hopeless chasing someone in a wood in the dark—especially someone who knew exactly where they were going. And even if I *did* carry on, I'd have to get across the stream. One last time, I swept the torch over the trees on the other side, but all it lit up were tree trunks and muddy footprints...

Muddy footprints?

I'd never been further than this side of the stream. This was weird. What were the chances of someone wearing exactly the same trainers as me? But now there was a trail to follow. I could track whoever it was to wherever they were going and when I found them I could make them tell me exactly what they were up to: why they left the message and why they wanted to scare us away.

I shone the torch over the rippling water. It was probably only a couple of feet deep. I was just about to pull off my trainers and wade in when I saw the footprints heading along the bank to my right. I followed them for a few metres until they stopped. There, four large stepping stones lay in the stream. I jumped from stone to stone until I was on the other side.

Whoever it was would be long gone, but now I had the footprints to follow. The prints ran on through the trees. Sometimes I thought I'd lost them, where the ground was harder, but then they reappeared. It felt like I'd been following them for ages. How big *was* this wood? I hesitated. What if Ar and Ma had woken from the howling, or from me calling out—and found the message? What if they'd discovered me gone?

Maybe I'd better go back. I'd get rid of the message—pick up the plastic stuff and hide it in my rucksack. Then I'd drop it into a waste bin on the way to school, and Ar and Ma would never know about it. And later, after school, I could tell them I was going to get water from the stream and follow the footprints to wherever they led—much easier in the daytime, and much less scary.

I was about to turn back when a sound up ahead made me stop: the last sound I'd expect to hear in a wood.

The sound of a door slamming.

FEROCIOUS:

savagely fierce

A slamming door? If there was a door here, in the middle of the wood, it might belong to a house. And if there was a house here, then it most likely belonged to the person who was trying to scare me. I shone my torch on the ground. There were the zigzag footprints in the mud, dodging round trees and disappearing into the darkness ahead.

I listened. Everything was silent. I trained my torch on the footprints. The trees seemed to grow even closer together here and I had to duck under low-hanging branches to follow the trail.

Gradually the branches thinned out. I must be coming to the edge of the wood. Up ahead, in a clearing, was something tall and black and solid-looking, like a wall, with pale rectangular shapes on it. I tiptoed across the clearing and shone my torch over it. It wasn't a wall—it was a high fence, made of rough pieces of wood bound together with rope. And the rectangular shapes were white-painted signs, peppered with nail-heads and scrawled with lettering in black paint. The first said:

NO TRESPUSSING

On another was written:

PRIVAT - KEEP OUT

And a third one said:

BEWARE OF THE
FUROSHUS DOG

Whoever lived here couldn't spell *ferocious*. Or *private*, or *trespassing*. I stared up at the fence. Could I climb over it? *No.* It was at least twice my height. And anyhow, if there really was a *furoshus dog* prowling round, no *way* was I going to try.

Maybe if I followed the fence round, there'd be a door—the one I'd heard slam. I tiptoed on, keeping my ears peeled. Just as I thought I must be back where I started, my torch flickered over a gate. I reached out to push it. It didn't move. Then there was a sharp rattle—making me jump—as my hand hit a chain, with something heavy and square on the end. *A padlock.* Someone wanted to make very sure that they had no visitors. Between the fence and the gate there was a tiny gap, just a few centimetres wide. I bent down and peered through it, but all I could make out was the dim, pale shape of a building. No way was I going to shine my torch there. Better to come back in daylight. But just as I stood up to head back for the wood, a huge white moon slipped from behind the clouds and hung above

123

the fence like a lantern. I bent down again and peered through the gap.

A small, squat house, like a bungalow but perfectly round, gleamed in the moonlight. Its rough walls were painted white, and it had tiny arched windows like surprised eyes. A plume of pale smoke drifted from a small chimney. Beside the house was stacked a neat pile of chopped wood.

A sweet scent seemed to wind through the gap in the fence. I shifted around so I could see where it was coming from. *A garden.* There were beds of flowers and fruit bushes and vegetables: neat rows of lettuces, and the lacy tops of carrots. A spade stood upright in the ground.

We'd never had a garden—never stayed in one place long enough to grow one. And Ar would have made a useless gardener—he was far too impatient and would probably roar 'GROW!' at the plants to hurry them up, while Ma would be so sure they'd never flourish that she wouldn't plant them in the first place.

Thinking of Ar and Ma reminded me I'd better get back. It'd be dawn soon, and I didn't want them finding the message. I was just about to stand up when I noticed something else, built up against the fence at the end of the garden. It looked like a large storage shed with a wooden roof and stone walls on three sides. The fourth side, facing me, had no wall. The store was filled to bursting with white sacks, gleaming in the moonlight. I screwed up my eyes to make out what was written on them.

PRATT'S PLASTIC PELLETS

Sacks of plastic. Like the sacks the lorries took to the factory. Like the empty ones floating in the sea. Like the one some-one used to make the ◇ in

G◇
AWAY

One of the sacks had toppled over and plastic spilt out on to the ground. Only it wasn't plastic pellets. It was plastic *junk*—squashed empty drinks bottles and plastic drinking cups and plastic buckets and bowls. Like the junk in the sea. I stared at it, my mind whirring.

Suddenly, Professor Potkettle's words flashed into my mind.

And if there's too much plastic for our incinerator to deal with, then it can be dumped...

Could whoever lived here be in the pay of Professor Potkettle—doing his dirty work for him, storing his leftover plastic junk for him and secretly dumping it in the sea? I shifted around again to get a better look... and froze.

Because hanging in mid-air beside the storage shed was the Ghost from the Sea.

For a long moment, I just stared at it, not breathing. It stared back at me with its empty, goggle eyes.

Then I got it.

It wasn't a ghost at all. It was certainly the thing that rose out of the sea and frightened me, but it was a mask. It had plastic goggles for eyes, and a long stream of plastic-and-seaweed hair. And it wasn't hanging in mid-air: it was hanging from a hook on one wall of the storage shed.

So whoever lived in this house not only left the message made of plastic junk warning us to go away: they'd also tried to scare me away from Stopford Cove by dressing up as the ghost. But why?

Suddenly, the shed and the mask were blotted out. Two enormous eyes stared right into mine. A low, fierce growling filled my ears. I gasped and fell backwards into the mud. The growling got louder. I picked myself up and ran for my life, across the clearing and into the trees.

It-can't-get-out-It-can't-get-out-It-can't-get-out, I told myself. But I wasn't going to hang around to find out. I blundered through the wood, hardly feeling the branches and leaves scratching my face. After a bit, I stopped, panting, and listened. Nothing seemed to be following me. I fumbled in my pocket for my torch. Its light wavered over the footprints and I followed them, one by one, until at last I reached the stream and jumped over the stepping stones to the safety of the other side.

Back in our clearing, the plastic message still lay on the ground beside the Pantechnicon. Silently, I gathered up all the plastic objects and carried them down to the lane. I left them in a neat pile, ready to stuff in my rucksack on my way to school. Then, I brushed the mud off my pyjamas as best I could and went back to the Pantechnicon. I managed to open the door without waking Ar and Ma and wriggled into my sleeping bag.

But I couldn't sleep. A jumble of pictures ran round and round in my mind—messages made of plastic, footprints in the mud, fences with warning notices, round houses, hanging ghostly masks and sacks of plastic rubbish. Only one thing was clear.

Someone wanted us out of here.

And I was going to find out who, and why.

ESTRANGED:

a loss of affection

It only seemed a moment later that Ma woke me.

'Ophelia! Wake up—quickly! We've *overslept*!'

I rubbed my eyes. Through the windscreen, the sun dappled the muddy ground where the message had been. Everything that happened last night seemed far away, as if it was a dream. Maybe it *was*. But when I wriggled out of my sleeping bag and sat up, I'd still got my trainers on, and my pyjamas were streaked with mud.

'What time is it?' I threw off my pyjamas and pulled on my uniform.

'Almost nine o'clock!' growled Ma, shaking Ar's shoulder. 'Get *up*, Arthur Bottom! Ophelia's late for school and you need to move *that leg* out of the way.'

But Ar just turned over in his bunk and started snoring again. Ma's eyebrows crossed together. She climbed over Ar's plaster cast and hurried to the larder box.

I decided to give washing a miss, since all our water was outside in the witches' cauldron.

'Wait, Ophelia! Your *breakfast*!'

'No time, Ma—I'm going to be really, really late for school!' I grabbed my rucksack and pushed open the door of the Pantechnicon.

But Ma wasn't having any of it. 'Come *back here*, Ophelia! *Now!*'

Reluctantly, I climbed over the driver's seat, and over Ar's plaster cast. He didn't stir. This was *so* annoying. Just when I'd started to fit in at school, I'd have to turn up late—and *different* again. I sat on the edge of Ar's bunk and watched Ma searching in the larder box.

'There's no bread, Ma—we had the last of it yesterday for supper, remember?'

'There were biscuits—a whole packet. I hid them right at the back.'

'S'OK...I'm not hungry.' My heart sank. I saw Ar scoffing biscuits yesterday, while Ma was making supper.

'You're not going to school without *eating*!' There was a pause, and Ma pulled out an empty biscuit wrapper.

'*Ophelia.*' She glared at me, holding the wrapper between two fingers as if she'd found a mouse. 'Did *you* eat them?'

'N-no, Ma.'

'In *that case*,' Ma hissed, turning to Ar's sleeping hump in the bunk, 'I *know who did.*'

Every bit of me wanted to vault over the driver's seat, jump out of the Pantechnicon and race away up the lane. But I knew better than to disobey Ma when she was in this mood.

'Don't be mad at Ar,' I muttered 'He's bigger than us and he needs more f—'

'Quiet, Ophelia!' Ma grabbed Ar's blanket and pulled it off him. Then she yelled in his ear. '*Arthur Bottom!* How *dare* you eat the last of the biscuits!'

Ar opened one eye, saw the expression on Ma's face and quickly closed it again.

'I've had *enough* of this!' Ma hissed. 'How are we supposed to *survive* for the next five weeks without *food*, just tell me that!'

'Ma—don't worry,' I said. 'I'll get something from the shop on my way, and I can get some bread, too, and milk—'

Ma's face was a thundercloud. She turned to the small pile of coins by the sink and handed me a few pounds.

'Thanks, Ma!' I climbed back over everything and pushed open the door. As I ran across the clearing and towards the lane, Ma's voice followed me, shouting at Ar.

'If you mess up *one more time*, Arthur Bottom, I swear I'll *divorce* you.'

A shiver crept down my spine. Ma had never said that word before. Did she mean it, or was she just sounding off? But there was no time to think about this. I picked up the pile of plastic stuff I left by the roadside and stuffed it into my rucksack.

I was going to be so, *so* late for school.

The class was working silently as I pushed open the door. Miss Smith had her back turned, scribbling dates and names on the whiteboard. I slipped into the classroom and tiptoed over to my desk. I was almost there when Chloe glanced up and spotted me. Her hand shot in the air.

'Miss—Miss!'

Miss Smith turned. 'Yes, Chloe?'

'Ophelia Bottom's *late*, miss!'

Everyone stared at me.

'O-*failure!*' snapped Miss Smith. 'Where have you been?'

'S-sorry,' I muttered. 'We, um, overslept.'

'Sit down!'

I plumped down into my seat and pulled open my rucksack. A plastic flip-flop fell out on to the floor. Miss Smith glared at it.

'And *what*, may ay ask, is *that*?'

Why didn't I remember to empty out all the plastic stuff into a bin?

Miss Smith marched over to me, grabbed my rucksack and upended it on the desk. Chloe and Zoe sniggered. Miss Smith gave me a strange look.

'O-*failure*, *w*here did you get all this?'

'I—um, picked it up, miss.' At least this was the truth.

Miss Smith gathered the junk together, pursing her lips, and dumped it in the bin.

'Perhaps we should concentrate less on picking up rubbish, and a little more on getting to school in time.'

'Yes, miss,' I said. Merry winked at me, and I felt a bit better.

But it was impossible to concentrate on lessons, there were so many things whizzing round in my mind—the warning message, the mysterious house in the woods, and Ma threatening to divorce Ar—and I kept getting told off by Miss Smith for daydreaming.

At breaktime, Merry pulled me aside.

'What's going on, Fee? Are you OK?'

I opened my mouth to tell her, then shut it again.

Merry nudged me. 'C'mon, Fee, I know there's something wrong. Tell me!'

It felt *so* nice to have a friend—someone who was on my side and who wanted to know about me because they were interested, not because they wanted to make fun of me. If *only* I could tell Merry everything. But I couldn't. She thought I lived in Magnolia Drive, in a house just like hers. Whatever would she say if she knew that I lived in a Pantechnicon in the woods?

Merry was still staring at me, looking worried.

I took a deep breath. 'What do you do when your mum and dad argue?'

Merry looked surprised. 'Argue? How d'you mean?'

'When they disagree about stuff all the time... and yell at one another.'

Merry looked blank. Maybe Stopford parents didn't behave like Ar and Ma.

'Never mind,' I muttered. 'It's not important.'

Merry grabbed my hand. 'Course it's important, Fee! It's just that my mum and dad don't really argue much.'

I hung my head. Another way that my family was different and odd.

'Do your parents row a lot, then?' asked Merry.

I sighed. 'Yeah. A bit. I mean, they always row, cos they're sort of noisy people. Only since...' I was about to say *since Macbeth*, then remembered Merry didn't know they were actors, and quickly changed it to: '...since we arrived here, it's got a lot worse.'

'It'll be cos of all the stress, I expect,' said Merry. 'What with moving, and everything.'

I nodded. If *only* I hadn't lied to Merry. But it was too late now. Merry suddenly grinned, her dimple appearing. 'I bet we can stop them rowing!'

'What? How?'

'I read about it,' said Merry. 'In one of my mum's magazines. 'When people have lots of rows, it's because they've sort of forgotten that they love one another. It's called being *estranged.*' She looked at me, her head on one side. 'Do your mum and dad love one another, Fee?'

Did Ar and Ma love one another, under all the crossness and shouting? Were they estranged—or just *strange?*

'Maybe they do,' I said. 'Only they've got a funny way of showing it.'

Merry grinned again. 'You've just got to make them remember that they love each other, and then everything'll be all right again.'

'How?'

'In the magazine, it says you've got to bring romance back into your lives.'

'Romance?' Somehow, I couldn't imagine Ar and Ma being romantic.

'Y'know—writing love letters and stuff.'

I thought about this. 'I don't think Ar—I mean, my dad and mum—would be likely to do that.'

'Oh, they won't do it by themselves!' Merry said. 'What they need is a little helping hand... from you!'

'Me?'

'Uh-oh!' Merry suddenly nudged me. '*Perfect alert!*'

Zoe and Chloe marched towards us, perfectly in step, their Prefects' badges gleaming.

'I'll dash home at lunchtime and get the magazine,' Merry whispered, her green eyes sparkling. 'And then we'll make a plan to bring your mum and dad back together.'

RENDEZVOUS:

an arrangement to meet someone, especially
secretly, at an agreed place and time

'**Y**ou keep watch for the Perfects,' said Merry, 'and I'll find the article.'

She licked her finger and flicked over the pages of the magazine. It had lots of photos of pop-stars and soap actors, and headlines saying things like 'Don't Worry, Be Happy!', 'How to Stay Calm in a Crisis' and 'Easy Microwave Menus'. Maybe if Ma read magazines like this, she'd be a bit calmer and more organized.

I kept my eye on the classroom door. Merry said we weren't allowed magazines in school, and we were supposed to be at lunch. My tummy was growling with hunger after having no breakfast, but at least Zoe and Chloe would be busy eating.

'Here it is.' Merry flattened the magazine on her desk and began to read.

'*Three Ways to Restore Romance. One: Say it with Flowers.*

Show your loved one how much they mean to you by giving them a single red rose. The scent of a rose softens hearts and restores love.'

Wherever would I get a red rose? Then I remembered Merry's garden.

'Can—can I have one of your roses? From your garden?'

Merry bit her lip. 'All the flowers in our garden are made of plastic. Same as the grass.'

'Oh.' The flowers and grass had looked so real. But it was no good giving Ma a plastic flower with no scent.

'How about this?' Merry traced her finger down the page. '*Two: Write a Love Letter.*'

I bit my thumbnail. It was all very well telling people to write love letters, but they'd got to *want* to—and Ar and Ma obviously didn't.

Merry went on reading. '*Write a love letter to your partner, telling them all the things you appreciate about them.*'

'Er, I don't think this'll work, Merry,' I said. 'Ma—I mean my mum—doesn't appreciate *anything* about my, um, dad at the moment.'

Merry turned to me. 'This is where you come in, Fee! You must play Cupid—'

'Cupid?'

'The god of love,' said Merry. 'Cupid brings estranged people together again. You must write the love letters and pretend they're from your parents!'

I thought about this and shook my head. 'They'd never be fooled. They'd spot my writing straight away!'

'Um,' Merry frowned. 'I s'pose they would.' She brightened. 'But you could write the love letters on your computer and print them out!'

'We, er... don't have a computer at—at home.'

Merry stared at me. 'You don't have a—?'

'I mean, it's not working at the moment.' *More lies.*

Merry shrugged and turned back to the magazine. 'OK, let's try the last one. *"Three: Organize a Date Night. Surprise your loved one with a romantic meal in a beautiful setting."'*

I tried to imagine Ar and Ma on a date night, eating a romantic meal. But what would they eat? I fingered the pound coins in my pocket. I was supposed to be getting bread and milk for Ma—could I buy something more romantic with a few pounds? And even if I could, how would I find a beautiful setting? The woods were muddy and dark and definitely not romantic. I shook my head.

'You can do it, Fee!' Merry urged. 'You've just got to think outside the box!'

My tummy growled again and an idea came. What if I smuggled my lunch from the canteen and took it home in my rucksack? Then I could use it for a romantic meal for Ar and Ma.

'Maybe...' I said, 'I could tell my mum that my dad wants to meet her down on the beach, and—'

'The beach?' Merry frowned. 'But what about the Ghost from the Sea?'

If only I could tell her that there *was* no ghost—that it was just a scary mask made of plastic. But I couldn't.

'My mum and dad are pretty brave,' I said. 'I don't think a ghost will bother them.'

Merry looked doubtful. 'OK... if you say so.'

'I can take a table and chairs down to the edge of the sea,' I said, feeling a bit more cheerful. 'And I can put some nice food on it. And they'll each think the other has done it...'

'...and then they'll fall back in love with each other!' said Merry.

We high-fived, and I jumped to my feet. 'Now—let's run to the canteen before they stop serving lunch!'

When I got back to the Pantechnicon after school, everything was strangely quiet. The witches' cauldron was missing. Ma must have gone to get water from the stream, and Ar was probably getting in her way. *Good.* I could start playing Cupid and get things organized for the date night.

I jumped into the Pantechnicon, wriggled out of my uniform and into my sweatshirt and jeans and checked inside my rucksack. The two slices of pizza were a bit squashed, but they smelt good. I was *starving*, what with not having any breakfast or lunch, but it'd be worth it if Ar and Ma stopped being estranged. With the coins Ma gave me, I'd bought two pink cupcakes made in the shapes of hearts.

I hurried to the back of the Pantechnicon, pulled open the doors and hunted among the scenery until I found a small table. And I could use two folding chairs from the audience seats. Somewhere among the props were some plates for the pizza, and there was a candle, used for *Macbeth*. One by one, I pulled out the table, the chairs, the plates and the candle and lugged them down the lane to the cove.

The tide was going out, leaving behind lots of junk on the wet sand: plastic forks, fruit punnets, strands of cellophane, even a plastic rubbish bin. *Not very romantic.* I picked up as much of it as I could and cleared a space on the sand. Then I arranged the table and chairs close to the edge of the sea, and set the candle in the middle of the table. I put the pizza slices on the plates in front of each seat. They were a bit squishy, but they'd have to do. Then I placed the pink cupcakes on either side of the candle and stood back to look at it all. Later, with the sun sinking into the sea, the sky full of red and orange clouds, the whisper of the waves and the flickering candle, it really *would* look romantic. All I had to do now was to somehow persuade Ma and Ar to come down here.

There was a sudden scream and a gull swooped down at the table, its yellow eye fixed on the pizza.

'SHOOO!!!!' I yelled, waving my arms, and the gull swerved away.

All this playing Cupid was *hard.* I couldn't leave the food here—the gulls would gobble it up way before Ma and Ar did. I pushed the plates of pizza back into my rucksack, and carefully balanced the cupcakes on top. I'd have to bring them back later, just before Ma and Ar arrived.

'You're SPILLING IT, Marina!'

Ma dragged the cauldron of water into the clearing. Ar limped behind her on his crutches, shouting instructions. Ma's face was white with fury. My heart sank. The way Ma looked, the last thing she'd want to do was to spend any more time in close quarters with Ar. She stomped off to the Pantechnicon. Ar stayed outside. It was too much of a

139

hassle for him to keep climbing over the seats. I thought very hard. How could I persuade him to meet Ma in the cove?

'Um, Ar...' I began.

Ar plumped down into a chair with a gusty sigh, sticking his plaster-cast leg out in front of him.

'YES, Ophelia?'

I crossed my fingers behind my back. 'Ma told me to tell you that—that she's got a special surprise for you.'

Ar's big black eyebrows rose. 'A SURPRISE?'

'Yes. She wants you to meet her down at the beach at sunset.'

'WHATEVER FOR?'

'It's—it's a secret. But it's very important.'

'A SECRET RENDEZVOUS?' Ar's forehead wrinkled. 'Why didn't she APPRISE me of this HERSELF?'

'Because—because she wants to be... er... alone with you. And she—she wants you to dress in your very best.'

Ar stroked his beard. 'Very well, Ophelia. It shall be DONE.'

Yes. That should keep him busy for a while. The first part of my plan was going exactly as I hoped.

The second part would be much, much harder.

TRYST:

a private romantic rendezvous between lovers

This was the bit I wasn't looking forward to. But if it meant Ar and Ma falling in love again and stopping being estranged, it would all be for a Good Cause. And if Ma got mad at me, maybe she'd feel less angry with Ar. Except she already sounded pretty annoyed, banging saucepans around in the kitchen of the Pantechnicon. I jumped over the driver's seat and inside.

'Ma...'

'*What?*'

'Don't be cross with Ar. He doesn't mean to be bossy.'

Ma ignored this. Then she said the words I was dreading. 'Did you get the bread and milk?'

I hung my head. 'Sorry, Ma. I forgot.'

'*Forgot?*' Ma crossed her arms and looked daggers at me. '*Forgot?* Not with your memory! What's *going on*, Ophelia?'

I kicked the side of my bunk. When Ma was hungry *and* angry, she was not to be messed with. But instead of shouting any more, her face sort of crumpled up and she sat down on the bunk.

'I'm—I'm really sorry, Ma.'

'And just *what* are we supposed to have for supper?'

'Well, Ar's got a surprise—'

'You're just as bad as *him*! You neither of you *think* about me, trying to *hold everything together.*'

'That's not true, Ma,' I muttered. I took a deep breath. 'The thing is... there *will* be some food tonight.'

'What are you *talking about*, Ophelia?'

'Ar told me to tell you,' I crossed my fingers behind my back, 'that he wants to give you a lovely, romantic surprise.'

'I'll give him *surprise*!' growled Ma.

'No, really, Ma—he's arranged it all in secret, and—he wants to meet you for a date night—'

'A *what*?'

'A date night, down on the beach!'

'*Arthur Bottom!*' yelled Ma. 'What's all this about a—'

'Shhhhh!' I whispered frantically. 'It's got to be a secret! He—he wants you to know how much he really... er... loves you.'

'What nonsense!' But Ma's face went a bit pink and she pulled at a loose thread on her dress.

'And he wants you to go down to the beach and wait for him—right now!'

Ma looked up at me. 'Did—did he really say he *loves me*?'

I nodded, hardly daring to breathe. There was a long silence, then Ma stood up.

'Very well,' she said, at last. 'I'll *do it.*'

I followed her as she climbed over the seats and jumped down. She stopped and fiddled with her curls.

'You look fine, Ma. Very... very beautiful.'

Ma headed for the back of the Pantechnicon. 'I shall wear my costume from *Romeo and Juliet*,' she said.

'No!!!' I grabbed her arm. She mustn't find Ar in there. 'There's no time! It's almost sunset!'

Ma nodded reluctantly. I gave her a little push towards the lane. 'You look lovely, Ma! Enjoy your date night!'

She disappeared down the track.

In the back of the Pantechnicon Ar, wearing a cap with a long feather, was pulling out costumes. He draped a long velvet cloak around himself, the one he wore when he played Oberon in *A Midsummer Night's Dream*. When he saw me, he twirled around like a model.

'What do you THINK, Ophelia?' he said, looking very pleased with himself. The feather in his cap fell over his nose, and he gave a ginormous sneeze. 'Is this suitable ATTIRE for a secret TRYST?'

'You look *great*, Ar.'

And he did. He wore his blue velvet trousers from *Much Ado About Nothing*, his knee-boots from *Hamlet*, and his black shirt from *Othello*. With the cloak swirling from his shoulders and the feathered hat, he looked like the swash-buckling hero of a fairytale. The crutches and the plaster cast spoilt the effect a bit, but maybe they'd remind Ma to feel sorry for him.

I gave him a little push. 'Hurry up, Ar! Ma will be waiting!'

Ar limped towards the doors and lowered himself to the ground.

'TO THE BEACH!' he roared, and set off towards the lane.

I sighed. All this playing Cupid was *tiring*. Especially when I'd had nothing to eat all day. I jumped into the back of the Pantechnicon and rifled through the rack of costumes until I found the starchy black costume with its white apron. I threw off my jeans and sweatshirt and wriggled into it. It was rather big—Ma wore it when she played the maid in *Othello*—but it would do. Then I grabbed an old tin tray from the props store, arranged the pizza and the cupcakes on a couple of plates, and, balancing the tray, hurried down the track towards the beach.

I heard Ma and Ar before I saw them. Why were they talking so loudly? I tiptoed up the sand dunes and peered over.

Ma and Ar stood facing one another down by the sea. They didn't look as if they'd remembered their love. Ma pointed at something in the sand and shouted. Ar waved his arms about in a bewildered sort of way. What had happened? Balancing the tray, I hurried over the beach towards them.

As I got closer, I nearly dropped the tray. The table floated upside down in the sea, its legs in the air. The two chairs and the candle lay smashed and broken. And written in the sand in bits of plastic junk was another message:

I HATE YOU
GO AWAY FOREVER

I stared down at the sand, cold all over. All around the message were the zigzag footprints, just like mine. Only this time they disappeared off along the beach. Who was doing this? And why? But there was no time to think. Ar and Ma were fighting again.

'How *dare* you, Arthur Bottom!' Ma hissed. 'Asking me down here for a—a *date night*, just to tell me you *hate me*!'

'NONSENSE, Marina!' Ar shouted. 'It was all YOUR IDEA!'

'*Whaaaat?*'

I stumbled forward, the tray shaking in my hands. 'Ma—Ar! Stop fighting! It wasn't you, it was my—'

They both turned to me.

'*Stay out of this*, Ophelia!' snapped Ma. She turned back to Ar. '*Hate* me, do you, Arthur Bottom? Want me to *go away forever*, do you?'

Ar opened and shut his mouth like a fish.

'Well, I *will* go away! Yes—we'll go our separate ways, just as soon as I can get the money for a train fare!'

She turned her back on Ar and stomped away over the dunes, leaving Ar standing there. I dropped the tray and ran after her.

'Ma—wait!'

Ma swivelled to face me. I'd never seen her look so furious.

'I cannot *believe* you played a part in this, Ophelia. How *could* you?'

'I—I didn't mean—'

'Get out of that ridiculous costume and *do not speak to me*. You can speak to your good-for-nothing father instead.

145

Tell him he's to sleep in the back of the Pantechnicon from now onwards. Now *get out of my sight*!'

And she marched off, her shoulders looking stiff. As she headed up the lane, I thought I could hear her crying.

LOITER:

to hang around a place with no real purpose

All night, I lay awake, my tummy churning from lack of food and my mind churning too, like there was a washing machine-full of questions inside it. In her bunk, Ma tossed and turned.

How did everything go so badly wrong? Would Ma really leave Ar? And if they went their separate ways, which way would *I* go? Ma wouldn't want me with her now, and even if she did, how could I choose between living with her or with Ar? What would become of Bottom's? And how would I ever fit in at school, if I came from a Broken Home? Tears leaked out of my eyes and I brushed them away. I'd tried to help, and now everything was about as bad as it could be.

When morning came, Ma shoved a mug of black tea at me, her expression grim, and jerked her head.

'Drink this and *go to school*, Ophelia.'

I wriggled into my uniform and, holding the mug, climbed over the seats and jumped to the ground. From the back of the Pantechnicon, Ar limped out on his crutches. He must've slept in his costume because it was creased all over. He looked different somehow. Sort of smaller, like a balloon that had had the air let out. I ran over and took his hand.

'I'm sorry, Ar. I was trying to make it all right between you and Ma...'

'It's not your fault, Ophelia,' muttered Ar. 'Your mother's been INFURIATED with me for weeks.'

'But you'll make it up, won't you?'

Ar said nothing. I handed him my mug of tea.

'Have this, Ar. And be nice to Ma today?'

Ar shook his head. 'What can I do, if she won't CONVERSE with me?'

'Maybe she just needs some—some alone time.' I pulled on my rucksack and kissed him. His beard tickled my face, like it always did, and I felt all sad again. I turned away, so Ar couldn't see I was upset, and headed off towards the lane.

'Well? Did you do it?'

Merry waited for me outside school. We'd arranged to meet early so I could tell her what happened on Date Night. I nodded, but my eyes were drawn to the words carved above the entrance.

PLASTICUS STUPENDUS EST
DIVERSUS PERICULOSUS EST

Plastic *wasn't* fantastic—not when it was used to mess up the beach and the sea, or to spell out horrible messages.

'So, did it work? Are your parents in love again?'

I stared at the ground, so Merry wouldn't see my face. She took my arm. 'What's the matter, Fee?'

When I looked up, her eyes were so full of worry and kindness that I just couldn't go on being brave. The tears I'd held in since I woke up this morning leaked out of my eyes and ran down my cheeks. I hiccupped and stuttered and my nose ran, and I wiped it on my blazer sleeve—until I remembered it was Merry's blazer sleeve, and then I cried even more.

'What is it, Fee? What's happened?'

'I—I did it, only—only it all went wrong—and now everything's a million *trillion* times worse...'

'But what—' Merry's hand suddenly tightened on my arm. '*Perfect alert!*'

Zoe and Chloe marched up, their Prefects' badges gleaming.

'What's going on here?' said Chloe.

'Why're you two loitering outside?' said Zoe. 'Loitering is against the rules.'

Then they noticed my tear-stained face and their expressions changed.

'Awwww, diddums!' sneered Zoe. 'Is O-*failure* upset?'

Chloe grinned, her braces gleaming. 'Course she's upset! I'd be upset if I was *different*, wouldn't you?'

Merry's green eyes flashed. 'Shut *up*! And leave Fee alone.'

Zoe stared at her. 'It's your birthday today, isn't it, Merry Jones?'

Now I felt even worse. It was Merry's birthday, and I'd completely forgotten. And I'd no money to get her a card, let alone a present.

149

'So?' said Merry.

'After your Ceremony, you won't want to hang around with little crybabies like O-*failure*,' Chloe said.

And the pair marched into school, backs straight, perfectly in step.

'Don't let the Perfects get to you,' said Merry. 'They're not worth it.'

'But they're right,' I wailed. 'I *am* a failure. I forgot it's your birthday.'

Merry shook her head impatiently, but I couldn't stop now.

'And I tried so hard to make things OK with Ma—I mean, my mum and dad—and now—now they're going to—to separate!'

Merry went pale. 'Separate?' She pulled me away from the entrance towards the big wheelie bins at the side of the school. We crouched down behind them.

'What went wrong?' Merry asked.

'I got the food and—and I set up the table and chairs down by the sea—and I told Ar—'

'Who's Ar?' Merry looked puzzled.

'I mean—my dad—to meet my mum there, and I told my mum to meet *him* there... and then—then...'

'Then, what?'

I shook my head and stared at the ground. If I said anything else, I'd give myself away. Merry took my hand.

'You can tell me, Fee. I'm your friend. And friends can tell each other *anything*.'

A warm feeling stole into my chest. *My friend*. The first proper friend I'd ever had.

Merry squeezed my hand. 'You don't *have* to tell me. But if you want to, I swear I won't tell anybody else.'

And then I just couldn't hold it in any more, like I couldn't hold in the tears.

ASHAMED:

feeling guilty or embarrassed about something

'**S**omeone—someone hates us—' The words tumbled out of my mouth in a muddle. 'They—they left a message outside the Pantechnicon saying *go away*—and then they tipped over the table and broke the chairs and wrote *I hate you*—and—and Ma thought the message was from Ar—and she's going to leave—and Ar's leg's broken, so—'

Merry stared at me. 'Slow down, Fee! What's a Pantick-thingy? And what happened to your dad's leg?'

I took a deep breath, and pulled my hand away, in case she wanted to walk off when she heard what I had to say.

'I lied to you, Merry.' My face felt hot, and I couldn't look at her. 'I don't live in a house in M-Magnolia Drive. We live in an old furniture van in the woods—it's c-called the Pantechnicon. And my mum and dad won't be working at the factory. They're actors, in Bottom's Travelling Theatre. And—that's how Ar's leg got broken, during a performance of *Macbeth* on the Common...'

I stumbled to a stop. There was a long silence. I felt sort of empty, now all the lies were out. I stared at the ground, too scared to see Merry's face. Then, when the silence went on, I looked up. Merry stared at me, her mouth in the shape of a big O.

'That's—that's—' she stammered.

What was she going to say? *That's disgusting? That's horrible?*

'—that's FANTASTIC!' said Merry. She grabbed my hands and pulled me up, dancing me round and round. 'I've never met a real actor before!'

'I'm not an actor! I just do the backstage stuff. Ma and Ar—my mum and dad—are the actors.'

'Was it them who performed the Entertainment on the Common?'

I nodded. 'Yeah.'

'This is so exciting!' Merry eyes sparkled. 'I want to know *everything!*'

I glanced at the school entrance. Any minute now the bell would go. Which was a good thing, because I really didn't want Merry to find out too much about how we lived, and where. I stood up and changed the subject.

'What time's your Ceremony?'

Merry frowned. 'After school today. They'll come and collect me and take me up to the factory.' For the first time, I noticed that she looked strangely neat, for Merry. Her hair wasn't escaping from its scrunchy, and her tie was done up properly.

'Are you excited?'

'Well—just a little bit. Except... don't you think there's something a bit, well, *creepy* about Professor Potkettle?'

I nodded. 'All that stuff about plastic being better than people. And that weird plastic baby...'

'But what I'm *really* worried about is having to become a Prefect, like Zoe and Chloe.'

'You'll *never* be like Zoe and Chloe!'

Merry grinned. 'True. They can make me wear a stupid badge, but they can't make me into a *Perfect*.'

'What d'you think will happen at the Ceremony?'

'Dunno. Probably Professor Potkettle will show me round the factory, just like he showed us round the Potkettle Institute.'

'But why?'

'I reckon it's to make us want to work there when we're older, like our mums and dads do.' Merry stopped. 'Only I don't *want* to work in the factory, making plastic stuff, Fee! I want to be an actor, like your mum and dad!'

Would she, if she knew what life at Bottom's was really like? Luckily, at that moment the bell rang.

'I'm sorry,' I muttered, as we hurried through the entrance and headed for our classroom.

'Whatever for?'

'You—you've given me so many things. The uniform. The pizza. Being my friend. And I haven't even got you a birthday present!'

Merry grinned. 'Oh, yes you have!'

I stopped. 'What?'

Merry whispered. 'Once I've done my Ceremony, you're going to take me to visit your Pantechnicon and show me your theatre, and let me meet your mum and dad!'

I followed her into the classroom. Merry might think the acting life was exciting and adventurous, but if she saw the Pantechnicon and the way we lived, she'd soon change her mind. And with Ar and Ma at war, it would all be embarrassing and awful.

Miss Smith was writing on the whiteboard, and Chloe and Zoe sat to attention at their desks at the front. I leant over to Merry.

'I—I don't think visiting us is a good idea, Merry...'

Merry's face dropped. I stumbled on.

'It's—it's just, I don't think you'd—'

Merry turned to stare at me. 'Are you ashamed to introduce me to your mum and dad, Fee? Because I'm ordinary? Is that what it is?'

'*No!*' I whispered. 'It's not you... it's *them*. I mean—they're not like normal parents...'

'*Please*, Fee! It'd be such an adventure to go to the woods, and I've never seen a real theatre, or met real actors!'

There was nothing else for it. I owed Merry, big time, for everything she'd done for me, and the very least I could do was to give her this.

I sighed. 'OK...'

'*Yes!*' Merry punched the air, and Chloe and Zoe swivelled in their seats and glared at us. She grinned at me, her dimple dancing in her cheek, and whispered: 'It'll be the best birthday present—*ever!*'

HANGRY:

bad-tempered or irritable as a result of hunger

'**P***lasticus stupendus est,*
Diversus periculosus est...'

It was the end of the school day, and our class stood in a line outside the school entrance, hands clasped together, chanting the words of the Stopford motto. Beside me, Merry's face was pale. I reached down and squeezed her hand. It felt clammy.

'It'll be fine,' I whispered, trying to sound positive. 'It'll— it'll be an adventure.'

She nodded, but hung on to my hand.

There was a murmur of excitement from the class as an enormous silver limousine drew up to the pavement, driven by the two Boiler Suits. From the gleaming doors hung garlands of plastic flowers.

Miss Smith came over to us. 'Time to go, Merry.' She clapped her hands. 'Attention, children!'

Chloe and Zoe shushed everybody.

'As you all know, our generous benefactor, Professor Potkettle, has recently introduced the Ceremonies to our school. Each child who turns eleven is invited to the factory and will return as a Prefect, just as Zoe and Chloe Adams have done.'

Zoe and Chloe smiled proudly, their braces gleaming.

'So today it is the turn of Merry Jones,' said Miss Smith, 'to receive the greatest honour a Stopford School pupil can experience.' She looked sternly at Merry. 'And ay sincerely hope, Merry, that you will behave yourself during your Ceremony.'

As soon as Miss Smith turned to the limousine, Merry crossed her eyes and stuck out her tongue. I giggled. *Go, Merry.* Then she followed Miss Smith to the limousine. Green Boiler Suit got out and walked round to open the door, Merry stepped inside and Green Boiler Suit slammed the door.

Miss Smith led the clapping and cheering as Blue Boiler Suit started the limousine and it moved away from the pavement. As it glided up the road towards the distant factory on the hill, Merry's white face appeared in the back window. I waved to her, but I don't think she saw me.

When I woke up next morning, it was quiet. Too quiet. All my life, I'd wished that Ar and Ma would stop arguing and shouting. But now that they weren't speaking to one another, it felt all wrong—like my family wasn't my family any more. I rummaged through the larder box, but it was empty apart from a jar of pickled onions. Yesterday, I'd brought back two cold burgers from school for Ma and Ar. I'd told the dinner ladies I was really hungry (which

157

was true) and they'd given me the leftovers. But I couldn't *keep* doing that, or they'd get suspicious. Ar had wolfed his burger down in seconds and stared at me like a greedy dog. And Ma had been upset.

'This situation is *impossible*,' she'd said. 'How are we supposed to carry on without food, and without money to buy it with?'

And she'd gone very quiet for the rest of the evening.

I hopped out of the Pantechnicon. The witches' cauldron, half full of water, sat beside it on the muddy ground. However could I keep my promise to Merry, and bring her here? At least there was no sign of any more messages. I glanced at the trees. Was someone lurking in there, spying on us and planning their next move? Then, a flash of purple caught my eye. A figure hurried away from the Pantechnicon towards the lane.

'Ma?' I shouted. 'Where are you going?'

Ma's red curls were wilder than ever, and she wore a long purple dress from *Othello* with welly boots underneath, because of the mud. She brandished her phone.

'There's no signal in this *wretched place*. I'm going up to the Common.'

'Where's Ar?'

Ma's eyes went steely. 'Your *good-for-nothing* father is down on the beach.'

'On the beach?'

'Doing his *recuperation exercises*, he said.' And she stalked off towards the Common.

'How're things, Ar?'

Ar limped up and down the sand on his crutches. He frowned, his black bushy eyebrows almost squashing his eyes out of sight.

'Things are FRIGHTFUL, Ophelia,' he said. 'Your mother's BANISHED me! She says I mustn't GO NEAR HER.'

'She's probably hangry.'

'HANGRY?' roared Ar. 'Is this the PRONUNCIATION they teach you at that RIDICULOUS SCHOOL?'

'Hangry is when you're hungry, and it makes you angry,' I said. 'If we had more to eat, maybe she'd stop being grouchy.'

'What's she doing now?' Ar's eyes looked wistful.

'She's gone off to the Common with her phone,' I told him. 'Who d'you think she's trying to call?'

Ar shook his big head. 'I have no NOTION.'

I sighed. 'We'd better go on walking. It'll be good for your leg.'

'INDEED!' roared Ar. 'PERAMBULATION is the OPTIMUM EXERCISE!'

Up and down the beach we went. There was a lot of plastic about, but at least we had the beach to ourselves. After twenty minutes, Ar stopped.

'After all this exercise, we need REFRESHMENTS!' he said. 'Run back ahead and put on the KETTLE before your MOTHER returns.'

I nodded.

'And you could have a little peep in the LARDER, while you're at it,' he added, a greedy glint in his eye. 'There will perchance be the odd BISCUIT left.'

'Sorry, Ar, there's nothing—'

'I'm so hungry, my stomach thinks my THROAT'S BEEN CUT!' roared Ar.

I set off over the sand dunes towards the lane, leaving Ar limping more slowly on his crutches. It was Saturday, so I couldn't get any more food. And if Ar and Ma were hangry, they'd go on being mad at one another, and then they'd get divorced. As I hurried up the lane and through the wood, my shoulders felt like they'd got huge weights piled on them. And then I reached the clearing, and the Pantechnicon.

I'd thought things were as bad as they could get.

It turned out I was wrong.

RANSACK:

to go through a place, stealing or damaging things

A terrible sight met my eyes. The Pantechnicon's doors hung wide open, front and back, and the clearing was strewn with all our things. Torn costumes lay in the mud. Every piece of scenery had been slashed from top to bottom and tossed into the clearing. The tent was ripped all over, like someone had stabbed at it with a knife. The seats were smashed and splintered, the props broken, the CDs snapped and scattered over the ground. Our old mirror lay in fragments among Ma's saucepans and the crushed kettle. Our sleeping bags were streaked with muddy footprints. The windscreen of the Pantechnicon was shattered and one of the windows was cracked. And everything was covered with paint—the green paint we used for painting the tree scenery, the brown for painting buildings, the blue for sky. The sign for *Bottom's Travelling Theatre* was no more, obliterated with smeared paint. Empty, crushed paint tins lay everywhere, seeping their colours into the mud.

For a few moments I couldn't move or speak. I just stared

at our ruined home, icy cold all over. Then Ar limped up behind me, and his gasp echoed round the clearing.

'WHAT IN THE—'

But even Ar didn't have words for this.

Then I heard it. A shuffling among the trees, followed by the crack of a twig. Rage such as I'd never known before erupted through my body and I raced headlong into the wood.

There was no one to be seen. But... there in the muddy ground were fresh trainer-prints. Fury lent my legs speed. I crashed through the trees, scarcely noticing the branches whipping my face, dodging tree roots, slithering and sliding in the mud. The only thing I cared about was getting my hands on whoever had done this and making them pay for it. My trainers skidded on the stepping stones and I almost fell in the stream, but I managed to right myself and leap to the ground on the other side. Someone ahead of me, just out of sight, was running fast. I forced my legs to go faster, faster. I was almost on them now, so close I could hear their panting. I plunged ahead, the trees slipping past me like dark shadows. I burst out into the clearing, just in time to see a thin figure—with a PRATT'S PLASTIC PELLETS sack over its shoulder—racing towards the round house. My lungs bursting, I leapt forward like a rugby player and grabbed the person's legs. We rolled over on the ground, the sack bursting its plastic rubbish over us both. They kicked out hard, almost knocking out my teeth, but I held on tight. Then hot breath panted in my ear, something growled fiercely, and sharp teeth nipped at my fingers, so I had to let go. The person struggled to his feet.

It was a boy: the boy I'd seen on the beach the day my uniform disappeared; the day I went swimming and got scared by the Ghost from the Sea. Close up, he was much shorter than me, and skinny, but he looked older—maybe thirteen. Curly hair framed a thin face with piercing dark eyes, flashing with a rage to match my own. He bent and scooped the black-and-white puppy into his arms. Its front end growled, but its back end wagged, as if it wasn't sure whether I was a friend or an enemy. So much for the *feroshus* dog. For a long moment, we glared at one another, gasping for breath.

The boy's clothes looked very familiar.

My blazer, its arms made into a pair of shorts.

The sweatband tied around his hair.

My tie.

What he wore on his feet.

My trainers.

So *this* was who had stolen my uniform from the cave. *This* was the person whose footprints I'd followed—who'd scared me out of the sea with his stupid mask—who'd warned us away with his horrible messages—who was storing Professor Potkettle's leftover plastic junk and dumping it in the sea. Fury sizzled through my body and words scorched out of my mouth into the air, higgledy-piggledy.

'You—you—wicked *vandal*—wrecking our van—stealing my uniform—you *thief*—with your *horrible* plastic messages and your *nasty* plastic mask and, and—dumping *junk* in the sea—ruining date night—making Ar and Ma *divorce*—'

The boy just stood there, his face blank. When I finally stuttered to a halt, he said in a cold voice:

'Go away, *Plastic.*'

'Whaaat?' How dared he call *me* plastic, with his plastic sacks and his plastic mask and his plastic messages! But I was so angry that the only sound that came out of my mouth was a furious squeak.

'If you'd left when I told you to,' he said, 'none of this would've happened.'

'What g-gives you the—the right—to tell us to leave!' I stuttered. The puppy's eyes went from him to me, like someone watching a tennis match.

'I live here.' The boy turned to the gate. 'You don't.'

'We do now!' I spluttered. 'And you don't own the woods.'

The boy bent to the padlock and opened it. I *wouldn't* let him get away with this. I grabbed his arm.

'Why did you do it? Just tell me that! Why did you steal my uniform? Why did you dress up as the Ghost from the Sea to scare me? Why did you leave those hateful messages telling us to leave? And why have you destroyed our van?'

A strange expression flickered over the boy's face.

'Who says I destroyed your ugly old van?'

I stamped my foot. 'Don't play stupid games with me— you *did*!'

The boy stared at me, his eyes giving nothing away. How *dared* he stand there, in *my* uniform, and deny what he'd done?

'I *know* it was you who left the messages!' I hissed. 'Your footprints were all over the clearing. And they were down by the sea, too, when you overturned our table and chairs. And it was you who dressed up in your stupid plastic mask and scared me out of the water—and you who just attacked our home and—and slashed our things—and broke them—and emptied paint all over them—'

The boy's face went very still. Then he stepped towards me.

'Listen very carefully, Plastic. I don't give a whistle what you believe. But yes—I left the messages and I scared you out of the water. I don't want any of you Plastics camping in the wood, swimming in my cove, spying on me. But that's all.' He said every word very slowly, 'I—did—not—attack—your—van.'

'You liar—you *did*!'

The boy's eyes were suddenly full of hatred.

'Get *out* of my woods. Do you hear me?' he hissed. 'And *never* come back.'

He yanked the gate open so hard that it smashed against the fence. The puppy whined in his arms. Then the gate slammed shut behind them.

'OPHELIA!' Ar's voice echoed through the wood. 'WHERE ARE YOU?'

I hurried towards the sound. Ar was disentangling one of his crutches from the branch of a tree, his beard full of leaves. 'I'm here, Ar.'

'Are you SAFE?'

'Yes—yes, I'm all right.'

'Did you APPREHEND the vandal who RANSACKED our VEHICLE?'

'No. He—he got away.' There was no point in telling Ar about the boy. It'd mean telling him all the other stuff, about the messages and date night.

We walked slowly back, my mind spinning. The first thing we saw as we stepped into the clearing was Ma, staring at the ruined Pantechnicon, her face sheet-white.

'Who did this?' she whispered.

'VANDALS!' roared Ar. He limped over and tried to put his arm around Ma, but she shook it off.

'Don't you touch me, Arthur Bottom! I *told* you we should never have come here!'

'We'll clean it all up, Ma!' I whispered. 'We can—we can make it good as new!'

I hurried over to the mess on the ground and began to pick up the stuff. If we all worked together over the weekend, we could sort it all out. We could rebuild the Pantechnicon and make it home again. We *would*.

Then I saw them.

Footprints, leading from the clearing towards the lane. Not the zigzag trainer prints of the boy, but big, adult footprints made by heavy boots.

So the boy was telling the truth. But who left the prints? How did they know we were here? And why would anyone want to destroy our home?

PREFECT:

a school pupil in a position of
power over other pupils

Rain pattered on the roof of the Pantechnicon, and I pulled my sleeping bag over my head. I ought to get up and get ready for school, only I ached all over.

All weekend, the three of us had worked to clear up the mess. At first it was chaos, what with Ma moaning and picking stuff up and dropping it, and Ar shouting instructions and vowing revenge on the MISCREANTS who did it—until I suggested we got organized and do one job each. I sorted everything into three piles: one pile for washing and cleaning; one pile for mending; and one pile for things that were ruined beyond repair. Ma wiped the paint off things in the first pile and washed the muddy things in the stream, while Ar—his plaster cast propped on a chair—wielded hammer and nails, fixing the broken things. At least they were too busy to argue. Only then it began to rain again, and we had to carry everything into the Pantechnicon and start all over next day.

The only good thing about our stuff being ransacked was that I found three precious cans of food, lying in the mud among the battered saucepans—two of beans and one of spaghetti. Ar was all for wolfing them down immediately, but Ma insisted on doling them out a little each day, so we could keep our strength up.

I'd better get up. I'd be late for school, and today Merry would be back from her Ceremony. I wriggled out of my sleeping bag. The Pantechnicon seemed weird and dark: Ar had draped the shattered windscreen with a tarpaulin to keep out the rain. Beside me, Ma was asleep. I wouldn't wake her. She needed the rest and anyway, my head hurt too much to listen to her complaining and being cross. I tiptoed over to the bucket of water under the sink, dipped a mug into it and drank. Then I got into my uniform. The blazer was smeared and scabbed with mud from wrestling with the boy. Whatever would Merry say when she saw it?

I rubbed my aching forehead and clambered over the seats into the driver's cab. One of the windows had a giant crack in it, which Ar had sealed up with packing tape. The other was missing altogether. I pushed open the door and jumped down into the clearing, half expecting—like I'd done all weekend—to see another threatening plastic message on the ground. But no—there was only mud and puddles.

I swished my trainers about in an extra-large puddle to try and get off some of the mud. But my eyes kept returning to the Pantechnicon, with its broken windows and ruined paintwork. What if whoever did this came back? What if they did something even more terrible while Ma and Ar were asleep? I turned and ran to the back of the Pantechnicon, threw open the doors and climbed into the back. Ar was snoring loudly on a heap of cushions, his crutches beside him, surrounded by toppling piles of stuff. I shook his shoulder.

'Ar! Wake up!'

Ar sat bolt upright, his beard all over the place, grabbed one of the crutches and brandished it.

'ATTACK ME, WOULD YOU, MISCREANT!'

'Shhh, Ar—it's only me, Ophelia!'

Ar blinked.

'I've got to go to school, so—so it's up to you to look after Ma. She's still asleep.'

'SCHOOL, Ophelia?' Ar scratched his beard crossly. 'You can't go to SCHOOL!'

'I've got to, Ar. We've nothing left to eat, remember? I'll be back later, with some food from the canteen.'

Ar's stomach gave an enormous growl, and he nodded reluctantly.

'VERY WELL, Ophelia. Given the CIRCUMSTANCES...'

I kissed his cheek and hurried out, my own tummy growling in company. At the edge of the clearing, I turned. The Pantechnicon looked so sorry for itself, standing in the rain, the sign for *Bottom's Travelling Theatre* blotted out and spoilt. Was this the end of Bottom's? And if Ar and Ma separated, would it be the end of our family?

'*Never*,' I muttered.

I stared down at the large footprints in the mud. I didn't

know who'd done this to us, or why, but I wouldn't let them win.

'I'm going to find out who you are,' I whispered to the tracks. *'And when I have, I'll do whatever it takes to stop you.'*

Merry's desk was empty when I got to school. I shuffled into my seat, hoping no one would notice my muddy blazer and trainers. No such luck. Chloe and Zoe, their hair perfectly plaited, their ties perfectly straight and their shoes perfectly polished, nudged one another and stared.

'Look what the *cat* dragged in!' smirked Chloe, and Zoe giggled.

I ignored them, opened my rucksack and pulled out my books and pens.

'Been mud-wrestling, O-*failure*?' Zoe said.

I was just about to tell her to shut up, when Miss Smith came in, with Merry.

'Your attention, please, children!' Miss Smith said, and everyone stopped what they were doing. 'Ay have the pleasure of welcoming our new Prefect.'

Merry's face was pale. She must be cringing about being singled out in front of us all. A shiny Prefect badge gleamed from her blazer.

'Becoming a Prefect is a great responsibility,' said Miss Smith. 'And ay expect you to set an example to the rest of your classmates by your behaviour.'

Why wasn't Merry rolling her eyes and poking out her tongue? Instead, she stood very still, her face solemn.

'You may sit down,' said Miss Smith.

Good. Once Merry was next to me, we could make a plan to talk at breaktime.

Only Merry didn't come to sit beside me. Chloe and Zoe grabbed her by the arms and steered her into a seat between them at the front of the class. She didn't argue the way she usually would. She just sat down quietly, removed her blazer, draped it neatly over the back of her seat and got out her pencil case. She didn't even look at me. But Zoe and Chloe did. They smirked at me, their identical braces gleaming, as if to say: *See whose friend she is now!*

My tummy felt weird, like something dark and shadowy was creeping inside it. And suddenly, I knew what Ma meant when she said she had *a very bad feeling indeed.*

As soon as the bell rang for breaktime, I hurried over to Merry's new desk and reached out to tap her shoulder. But Zoe grabbed my hand.

'What are you doing, *O-failure?*'

'I want to talk to Merry.' Merry still had her back turned to me.

Zoe nudged Chloe, imitating me. '*O-failure wants to talk to her.*'

Chloe smiled. 'What if she doesn't want to talk to *you?*'

'Merry!' I said. 'What's going on?'

Then Merry turned to look up at me. Close up, she looked neater and cooler and paler than the Merry I knew. Where was the sparkle in her green eyes? Why didn't she look happy to see me? She looked at me—almost *through* me—as if I was a stranger.

'Merry?' I said again.

'Why are you calling me *Merry*?' she said, in a cool voice. 'My name is *Mary*.'

I gawped at her. 'What do you mean? I've always called you Merry.'

'Then you must have heard it wrong in the first place,' Merry said.

'That's why she's called O-*failure*! Because she gets everything wrong!' Chloe and Zoe grinned on either side of her.

Then, I got it. Merry must be playing some kind of joke on me—pretending to be a Perfect to see if I'd believe her. Any minute, she'd nudge me in the ribs, her dimple dancing in her cheek, and say, *Fooled you!*

I grinned. 'OK, Merry, enough's enough!'

Merry slowly picked up her blazer from the back of her chair and shrugged into it. The Prefect badge, pinned to the pocket, shone. Chloe and Zoe linked their arms through hers, just as if they were her best friends, and they set off across the room. I ran after them and grabbed her shoulder.

'Merry—wait!'

Merry turned. 'What do you want...O-*failure*?'

Did I hear right? She *couldn't* have called me that name.

'C'mon, Mary,' said Chloe. 'Let's go and play on the laptops.'

And Merry nodded, brushing past me as if I didn't exist.

BETRAYAL:

treachery or disloyalty

The rest of the morning passed in a blur. Miss Smith talked, Chloe and Zoe and the others put up their hands. But all I could concentrate on was Merry. I stared at her back as she sat up straight between Chloe and Zoe. Why was she being this way?

At lunchtime, I went to the canteen. It felt weird without Merry by my side. I wasn't hungry, even though I hadn't eaten anything since yesterday. But I had to pretend I was, so I could sneak some food home for Ar and Ma. I grabbed an extra couple of slices of pizza and two apples and hurried with my tray to a table in the corner. Making sure no one was looking, I wrapped the food in a paper serviette and slipped it into my rucksack. Merry, Zoe and Chloe came in soon after, linking arms like they'd been friends forever. I watched them as they formed a neat line at the serving hatch, then marched to sit together at a new table marked *Prefects* on the other side of the canteen. Miss Smith led us all in the chanting of *plasticus stupendus est, diversus periculosus est.* I bowed my head so no one could see I wasn't saying the words.

When the chant finished, I looked up. Chloe, Zoe and Merry sat in a huddle, munching and whispering. They must be talking about me because Zoe and Chloe kept glancing at me, their mouths wide open. I felt sick. I tried to eat my pizza, but it reminded me of the day I visited Merry at her home—when Merry was my friend. I wrapped it in another serviette and dropped it into my rucksack with the rest. At least Ma and Ar would eat well tonight.

I ought to go—leave the canteen and go out into the playground. At least then I wouldn't have to see Merry being pally with the Perfects. I got to my feet. But before I could hoist my rucksack on to my shoulder, Miss Smith marched over to the Prefects' table and said something to Zoe and Chloe. They nodded in unison, stood up together and went off with her, towards her study. Merry stayed where she was, her back to me.

I hesitated. This might be the only chance I'd have to get Merry on her own, away from Chloe and Zoe. Maybe when it was just us, she'd go back to being the Merry I knew. I walked slowly over until I was standing behind her.

'Merry—I mean, Mary?'

Merry turned round. 'Yes?' She didn't look sorry to see me, which was *something.*

'Can I—can I sit down?'

Merry shrugged. 'If you want.'

I walked round the table and sat down opposite her. She looked just the same, yet not. Sort of more grown up.

Maybe it was the Prefect badge. It gleamed on her blazer pocket like an extra eye.

'So, um... how was your Ceremony?'

Merry looked blankly at me. 'It was fine.'

'What did you do? Did you get shown round the factory? Did you meet Professor Potkettle again?'

Merry sighed, just like a grown-up does when a child asks too many questions.

'It was fine,' she said again.

'But what actually *happened*?'

Merry picked up her rucksack. 'The Ceremonies are secret,' she said. 'You'll have to wait until it's your turn—and the sooner, the better, in my opinion.'

'What do you mean?'

Merry stood up. 'You need to grow up, O-*failure*.'

How dare she talk to me this way? How dare she act as if we'd never been friends? I took a deep breath and stared at her.

'I won't be having my Ceremony,' I said.

Merry stopped. 'What?'

'I said, I won't be having my Ceremony. Not now I've seen what's happened to *you*.'

'You have to,' said Merry coolly.

'No, I don't! We'll soon be on the road again, just as soon as Ar's leg's mended...'

'But isn't it your birthday soon?'

She'd remembered that, at any rate.

I nodded. 'I'll just tell Miss Smith I'm not doing it.'

Merry stared at me. 'You mean, you want to be *childish* forever?'

'I'd rather be that way than be a—a *Perfect*!'

'Anyhow,' Merry shrugged as if she didn't care either way, 'you'd better make up your mind—If you want to be like us, you'll have to go for your Ceremony. If you want to go on being *different*, you and your weird family had better pack up and leave Stopford... before anything *worse* happens to your old van.'

'What—what do you mean?' I hadn't told Merry about the attack on the Pantechnicon, so how did she know about it?

Before Merry could reply, Chloe and Zoe marched over to us.

'Is O-*failure* bothering you, Mary?' said Zoe.

'Should we report her to Miss Smith?' said Chloe.

'Shut *up*!!!' I shouted.

'Ignore her,' smirked Zoe. 'She can't help being *different*.'

'With parents like *hers*, it's no surprise,' grinned Chloe. 'Hammy old actors living in a beat-up old van in the woods.'

How did they know?

I turned to Merry.

'You just *told* them, didn't you, Merry?' I stared at her. 'You promised me you wouldn't tell anybody! All this time, I thought you were my friend.'

'A fine friend *you* are—O-*failure*,' sniffed Chloe. 'You can't even remember Mary's name!'

Merry said nothing. She just stood there, her face cool. I took in a big hiccup of air and my eyes stung with tears. My face felt like it was crumpling up. I swivelled round and made for the door. No way would I show them I was upset.

'Crybaby!' called Chloe.

176

Then they began to chant. Quietly at first, then louder and louder and louder.

'*Diversus periculosus est... diversus periculosus est... DIVERSUS PERICULOSUS EST!*'

And in that moment I knew three things:

That I'd never fit in at Stopford School;

that I was walking out of school now and was *never* coming back;

and—worst of all—

that I'd lost the only friend I ever thought I had.

I stumbled out of the school entrance, tears rolling down my face. I wiped them away with my blazer sleeve. Then I remembered it was Merry's blazer sleeve, and the tears poured faster. I shrugged the blazer off and hurled it, as hard as I could, towards the wheelie bins. It landed on top, one arm hanging down. I ran out of school, past all the perfect little houses, over the Common, down the lane and through the wood. But however hard I ran, the cruel words followed me, winding about my neck like a noose. ...*you need to grow up... childish... a fine friend... leave before anything worse happens... different is dangerous... O-failure... O-failure... O-failure...*

I *was* a failure. If I hadn't said *Macbeth* when we arrived here, Ar wouldn't have broken his leg and the Pantechnicon wouldn't have been attacked and ruined. If I hadn't set up the date night, Ar and Ma wouldn't be splitting up. I'd failed at fitting in at school. And I'd failed at making even a single friend.

At the edge of the clearing, I stopped running and wiped my face to get rid of any streaks of tears. The Pantechnicon looked as horrible as I felt. The black tarpaulin draped over the windscreen made it seem blind. And the huge pile of things spoiled-beyond-repair sprawled on the muddy ground—a bashed-in frying pan, the torn and slashed velvet curtain, snapped CDs. Someone—probably Ar—had tried to clean off the paint splattered over the words **BOTTOM'S TRAVELLING THEATRE**, but they'd made it a hundred times worse. Cautiously, I pulled open the driver's door, keeping an eye on the cracked window, climbed in and over the seats. Ma sat alone, a large pair of scissors on the draining board beside her, sewing one of her costumes. She looked up as I came in.

'Ophelia? What are you doing back so early? And where's your *blazer*?'

Instead of answering, I shrugged off my rucksack and tipped a wrapped-up pizza slice on to one of the only not-broken plates.

'For lunch, Ma.'

Ma's cheeks flushed pink. 'Thank you, Ophelia. But this *isn't right.*'

'It's only for today, Ma,' I said. I was going to have to tell her that I wouldn't be going back to school. But I'd wait until she'd had something to eat, so she wouldn't be hangry.

Ma reached out for the pizza slice and began to nibble it.

'I'll—I'll just take a slice to Ar.' I picked up my rucksack.

'Wait, Ophelia.' Ma looked up from her pizza.

'Wh-what is it?'

'I need to talk to you about something. Something *important.*' Ma's face was serious. 'Sit down for a moment.'

I dropped my rucksack on to the bunk and sat down. That creeping feeling was back in my tummy.

And I was about to find out why.

EMPLOYEE:

a person who works for wages

Ma finished her pizza slice and pushed the plate away. Her face looked pale, and sort of thinner. Suddenly, I was scared. What was she going to tell me that was so important?

I cleared my throat, to get rid of the last bits of tears. 'What is it, Ma?'

'We can't go on living this way, Ophelia.'

'Wh-what do you mean? We can sort it all out. We can make the Pantechnicon as good as new!'

Ma shook her head. 'No. It's ruined. And *someone*—whoever did this—wants us out of here. Look at the damage they've caused. Think what they could do *next time*.'

'You mean—we just give in? Let them bully us into leaving?' I said. 'Anyway, how *can* we leave? Ar's leg won't be better for weeks, and you're not allowed to drive. And—and we've no money for trains or taxis.'

Ma nodded. 'Exactly. Which is why I've made a *decision*.'

The creeping feeling in my tummy got stronger. 'What is it?'

'I'm going to *take a job*.'

My mouth fell open. I hadn't expected this. What on earth could Ma do, apart from act?

'What sort of job, Ma?'

Ma picked up the scissors and fiddled with them.

'I'm going to work up at the factory.'

'You—you can't!' The words burst out before I could stop them.

'I rang them yesterday,' Ma said, 'and it's all decided.'

'But, Ma—'

Ma's head jerked up. 'What else can I do, Ophelia? We can't perform. We have no money for food. And I *will not* rely on you bringing us food from school! If I work at the factory, we'll have money. And I'm going to get us out of this *wretched place* if it's the *last thing I do!*'

'But—but—' Thoughts whirred round my brain. 'They'll never let you work there! Not when they... actually see you.'

'And *why not*, pray?' Ma's eyes flashed.

'Because—you're, well...' I tailed off.

'What exactly are you trying to say, Ophelia?' Ma had That Look on her face, the one you don't mess with. I took a deep breath.

'Ma, you look and—and behave... too *different* to the Stopford folk. And—the owner of the factory believes that, well, different is dangerous...'

Ma drew herself up. 'I am an *actor*. And as such, I can fit in *anywhere.*'

She stood up and brandished the costume she was working on. It used to be her costume as Portia, from *The Merchant of Venice.* Only now it was a white boiler suit.

'I shall assume a *disguise*,' said Ma. 'This is the outfit worn by Mrs Barbara Brown.'

I gaped. 'Who's she?'

'The factory's new employee,' said Ma.

'But, Ma—Ar will go mad if you work up at the factory!'

'*Let him!*' Ma retorted. 'It's all his fault that we're in this mess. And just as soon as I've made enough money, your father and I will *go our separate ways.*'

My heart clenched up. Whatever would Ar say when he heard this? How long would it be before Ma made enough money to leave, and they split up? And what would Ma say when I told her I wasn't going to school any more? In this mood, she'd make me. Then I thought of something.

'Ma... will you be working shifts at the factory?'

Ma nodded.

'Um... what time will you have to be there?' I asked.

'Seven in the morning, and I won't be back till after midnight.' Ma's face softened a bit. 'I know it'll mean I won't see much of you. But it'll only be for *a few weeks*. And you can get yourself ready for school on your own, can't you?'

I breathed out. 'Yes... yes, of course.'

If Ma left early to go to the factory, she'd never know that I wasn't going to school any more. And Ar wouldn't tell her—he'd be overjoyed that I'd stopped. Suddenly, my heart felt a tiny bit lighter. Things were still bad—very bad. Our home was still ruined, Ar and Ma were still estranged, and Ma was going to work at the factory. But I wouldn't have to go to school. I wouldn't have to go to my Ceremony. I wouldn't have to hear Miss Smith and the Perfects calling me O-*failure*.

Most important of all, I'd *never* have to see Merry Jones again.

After that, we settled into a routine. Ar slept in the back of the Pantechnicon, while Ma and I slept in the front. Ar grumbled all the time —'A BOTTOM doesn't work in a FACTORY'—but Ma ignored him. Every morning, she got up at six, brushed her wild curls and skewered them into a neat bun, put on her white boiler suit and left for the factory. All day, Ar and I worked on repairing the Pantechnicon, and our stuff. Sometimes it seemed like we were never going to finish, but I felt that if we could somehow get the Pantechnicon back to the way it was, maybe everything *else* would go back to being the way it used to be, too. When Ma returned from the factory after midnight, she was too tired and forgetful to ask me about school. She handed me her wages and I stuffed the money into one of the few not-bashed-in saucepans. Every few days—during school hours so no-one would see me—I sneaked into Stopford and bought food. I also secretly bought the things Ar needed to repair the Pantechnicon—fresh paint, wood, nails. Ma would probably blow a gasket if she knew we were using her wages for this, rather than saving them for train fares out of here. But luckily, she didn't seem to notice the changes to the Pantechnicon—it was always pitch dark when she got back. She still refused to talk to Ar. Instead, she said *you'd better tell your father...* so I was a go-between, running between her and Ar with messages. And then Ar huffed and puffed and shouted, so I had to calm him down as best I could.

At night, I tossed and turned in my bunk. A bit of me was always on high alert in case whoever attacked the Pantechnicon returned, or the boy left more messages. So far, when I woke up, everything was just the way it was when I went to sleep. But it took ages to actually fall asleep because my brain was full to bursting. Would Miss Smith try to contact Ma about me not going to school any more? Somehow, I didn't think so. She was probably glad I was no longer there, sticking out like a sore thumb. Zoe and Chloe would be triumphant and smug that they'd got rid of me. And Merry? Would she even care that I'd gone?

If I wasn't thinking about that, my mind scurried round like a mouse, trying to work out answers to three more questions:

1. Who attacked the Pantechnicon, and why?

2. Would Ma and Ar separate forever? and:

3. If they did, what would become of Bottom's—and me?

RESCUE:

to save someone from a dangerous situation

I painted the last letter—the E at the end of THEATRE—and stepped back to admire my handiwork. It had taken Ar and me ages to clean off the dried, smeared paint from the side of the Pantechnicon. After that, we had to sand it all down and repaint it.

Now the name shone, bright and beautiful in the afternoon sunlight, in red and blue and gold:

BOTTOM'S TRAVELLING THEATRE

'BRAVO, Ophelia!' Ar roared, his beard speckled with paint. 'Bottom's is RESTORED to its FORMER GLORY!!!'

I wiped my paint-smeared fingers on my jeans and used my sleeve to mop my sweaty forehead. I hadn't had a wash for *ages*—there didn't seem much point when I wasn't going to school—but suddenly I longed to run down to the beach and bathe in the cool water of the cove. I grabbed my swimming costume and towel.

'Back in half an hour!' I told Ar. 'I'm going for a swim.'

'WELL DESERVED, Ophelia!' rumbled Ar. 'And a much BETTER use of your time than attending that RIDICULOUS SCHOOL!'

The sea was calm as a pond. Tiny waves lapped gently at the shore and the sand was golden in the sunlight. Stopford Cove was empty, all mine.

Then my heart sank. All along the shoreline were the familiar zigzag footprints, and paw marks running beside them. I scanned the beach, half expecting to see the boy, his puppy dancing around his feet, the sack of plastic on his back. But apart from the prints, there was no sign of him.

I wriggled out of my clothes and into my costume. Then I walked down over the sand to the sea, and waded in.

When I was up to my shoulders, I shut my eyes, held my nose and dunked my head under the surface. My hair needed a good wash, though nothing would get the specks of paint off it. When my breath ran out, I resurfaced and began to swim. But the further out I went, the more islands of plastic junk appeared, spreading in clumps over the surface of the water. That boy must come down here with his sacks full of plastic every day—maybe several times a day—doing Professor Potkettle's dirty work. And making sure that everyone was too scared to come here, by frightening them off with his stupid plastic mask.

Something wet and cold brushed my arm, and I pushed it away. *More junk.* Then another. I turned on to my front, and froze.

Floating a few centimetres from my face was a fish. But it was the wrong way up, and its eyes were glazed. I turned and swam away. But there was another, and another—lots of fish, all floating, dead, on the surface of the water. Then something moved in the water ahead. A clump of plastic swirled and bobbed, dipping under the water and swishing to the surface.

It's the boy. Back with his mask, trying to scare me out of the water again. Fury filled me. I shouted, as loudly as I could.

'Don't you think you can frighten me, you—you *coward*!'

There was no reply. The clump of plastic swished. Then suddenly, a drenched white head appeared from the water. A pair of eyes stared into my mine. A terrible sound echoed over the water—a sort of howling, whining groan. And then the thing in front of me began to splash horribly, slipping under the water and bobbing to the surface again, its black eyes fixed upon me.

The puppy. It's the boy's puppy.

I saw the white plastic sack wrapped around the puppy's neck, and another strand of plastic wound over its front paws. The puppy gave another howl and wriggled frantically in the water, but it slipped under again, and this time it didn't come back up.

I held my nose and ducked under the water. The puppy struggled just under the surface, its tail wildly waggling and its back legs desperately paddling to keep it afloat. I grabbed at it, but it panicked—its frantic paws splashed and slipped out of my grasp. I bobbed to the surface and took a great lungful of air, then dived under again. This time I managed to grab the puppy's back legs. They kicked, but I held on tight. I pulled the puppy towards me, still desperately fighting, until I'd got it against my chest, its little heart racing against mine. Then, using my other arm and my legs, I struggled towards the shore.

At last my feet found the sand, and I waded to the edge of the water. The puppy lay still, a sopping bundle of fur in my arms, all the fight gone out of it. Its dark eyes stared up at me pleadingly, the plastic sack wound tightly around its neck, its little chest heaving for breath. I stumbled out of the water and laid it on the sand. The puppy whined, its eyes popping with trying to breathe. My fingers scrabbled at the slippery sack, trying to untangle it, but it was too tightly wound, like a noose. If only I had a knife, or some scissors... but I did have my teeth.

I ducked down and gnawed at the wet plastic, grinding my teeth on the slipperiness, until suddenly the sack tore open. I pulled it away and cradled the panting puppy in my arms. It just lay there, staring up at me. It must be in shock. I unwound the strand of plastic from its front paws, but it still didn't move. I stumbled over to my pile of clothes, knelt in the sand and wrapped the shivering puppy in my towel. Then I rubbed it gently, over and over, whispering, *'It's all right, you're free now, it's OK,'* over and over, until its little paws scrabbled in my arms and it gave a weak bark. I bent down to kiss its nose and it gave my face a wet lick. Down on the sand lay the plastic sack, the words PRATT'S PLASTIC PELLETS jagged and torn.

Inside me, anger boiled.

The puppy almost died—*would* have died, if I hadn't come here to swim—and it was all because of the boy's plastic junk. How *dared* he do this! Holding the puppy close to me with one arm, I managed to squeeze my feet into my trainers and struggle into my jeans. I shook with cold and anger, and my hair dripped in rat's tails. The towel was sopping wet, so I wrapped the shivering puppy in my sweatshirt. Then I staggered to my feet. I'd go to the round house and have it out with the boy once and for all—make him stop filling the sea with his horrible trash.

Holding the trembling puppy close, I set off for the wood.

ACCUSE:

*to claim that someone has done
something illegal or wrong*

I'd almost reached the clearing when a piercing whistle echoed through the trees. The puppy in my arms went still, its ears twitching. Then it gave an excited yap and scrabbled weakly in my arms. But I held on tight. The whistle came again, closer now. And a voice—sounding scared—called out.

'Jack! JACK!'

I ran towards the clearing and almost collided with the boy. He glared at me.

'What's up, Plastic?' he said, with a sneer in his voice.

His gaze dropped to the bundle in my arms. He reached out and grabbed the puppy—Jack—from my arms. It yapped and wriggled against him, licking his face again and again. But the boy went on glaring at me.

'Stay away, d'you hear me? Stay away from my house—and stay away from my dog, you—dog-napper!'

He turned on his heel and set off for the round house, Jack squirming in his arms. For a second or two I stood, frozen with fury. Then I raced after him. As he bent to unlock the padlock on the gate, I grabbed his arm. He swivelled round, his face a mask of hatred.

'Don't you touch me, Plastic!'

He tried to shake me off, but I held on tight. At last, I found some words.

'Stay right where you are and listen to me!'

'Who's going to make me?' There was a nasty glint in the boy's eyes. I stamped my foot and all my anger poured out.

'How *dare* you accuse me of stealing your dog—standing there in my uniform that *you* stole! And anyhow, you've got a nerve calling me a *Plastic* when you do what you do!'

'What do I do?' The boy stared at me, his face a blank.

'I know exactly what you're up to—I've seen you down on the beach—and I've seen your shed stuffed full of plastic! You're in the pay of Professor Potkettle! You get rid of his horrible junk for him every day—dumping it in the sea—m-murdering the fish—'

The boy's eyes flared with anger. There was a long, hate-filled silence. Then, he shifted Jack under one arm, deliberately turned his back and unlocked the padlock.

But I hadn't finished.

'Too ashamed to admit it, are you?' I yelled. 'Well, you *should* be ashamed! Your very own puppy nearly *died*, thanks to you—strangled and drowned in the sea, because of your rotten plastic sack wrapped around his neck! And if I hadn't—'

'What did you say?' The boy turned, tightening his grip on the puppy in his arms. 'Jack was in the water?'

I stamped my foot again. 'I just said so, didn't I?'

'Calm down, Plastic.' The boy looked from Jack to me and back again. 'Just what are you accusing me of now?'

I folded my arms. 'I'm not saying another word until you swear *never* to call me that again!'

'I call things as I find them, Plastic.'

He sniffed and wiped his nose on his shirt sleeve—*my* shirt sleeve. My hair dripped cold water down my back and I started to shiver. There was no point in arguing with someone so rude and stubborn. I'd done what I came here to do—said what I needed to. I clenched my jaw to stop my teeth from chattering and wrapped the sodden towel round my shoulders. Then I turned my back on the boy and marched towards the wood.

'Wait!'

I stopped. What now? The boy stood very still, staring at me, Jack in his arms. I stared right back. Suddenly, Jack wriggled wildly. He jumped down and wobbled over to me, his stumpy tail wagging fit to bust, yapping and squeaking around my legs. I bent to stroke him and he wriggled into my arms, his tongue rasping over my nose in a warm, wet lick. When I looked up, the boy was still staring at me, but with a different expression on his face. He slowly pushed the gate open and jerked his head towards the round house.

'You'd better come in.'

It was said so grudgingly that he couldn't mean it. Or it was a trick. I stayed where I was. Jack squirmed against my chest, warm and alive.

'Get a move on,' said the boy. 'Before I change my mind.'

'Forget it.' I shook my head, and more cold droplets snaked down my back. 'I've got better things to do than argue with *you*. And I need to get dry.'

The boy jerked his head at the round house again.

'The stove's hot,' he said. 'You'll dry out in no time.'

I hesitated. 'I don't get it. Why've you suddenly changed your tune?'

The boy narrowed his eyes. 'I won't be accused of stuff that isn't true—not when it comes to Jack.'

'So we *will* argue.' I lowered Jack to the ground and gave him a shove towards the boy.

'Not if you listen to me,' the boy said.

Did he really think I was going to listen to him calling me Plastic and telling me that I was wrong? I turned back towards the wood.

'Anyhow—I know who attacked your van.'

I stopped. If he knew *that*, then I was all ears. The boy picked up Jack and carried him through the gate.

I slowly crossed the clearing and followed him in.

RECYCLER:

*a person who converts waste materials
into new materials and objects*

The boy carried Jack up the path to the wooden door of the round house, put him inside and closed the door. Then he walked past me, back to the gate. As he bent to lock the padlock, my heart beat fast. Had this been a trick to get me inside?

'Don't lock that!'

The boy looked up at me. 'Why not?'

'How do I know I can trust you?'

'Trust goes both ways,' he said. 'And I don't want any other Plastics breaking in and stealing my stuff.'

We glared at one another again. Then the boy sighed.

'All right, Plastic. I'll not lock it.'

He pushed past me and marched through the green door. I followed him in.

At first, I couldn't see much at all. The light inside the round house was very dim because of the tiny arched windows. The room wasn't much bigger than our living quarters in the Pantechnicon, and it smelt of smoke, but it felt sort of cosy and lived in. The walls were rough and round; the floor was made of old planks of wood, scuffed and stained. Something ticked against the wall. As my eyes grew used to the dim light, I made out a tall, carved grandfather clock with a pendulum swinging under its face. Beside it, the steps of a spiral staircase disappeared into darkness above. Under one window was a wooden table and three wooden chairs. Books were stacked from floor to ceiling against the wall on one side of a glowing stove, with a wicker basket of chopped logs on the other side. Jack trotted over to the stove and collapsed in front of it with a contented sigh.

The boy crossed to a rough wooden cupboard. He pulled out a sweatshirt full of holes and an old, frayed towel.

'Here.' He tossed them to me. I wriggled into the sweatshirt. It was warm and dry, and smelt of woodsmoke. Then I rubbed at my wet hair.

The boy marched over to the other window, where there was a stone sink with a bucket of water beside it and a little wooden cupboard. He took two mugs from the cupboard. Then he went over to the stove and scrabbled in the wicker basket. He found a yellow candle and pulled on a pair of leather gloves which looked too big for his hands. He opened the door of the stove and lit the wick of the candle from the flame. Light glimmered over his thin face and sent dancing reflections over a battered metal kettle on the stove, a stream of steam pouring from its spout. He set the candle in a saucer on the table. Back at the stove, he picked up the kettle and poured hot water into the two mugs.

'Sit down, Plastic.'

I frowned but took a seat. It creaked as I sat down. I ran my fingers over the wood of the table. It seemed to be made of driftwood, softened by the sea. The boy pushed a mug towards me and sat down opposite. I looked at the three chairs.

'Who do you live with?'

The boy's face was closed. 'I live on my own.'

'On your own? What happened to—'

'*I live on my own, Plastic.*' The furious look was back in his eyes. I blew on my mug of water. I was right. We were just going to argue. The sooner I found out who ransacked the Pantechnicon, the sooner I could get out of here.

'So,' I put the mug down on the table, 'you said you'd tell me who attacked our van?'

'Not so fast, Plastic. First, I want to hear what happened to Jack.'

Jack's floppy ear twitched at the sound of his name. He padded over to the boy's chair and jumped up into his lap.

'I'm not telling you anything,' I said, 'until you stop calling me Plastic.'

The boy's lip curled. 'You wear a Plastic uniform, which means you go to the Plastic school. And I bet your mum and dad work up at the factory.'

My face went hot. 'Only Ma—my mother.'

A triumphant smile flitted across his face. 'If someone dresses like a Plastic and acts like a Plastic, then she most likely *is* a Plastic.'

I stared down at his shorts, made out of my blazer. 'If someone dresses like a thief and acts like a thief, then he most likely *is* a thief!'

'I'm not a thief.' He grinned, suddenly. 'I'm a Recycler.'

The cheek. But I swallowed down my anger and tried to speak calmly. 'Well, you're wrong about me. I'm *not* a Plastic. And anyhow—why do you call them Plastics?'

The boy sniffed. 'Because Plastics all look the same and act the same. Because Plastics work at the factory, making things out of plastic that look just the same. Because Plastics live in just-the-same houses with just-the-same plastic furniture and gardens full of just-the-same plastic flowers and plastic grass...'

'Well, I don't—I live in a Pantechnicon!'

'A what?'

'Our van in the woods. And my mum and dad are actors.' I lifted my chin. 'We are Bottom's Travelling Theatre.'

'Bottom's?' The boy smirked. 'Why did you say your mum works up at the factory, then?'

'Because she does. But only for a few weeks, until we can perform again. Ar—my father—broke his leg. And we need the money for food.'

The boy looked at me, and this time his expression wasn't mocking.

'So you're not a Plastic.' One thin hand stroked Jack's fur, over and over. 'What's your name?'

'Ophelia... Fee. What's yours?'

'Seal.'

'Seal? As in sea lion?' He nodded. Then he glanced down at Jack.

'So what happened? With Jack?'

I took a sip of hot water.

'I went down to the sea for a swim. It was full of plastic junk and—and dead fish. Jack was struggling in the water, with one of *your* plastic sacks round his neck. I swam back to the beach with him and got the plastic off. Then I ran here.'

Seal buried his face in Jack's soft fur and mumbled something.

'What did you say?'

'Thanks. For saving Jack.'

'That's all very well,' I said. 'But I wouldn't have *had* to save him, if you hadn't dumped the plastic in the sea.'

Seal glared, then gave a huge sigh.

'Look,' he said. 'I got it wrong about you being a Plastic. And about kidnapping Jack. And you've got it all wrong about *me*.'

'What do you m—'

A chime echoed round the room, making me jump. The hands on the grandfather clock showed six o'clock.

I jumped to my feet. 'I told Ar I'd only be half an hour—and that was two hours ago! He'll think I've—I've drowned!'

I tossed the towel on to the table and began to wriggle out of the sweatshirt.

'Keep it.' Seal nodded at his shorts. 'In exchange.'

I ran towards the door. Behind me, Jack whined.

198

'Wait!'

I turned. 'What?'

'We'll do a deal. I'll tell you who attacked your van—if you listen to the truth about me.'

I hesitated. Ar could be limping down to the cove—staring out at the empty sea, thinking the very worst.

'I've got to go—now!' I pushed open the door and ran down the path to the gate.

'Meet me tomorrow at the beach,' Seal called after me. 'At eleven. Deal?'

I nodded and raced towards the trees.

MALEFACTOR:

a person who does bad or illegal things

'**O**PHELIA!... OPHELIA!!!'

Ar's voice was hoarse, like he'd shouted so much he'd almost worn it out. He stood at the water's edge, leaning on his crutches and staring out to sea, just like I'd imagined. I stumbled over the sand dunes and down the beach.

'AR! I'm safe!'

Ar turned, and I ran as fast as I could to him and threw my arms around him. When I looked up, tears were running down his face and into his beard.

'I thought... I thought you'd PERISHED!' His huge hand shook as he stroked my hair. 'And how it would have BROKEN MY HEART. And how I'd have to tell MARINA!'

'I'm sorry, Ar!'

'Where did you VANISH TO?'

I took his arm and we set off towards the lane. I told him about saving Jack, and going to the round house, and Seal. 'I just forgot the time—and Seal was going to tell me who attacked the Pantechnicon.'

Ar's face darkened. 'If I ever get my HANDS on the MISCREANT who did it, I'll...'

'I'm meeting Seal on the beach, tomorrow morning,' I said. 'And then I'll find out.'

'I will ACCOMPANY YOU!' said Ar.

I hesitated. 'No, Ar. Seal doesn't trust strangers—he's only just starting to trust me. I'll meet him, and I'll tell you what he says.'

'Very well. But when I discover who the MALEFACTOR is, he will PAY for his ACTIONS!'

Back at the Pantechnicon, Ar and I made supper of baked beans with slices of cheese and bread and butter. Afterwards, I sat in my bunk in the dark, waiting for Ma to come home. My eyes were just starting to close when torchlight wavered over the driver's cab and Ma climbed over the seat.

'Ophelia... you're still *awake*.' Ma looked pale and exhausted, like she always did these days. She pulled out her wages from a pocket of her boiler suit and handed them to me.

I scrambled over to put the money into the battered saucepan. Then I took the bread from the larder box and got the butter and the leftover beans from the fridge.

'No, Ophelia, it's all right.' Ma shook her head and sagged down on to her bunk. 'I'm not hungry.'

'But you've got to eat, Ma! You've got to keep your strength up!'

'I'll have some breakfast. All I want to do right now is *sleep*.' And she curled up, still in her clothes, on the bunk.

'Don't they give you a day off, ever?' I whispered.

'No.' Ma gave a weary shrug. 'Though tomorrow, I'll probably be *out of a job.*'

'What—what do you mean?'

'I got so tired, I made a *big mistake,*' Ma sighed. 'I had to sign my wage slip to get my money. And for a moment, I forgot I was supposed to be Barbara Brown, and I signed it with my *real name.*'

That creeping feeling was back inside me.

'Ma—' I whispered. 'Don't go back tomorrow. Professor Potkettle—'

But Ma was already asleep. I put the food away again. Then I gently pulled Ma's blanket over her shoulders and tiptoed to my bunk.

When I woke up next morning, Ma was gone. There were breadcrumbs in the sink, and an upturned mug, so at least she'd had something to eat and drink. But what would Professor Potkettle do, now he knew she was a Bottom?

At ten to eleven, I set off for the cove. Ar was banging at the wooden stage with a hammer.

'FAREWELL, Ophelia!' he called. 'And GOOD LUCK!'

I hurried through the wood, down the lane and over the dunes. Would Seal be there? What if he'd changed his mind? The sound of barking carried over the sand. Jack danced about at the water's edge, yapping. He seemed to be recovered. But each time a wave lapped in, he skittered back. He must still be scared of the water, after what happened to him yesterday.

Seal was wading waist-deep in the sea, a white plastic sack over his shoulder. The water around him heaved with plastic junk. Anger fizzed in my chest. How *could* he go on doing this, after what happened to Jack? What was I doing, trusting someone who stole uniforms and left cruel messages—someone who was in the pay of Professor Potkettle—someone who couldn't care less about the sea, and the fish? But I *had* to find out who attacked the Pantechnicon—then I'd make sure I never saw Seal again. I glared at him, willing him to hurry up and come out...

Only the more I stared, the more something niggled. And then I realized.

Seal *wasn't* emptying his sack into the sea.

Instead, he was gathering armfuls of plastic junk and shoving them into the sack. When the sack was full, he hefted it on to his shoulder and waded out of the water.

I gawped at him, my mind whirring. Then, Jack saw me. With an excited yap, he raced up the sand, jumping around my knees until I picked him up and gave him a cuddle. He wriggled around in my arms, licking any bits of my face and hands he could reach. I hurried down to join Seal.

'I'm sorry,' I said.

Seal hauled the sack from his shoulder and dumped it on the beach, looking wary.

'I'm sorry,' I said again. 'I got everything wrong.'

Seal gave a gruff nod.

'But why?' I asked. 'Why do you collect plastic junk? And why do you keep it in the shed in your garden?'

Seal jerked his head at the water. 'Better there than in the sea.'

'But—but where does it all come from? And why does it end up here?'

'Where does it come from?' Seal grimaced. 'The factory, of course. You've seen the chimney?'

'The incinerator?'

Seal nodded. 'Every time it burns plastic, it poisons the air. Except,' he picked up a long strand of cellophane, 'that lately there's too much plastic for the incinerator to handle.'

'Professor Potkettle said they could bury the leftover stuff... or dump it.'

'Which is exactly what he's up to now,' said Seal. 'Dumping it.'

'Then we must stop him! We can wait for them to come here, and—'

'Professor Potkettle never comes here,' Seal interrupted. 'And nor do the Plastics.'

'I don't get it.' I stared at him. 'How *does* the junk get into the sea, then?'

'I'll show you.' Seal headed off across the sand, Jack and I trotting behind him. When we reached the far end of the cove, he stopped.

'*Now* do you get it?' He jerked his head at the river. A plastic bucket bobbed in the current. Empty plastic drinks bottles floated, half full of water, like little boats. PRATT's sacks wound in the water like white seaweed, catching on rocks before continuing their journey into the sea.

'You mean...'

'The river runs past the factory. They chuck the leftover plastic into the river and it does the job for them—carries it down to the sea.'

'And you go and...'

'...pick it up. Yes. Every day. Except there's always more.' He glanced down at Jack, panting at his feet. 'What happened to Jack is what happens to the fish and to the seals and to the dolphins and the—'

'The plastic strangles them?'

'Either strangles them or they eat it by mistake and it kills them that way—their stomachs full of bags and food wrappers. I've seen dolphins with their flippers tangled in it so they can't swim. And seals with plastic tubs stuck on their heads so they can't breathe.'

I shivered. What other animals were suffering in the sea, under the surface?

'But—but...' I began, thinking hard.

'But what?'

'It's no good just—just picking it all up—not when it's going to go on being dumped...'

'No good?' Seal fished a dripping plastic bag out of the river. 'This might be the next one to wind itself around Jack's neck. Or be eaten by a whale or a dolphin.'

'No—what I mean is, we've got to stop it where it begins. Inside the factory.'

Seal glared at me. 'Have you ever been near the factory?'

I shook my head.

'It's surrounded by high brick walls, with barbed wire on the top. You can't get in without a pass code. Anyhow, the factory's evil. No one but the Plastics goes near it.' Seal avoided my eyes. 'Bad stuff happens up there.'

'Yes! Making plastic—'

'No—other bad stuff. People go up to the factory and...' Seal kicked at the sand.

'And what?'

'...and they never come back.'

ABOMINATION:

something disgusting or hateful

I swallowed. I couldn't help thinking about Ma. '*Who* never comes back?'

'Never mind.' Seal rubbed his eyes with his fist. 'Anyhow, I thought you wanted to know who attacked your van?'

'Who was it, then?'

Seal bent and scratched Jack's ears. 'It was the Plastics.'

'Which Plastics?'

'The green one and the blue one.'

'You mean... the two security guards?'

Seal nodded. 'I came to leave another message, telling you to go, when I heard a noise from the lane. A truck, it sounded like. So I ducked into the wood and watched. The two Plastics marched into the clearing. They were armed.'

I gasped. 'They—they had guns?'

Seal shook his head. 'The green one had an axe. And the blue one had a crowbar and a knife. They crept up to your van to see if anyone was there. Once they knew it was empty, the green Plastic swung her axe at the windscreen, while the blue Plastic went round the back and used the crowbar to get the doors open and started pulling out all your stuff.'

I clenched my fists. 'Why would they attack our home?'

'They wanted you gone, like I did,' said Seal. 'And that was their way of persuading you.'

'But *why*? What harm were we doing?'

'It's not about what you were *doing*,' said Seal. 'It's about what you *are*.'

'What?'

'You're *different*. And the Plastics hate different.'

A shiver whispered down my spine. So that was why the Boiler Suits ordered us off the Common—because we were different. But how did they find out we'd moved to the wood? And what would they do next, if we didn't leave for good?

I grabbed Jack and pulled him close to me. Only one person could have ordered the Boiler Suits to attack the Pantechnicon—Professor Potkettle. And if he hated us so much, what would he do now—if he'd found out who Ma really was?

I had to tell Ar. Between us, we had to persuade Ma to stop working there—even if it meant her and Ar splitting up. I let go of Jack and stood up.

'I've got to go.'

I ran. Up the beach, over the sand dunes, along the lane. All the way, Seal's words echoed in my head.

The factory's evil… stomachs full of bags and food wrappers… incinerator… poisons the air… bad stuff happens… people go up to the factory and they never come back…'

I burst out of the woods into the clearing. The Pantechnicon stood just as I'd left it, its newly painted lettering gleaming in the morning sun. The wooden stage lay abandoned on the ground, the hammer and nails scattered beside it.

'Ar? Where are you? AR!!!'

I ran to where the back doors of the Pantechnicon hung open. Ar sat inside on a folding chair among the hanging costumes, drinking a mug of tea. He looked up and saw me, his face breaking into a smile.

'WHAT HO, OPHELIA!'

I vaulted up into the Pantechnicon and grabbed his huge hand.

'Ar—you're all right! I was so worried—'

Ar put down his mug, his bushy eyebrows wrinkling. 'What is your CONCERN, Ophelia?'

My words came rushing out, higgledy-piggledy.

'Oh, Ar—Seal's told me about the factory—it's a bad place—and people don't come back—and Ma's up there—and we've got to—'

'HOLD UP!' Ar said. He pointed his crutch at another folding chair. 'Sit down and start at the BEGINNING!'

I unfolded the chair with shaking hands and plumped down on it. Then I took a deep breath and told Ar everything Seal had told me. Ar's face went red with anger when I told him about the Boilers attacking the Pantechnicon, and about the plastic killing the sea creatures. But when I told him about the factory, and how people didn't come back, and how Ma had given herself away, his face went pale.

'MARINA! I told her and told her that that place was an ABOMINATION!'

'Ar, we've got to stop her working there! Now—tonight!'

Ar nodded, his bushy beard shaking. 'INDEED we shall!'

'And—and we've got to get the Pantechnicon out of here! The Boiler Suits could come back any time, and—'

'But I can't DRIVE. And your mother's lost her LICENCE!'

'I know...' My mind turned somersaults. So this was what the motto meant—*diversus periculosus est*. Being different really *was* dangerous.

Ar hauled himself to his feet and made for the doors.

'Where are you going?'

'Bring me the SPEAR!'

'W-what?'

'The SPEAR! From *Julius Caesar*!'

I hurried to the props area, found the spear and jumped down with it. Outside, Ar lowered himself to sit on the stage and held out his hand for the spear.

'What—what are you doing, Ar?'

'I shall KEEP LOOKOUT for the MISCREANTS!' Ar shook the spear at the trees. 'No one gets past ARTHUR BOTTOM! The Pantechnicon, and all within it, will be SAFEGUARDED!'

I shivered. What chance would Ar stand against two burly Boiler Suits, when he couldn't even walk properly?

But Ma would be home after midnight, and once we'd persuaded her never to go back to the factory, we could all make a plan to get out of here.

TRESPASSER:

*a person entering someone's
land without permission*

In the dark, the wood flapped and rustled and whispered. My ears felt like they were out on stalks, checking on every sound. Beside me, Ar was unusually silent. He gripped the spear in one hand and the hammer in the other, scanning the trees for intruders. Any minute now, Ma's footsteps would come, with a flicker of torchlight. Any minute, she'd walk into the clearing, tired and hungry. Then Ar and I would tell her everything.

'It must be almost midnight,' I whispered. Ar glanced at his watch.

'It's QUARTER TO TWELVE,' he whispered hoarsely back.

'Ma'll need some food and a hot drink. We don't want her being hangry.'

Ar grunted, and I hurried back to the silent Pantechnicon. I got out bread and milk. Ma liked peanut-butter sandwiches, so I cut some bread and slathered it on. As I filled the kettle with water, I couldn't help looking at the money in the battered saucepan. What would Ma say when she found out we'd spent almost everything she'd earned on repairing the Pantechnicon? She'd probably be furious. If Professor Potkettle didn't give her the sack, she might be even more determined to go on working there. When Ma had her mind set on something, she was very hard to budge. But if Ar and I told her about the Boiler Suits attacking the Pantechnicon, and about how the factory was killing the sea creatures and spoiling the air, and about how sometimes people didn't come back from there—surely she'd agree not to work there any more?

I finished making the sandwiches and stuck a tea bag into a mug. Then I sat on the bunk, wrapped my sleeping bag round myself, and waited.

I was almost asleep when footsteps trudged up to the Pantechnicon.

'Ma? I got you peanut-butter sandwiches and—'

But it wasn't Ma. It was Ar, hoisting himself into the driver's cab on his crutches.

'There's no SIGN of her,' he whispered. 'And it's HALF-PAST MIDNIGHT!'

'Maybe—maybe she got held up...' But Ma was *always* back soon after midnight.

I climbed over the seat to sit beside Ar. We stared through the new windscreen of the Pantechnicon at the darkness of the trees. Every so often, I grabbed Ar's wrist and looked at his watch. One o'clock... one-thirty... My heart rattled round in my chest in time with Seal's words.

They never come back... never come back... never come back...

Two o'clock.

'She's not coming, Ar.' My eyes filled with tears. 'What shall we do?'

Ar shuffled out of the Pantechnicon and limped over to pick up the spear. Then he set off towards the lane. I ran after him.

'Where are you going?'

'To that DAMNABLE PLACE! I'll get your mother back if it's the LAST THING I DO!'

'Wait, Ar!' I grabbed his arm. 'You can't walk that far on your crutches!'

'I can and I WILL!'

'No, Ar!' I hissed. 'You won't be able to get in—Seal told me you need a pass code.'

I dragged him back to the wooden stage and pushed him down on it. 'I'm going to wake Seal—make him explain what he meant about people not coming back from the factory. Then we can make a plan to rescue Ma.'

'I'll ACCOMPANY you!'

'No—I can run faster by myself. You keep watch, in case Ma comes back.'

And before Ar could reply, I dashed into the wood.

The round house was shadowy and silent. I hurried to the gate. It was shut, the padlock fastened. I grabbed the gate and rattled it.

'Seal!' I called quietly. I didn't want to make too much noise, just in case the Boiler Suits were wandering about

213

the wood. There was no reply. It must be almost half past two. He'd be fast asleep.

'SEAL!' I called, a bit louder.

Something scrabbled and whined on the other side of the fence. Then Jack began to yap loudly. After a few moments, the door opened and footsteps approached the gate.

'Read the signs, Trespasser,' Seal's voice hissed. 'I have a ferocious dog, so beware!'

'Seal—it's me—Fee! I need to talk to you!'

The padlock rattled and the gate swung open. Seal appeared, holding a lantern, his hair over his face and dressed in a long T-shirt and his shorts. Jack threw himself at me, covering my face in licks.

'What's going on?' In the flickering light, Seal's face was wary.

I took a deep breath. 'It's Ma—she hasn't come back from her shift at the factory!'

'What?'

'And Ar wants to go there and get her back, only he can't because of his leg—so you've got to tell me what you meant about people disappearing...'

Seal stared at me blankly.

'*Please*, Seal! Ma could be in danger!'

'Why do you think *I* can help?'

'Because you know something about the factory—I know you do! And it might help me to find out what's happened to Ma!'

'You're wasting your time.' Seal picked Jack up. 'Once people disappear up there, they're gone for good.'

'N-no! I don't believe it!' I rubbed my eyes to get rid of the tears, but they kept leaking out.

'Well, you'd better start believing it.'

'I'll make up my own mind about that, when I know the truth!' I said. 'All you've got to do is *tell* me it.'

Seal gave a deep sigh. Then he jerked his head at me. 'You'd better come in, then.'

Inside the round house, the stove glowed red. Seal added a couple of logs from the pile and flames licked around them. I stood close to it, shivering. Jack's tail wagged against my legs, which was sort of comforting. Seal placed the lantern on the floor and sat cross-legged beside it, the light flickering over his wild black hair.

'Sit,' he said.

Jack obediently sat too, his tongue lolling. I lowered myself to sit down opposite Seal, and Jack rolled on to his back, wanting his tummy tickled.

'So.' Seal said, 'what do you want to know?'

'You said the factory is an evil place—that people sometimes don't come back. What did you mean?'

Seal stared into the flames for a long time. Then he looked up.

'I meant... that's what happened,' he said, his voice so low I could hardly hear him. 'It's what happened to my mum and dad.'

TROJAN HORSE:

*something that is used to hide in,
in order to trick an enemy*

'**Y**our parents?' I looked at the table and the three empty chairs. 'When—how?'

Seal pulled Jack onto his lap. 'Nine months ago.'

'Nine *months*?' I swallowed. No way was I going to let this happen to Ma. 'What happened?'

'My mum and dad were... are... ecologists.' Seal stroked Jack's ears and he wriggled his tail.

'What's an eco... um...?'

'Eco means... well, home. My mum and dad said that the Earth was our home, and we should look after it and all its creatures, and stop anything bad happening to it. They built this house with their own hands, out of straw bales and earth. And they made the garden for growing vegetables, with flowers for the bees and insects. We bathed in the sea every day. And we lived here, just us three, with no one else for miles around.'

'But what about Stopford?'

'Stopford didn't exist, then. We had the woods and the sea all to ourselves. Only when I was ten, everything changed. Bulldozers and cranes and cement mixers came, and they built the factory on the hill. Then the Plastics arrived to work there. And soon after that, they built Stopford, so the Plastics had houses to live in. When that happened, my mum and dad put up the fence around our house, just in case any of the Plastics discovered where we lived.'

'And did they?'

'No. The Plastics weren't interested in real stuff, like the woods and the beach and the sea. All they wanted was plastic, and more plastic.'

I shivered. 'So what happened—to your mum and dad, I mean?'

'Things got worse and worse. The incinerator poisoned the air with its smoke and fumes, and then, late last summer, the factory started chucking the leftover junk in the river. My mum and dad hated everything about the factory and what it was doing. So they made a plan to stop it. They were going to get into the factory one night and—'

'But how? You said no one could get in!'

Seal suddenly tipped Jack on to the floor and walked over to the books stacked against the wall. He pulled one out and tossed it to me. It was heavy and dusty smelling. The title said:

GREEK MYTHS

'Ever heard of the Trojan Horse? How the Greeks built a wooden horse and hid inside it so they could attack the city of Troy?'

I shook my head.

'Well, my mum and dad did what the Greeks did. You've seen the lorries driving up to the factory every day?'

I nodded. 'Pratt's Plastic Pellets.'

'My mum and dad made a plan to sneak inside a lorry and get driven into the factory. Then they were going to try to stop the factory making plastic—'

'How?'

'I don't know. It was all a secret. I heard them whispering, the night they left, when they thought I was asleep. They planned to get out again in an empty lorry before morning. Only something must've gone wrong, because when I woke up, they were gone...' Seal buried his nose in Jack's fur, his voice almost disappeared. 'And they never came back.'

In spite of the heat from the stove, I felt cold all over.

'You mean—you've been living here all alone since then? For nine months?'

Seal nodded and blinked a few times. 'It was better after I found Jack—left on the Common in a packing box to starve.'

I reached out and stroked Jack's warm fur. 'How could anyone do that to a puppy?'

'That's Plastics,' said Seal.

'So—so your mum and dad are still up there, inside the factory?' Suddenly I felt angry. 'Haven't you tried to find them? Have you just given up?'

Seal's head jerked up, his eyes sparking with fury. 'I've sneaked up there, night after night. It's a fortress, like I told you. High brick walls and huge metal gates. It's just a huge block of cement—no windows, nothing. The lorry drivers and the workers have a pass code to get in.' He suddenly looked at me. 'Did your ma tell you the pass code?'

I shook my head. 'She doesn't say much at all when she gets home. She's always tired.'

The spark of hope died in Seal's eyes. 'Then there's no way in.'

I couldn't sit still any longer. I jumped to my feet and paced around the room. I'd come here for answers. But not these.

'There *must* be a way! I've got to get Ma back!'

'There isn't,' said Seal. 'If there was, I'd have thought of it by now.'

He buried his face in Jack's fur. The firelight played over the red and gold of his shorts and over the book lying on the floor beside him.

And then, an idea popped into my head.

A very, very dangerous idea.

'The Trojan Horse...' I muttered.

Seal looked up. 'What?'

'There might just be a way to get into the factory,' I said slowly. 'And if I can get in there, I can find out where Ma is. And then Ar and I can rescue her.'

'Oh yeah? How, exactly?'

'I've got to work it all out, while I'm sewing.'

'Sewing?'

'Where're your scissors? And your needle and thread?'

Seal narrowed his eyes. 'What are you playing at?'

'My plan,' I said. 'Operation Trojan Horse.'

'Stop talking in riddles! If you know how to get into the factory, I'm coming too!'

'All right. But first I need the scissors and sewing stuff.'

Seal went to a drawer under the sink. He returned with a bobbin of cotton, a needle and a pair of scissors.

'Now—take off your shorts.'

Seal's mouth dropped open.

'I won't look,' I said. 'Just take them off.'

'What for?'

'D'you want to get your mum and dad back, or not?'

'Yes, but—'

'Well, get on with it, then!' I turned my back on him. There was some shuffling and rustling, and the cupboard door opened and closed.

'All right. I've done it. But I don't see...'

I turned back. Seal wore an ancient pair of jeans. He tossed the shorts over to me.

'Thanks.' I lifted them into the light from the stove and inspected them. They were pretty dirty, and the stitching was a mess, but with a bit of work...

I pulled the lantern near me, picked up the scissors and began to cut the stitches. Luckily I was used to altering and mending costumes at Bottom's.

'What're you doing?'

'Putting my blazer back together.'

'What for?'

'I'm going to get into the factory and find out where Ma is—and where your mum and dad are, too.'

Seal stared at me, a flicker of hope in his eyes. 'Then I'm coming with you!'

'You can't. This part I've got to do on my own. Your bit will come later on, when I get back.'

'What will I have to do?'

'Ever driven a van?'

Seal's mouth dropped open. 'No.'

'Well, that's what you're going to have to learn. From Ar.'

Seal looked wary. 'Ar? Your father?'

'It's OK,' I said. 'He's very noisy, but you'll like him.'

And as I told him my plan for Operation Trojan Horse, Seal's eyes got wider and wider.

I heard Ar's gigantic snoring before I saw him. He lay sprawled on the stage in the clearing, still clutching the spear. *Fat lot of good as a sentry.* I ran over and shook his shoulder.

Ar leapt to his feet, brandishing the spear. 'HAVE AT YOU, MISCREANT!'

'It's only me, Ar. You were fast asleep.'

Ar blinked. 'NEVER, Ophelia! I was merely RESTING MY EYES!'

I glanced back at the dark Pantechnicon. 'Any sign of Ma?'

Ar shook his great head mournfully. 'Your mother is still MISSING.'

I grabbed his wrist and looked at his watch. *Five in the morning.* I took Ar by the arm and steered him to the back of the Pantechnicon.

'Get some proper sleep,' I told him. 'Tomorrow, we're going to get Ma back.'

Ar drew himself up and puffed out his massive chest.

'SLEEP, Ophelia?' he roared. 'NEVER! I shall not REST until your mother is RETURNED!'

Before I'd reached the driver's cab, massive snores echoed around the clearing.

I climbed up on to the seat and rifled through the front compartment, holding my breath. The next part of my plan depended on two things being here. *Please don't let Ma have taken hers with her.* My fingers found the flat shapes of the two phones. I grabbed one of them and set the alarm for eight, then climbed over the seats to my bunk. Ma's peanut-butter sandwiches sat untouched on the sink.

What was happening to her? Was she safe?

I shook myself. It was no good asking questions I didn't know the answers to. I wriggled down into my sleeping bag. I had three hours to sleep, then I must start sanding the paint off the side of the Pantechnicon before Seal arrived.

There were so many things that could go wrong with Operation Trojan Horse. So many dangers to face.

'I'm going to get you back, Ma,' I muttered. 'I promise. You see, Seal and Ar and I are going to...'

Before I could finish the sentence, my eyes fell shut.

PLAYING TRUANT:

staying away from school without permission

By midday, my back felt like it was breaking, and sweat poured down my face. Ever since Seal arrived at the Pantechnicon that morning, we'd been preparing it for Operation Trojan Horse. First, we'd unloaded our bulkiest stuff—the stage, the costumes, the scenery—and piled it in the clearing. I'd draped a tarpaulin over it in case it rained. Then, we'd gone back to the shed at the round house and lugged all the Pratt's Plastic Pellets sacks of junk, one by one, through the wood and into the back of the Pantechnicon, Jack trotting at our heels.

Seal hefted the last sack from his shoulder and pushed it into the Pantechnicon to join the rest. I did the same with mine.

'That took *forever*,' he growled.

So far, everything was going according to plan—just so long as the Boiler Suits didn't come back. Of course, it would all have been so much easier if Ar could have carried stuff too, as Seal kept on reminding me.

'Well, he can't,' I said. 'Not with his leg in plaster. And anyhow, he's got his part of the plan to carry out.'

The Pantechnicon was unrecognizable. The name on its side, that Ar and me had so carefully painted, was gone. Ar had painted a new one, copied from Seal's plastic sacks.

PRATT'S PLASTIC PELLETS

Bottom's Travelling Theatre was no more, and in its place was our 'Trojan Horse'.

From the back of the Pantechnicon, a chunky figure appeared from behind the stacked sacks, and Jack gave a low growl. For a moment, I froze. Had a Boiler Suit somehow sneaked inside the Pantechnicon? Then the figure roared:

'WHAT HO, Ophelia! WILL I DO?'

Jack's growl turned into a squeaky bark, and he hurtled towards Ar, his tail wagging like crazy. Ar swung him up into his arms, and Jack covered his bare face in licks.

Seal gaped. 'Is that *you*, Mr Bottom?'

Without his huge black bushy beard, Ar looked like a stranger. He wore a cap, a checked shirt from the costume store, and a pair of corduroy trousers held up by red braces.

'You look *brilliant*, Ar.' I wiped my forehead on my sleeve. 'Really... well, normal.'

'NORMAL?' Ar growled. 'A Bottom is NEVER NORMAL!'

'Remember, you're playing a role,' I told him. 'The most important role ever. Now, I've got to go soon...'

Ar frowned. 'I have GRAVE RESERVATIONS about you doing this, Ophelia. You may be putting yourself in DANGER.'

'I've told you, Ar,' I said. 'This is the only way I can discover what the pass code is, to get into the factory—and find out what's happened to Ma. Once we know where she is, we can carry out Operation Trojan Horse.'

Ar harrumphed. 'Very well. But be VIGILANT at ALL TIMES!'

I nodded. 'Before I go, why don't you and Seal have one more practice?'

Seal groaned. 'Have we *got* to?'

'Yes! It has to work perfectly when you do it, or else they'll smell a rat.'

'PRACTICE makes PERFECT.' Ar put Jack down and hoisted himself up into the driver's seat. He clicked on his safety belt. 'Get in, Seal, and get READY!'

Seal wriggled reluctantly into the driver's cab, down by Ar's enormous boots.

'You need to crouch down lower,' I said. 'I can see your hair.'

'*You* try it,' muttered Seal.

'We've been through this,' I said. 'And you're the only one small enough to do it.'

'Huh,' grumbled Seal, but ducked down until he was invisible.

'Are we READY?' bellowed Ar.

A muffled *yeah* came from below.

Ar turned the key in the ignition and the Pantechnicon's engine rumbled into life.

'LEFT PEDAL DOWN!' he roared, then wiggled the gear lever. 'Now, gently press down the RIGHT PEDAL.'

225

'I *know*,' hissed Seal's muffled voice. 'We've done it enough times.'

'Lift the LEFT PEDAL...' Ar unbraked the Pantechnicon and it began to move slowly forward. 'And gradually INCREASE the PRESSURE on the RIGHT PEDAL.'

The Pantechnicon lumbered towards the lane, with Jack and I running beside it.

'Lift the RIGHT PEDAL and PRESS the MIDDLE one!'

The Pantechnicon slowed and stopped. Ar grinned from ear to ear. Seal crawled out, looking hot and cross.

'It's OK, Mr Bottom. You don't have to tell me any more. I know what to do.'

'Call me AR!' roared Ar. 'We're COMRADES, remember!'

'Um, Ar...' I said. 'You're doing a fantastic job. But could you possibly practise... um... talking quietly?'

'NEVER FEAR, Ophelia! I shall be QUIET as a RODENT on the night!'

Ar was used to making his voice reach the very back of a crowded theatre. Could he possibly change the habit of a lifetime?

'I'll be back tomorrow morning.' I crossed my fingers behind my back. 'Keep practising!'

Seal grimaced.

'We shall await your return with BATED BREATH!' Ar held out his arms to me and I ran into them. It was a bit like being hugged by a gorilla.

'Be CAUTIOUS, Ophelia,' he said. 'I could not ENDURE it if you came to any HARM.'

'I'll be careful, I promise,' I whispered.

'Good luck,' Seal muttered, clutching Jack just in case I tried to hug him too. I gave Jack a pat instead. Then I set off up the lane towards the Common.

'Oh, and, OPHELIA—' Ar's voice echoed through the trees.

'Yes?'

'HAPPY BIRTHDAY!'

The Common was empty. Up on the hill, the factory stood beside the river, grim and alone. Somewhere in there was Ma—and hopefully Seal's mum and dad, too. I bit my thumbnail. I'd got to concentrate on my part of the plan now. If this didn't work, then Operation Trojan Horse was doomed.

A gust of wind sent smoke and ash drifting from the incinerator chimney over the Common. My eyes burned and my nose itched with a sneeze. I pulled out the phone from my blazer pocket and checked there was a signal. Then I scrolled down *Recent Calls* until I found the one I was looking for. I tapped on it and waited. The ringing went on and on, but at last someone picked up.

'Seraphina Smith speaking.'

Ar always said that the way to take on the role of someone else was to imagine you *were* them. I closed my eyes and thought of being Ma.

'Good morning, Miss Smith,' I said. 'This is *Marina Bottom*.'

There was a pause. Surely Miss Smith hadn't forgotten who Ma was? Then she cleared her throat and said coldly:

'Mrs Bottom? How may ay help you?'

227

'I'm ringing to *apologize profusely*,' I said. 'I have just discovered that Ophelia has been *playing truant* from school.'

'Indeed, Mrs Bottom. 'O-*failure* has not attended school for two weeks now. Ay expected a call from you to explain her absence.'

'I only discovered this *yesterday*. I've been working *long shifts* at the factory, you see...'

'The factory?' Miss Smith's voice warmed a little bit.

'A *wonderful* place to work,' I said, trying to make it sound true. Suddenly, a gust of foul air filled my lungs and I started to cough.

'Are you all right, Mrs Bottom?'

'Yes... yes.' I swallowed and wiped my eyes. 'Just a frog in my throat. Anyway, Ophelia will be returning to school today. Furthermore, it is *her birthday*, and I wish, of course, for her to attend her *Ceremony* at the factory. Will you please arrange it?'

Miss Smith sniffed. 'This is extremely short notice, Mrs Bottom.'

'I do understand, Miss Smith. But I feel that *becoming a Prefect* will be the making of Ophelia.'

Silence. Then:

'Very well, Mrs Bottom. Ay will call the factory and see what can be done for O-*failure*.'

I breathed out.

'Thank you, Miss Smith. I shall be *eternally grateful* to you.'

As soon as the call was over, I screwed up my face and stuck out my tongue, as far as it would go, at the phone. But sticking out my tongue made me remember Merry and

I felt angry and sad all over again. I gave myself a shake. *Concentrate, Fee. You have a plan to carry out.*

I slipped the phone back into my rucksack and set off across the Common towards Stopford School.

CEREMONY:

a celebration of an event or achievement

At four o'clock exactly, the silver limousine, decked with plastic flowers, glided up the road and stopped outside the school. I tugged my plaits straight and stood up as tall as I could.

I'd never felt so alone. I'd expected Chloe, Zoe and Merry to be nasty, but they'd acted as if I simply didn't exist. Everyone else had kept away, too. Now, the whole class was lined up in front of the school entrance. Chloe, Zoe and Merry stood together, their Prefects' badges sparkling. Miss Smith addressed us.

'Children, today is the Ceremony of O-*failure* Bottom—an honour which ay hardly feel she deserves.'

Chloe and Zoe smirked. Merry stared through me as if I was invisible. Miss Smith went on.

'At Stopford School we obey the rules. And truancy breaks those rules. Ay sincerely hope that, following her Ceremony, O-*failure* will return a more grown-up and well-behaved child.' Miss Smith clasped her hands and shut her eyes, and we all did the same.

'*Plasticus stupendus est...*' the chant hummed. '*Diversus periculosus est...*'

I opened one eye. Merry was chanting along with everyone, her conker-brown curls neatly tied back, her uniform immaculate. Whatever had happened to the Merry whose tie was always undone, whose hair always escaped from its scrunchy and whose face was always full of life and dimples? This Merry was a stranger. A Perfect. My knees began to shake. The very last thing I wanted was to end up like that. But I'd *got* to get into the factory and find out where Ma was.

The chant came to an end, and Miss Smith pushed me towards the limousine. Green Boiler Suit got out and opened the door. Inside, it smelt of hot plastic. Green Boiler suit slammed the door and went round to join Blue Boiler Suit in the front seat.

The limousine glided slowly away from Stopford School. It headed through the maze of little roads until it turned on to the main street. Soon we were out of Stopford and driving up the hill towards the factory. To take my mind off the scary feelings, I ran through my plan.

1. Memorize the pass code to get into the factory.

2. Find out where Ma and Seal's mum and dad are.

3. After my Ceremony, go back to Stopford in the limousine.

4. Set off on Operation Trojan Horse with Ar and Seal.

Ahead of us, the factory reared up, grim and menacing, the dark river running beside it. A building without windows was like a face without eyes and mouth. It gave no clue about what—or who—was inside it. The limousine drew up to a great metal gate, with a red-and-white painted sign:

ENTER PASS CODE FOR ENTRY

Set into the wall was a keypad with rows of numbered buttons, from 1 to 26. Blue Boiler Suit leant out of the limousine and began tapping the buttons. I pressed my nose against the window and watched the numbers flash up on the screen, concentrating hard on the sequence.

16... 12... 1... 19... 20...9... 3... 21... 19

I whispered it under my breath three times, to make sure my sticky memory had it safe. The metal gate opened and the limousine drove through into a courtyard. Ahead, set into the wall, was a giant sealed door. Beside it was another keypad. As Green Boiler Suit punched in the pass code again, I silently repeated it, number by number. The door slid open, and the limousine drove through.

We were in the loading bay I'd seen in the video. A huge PRATT'S PLASTIC PELLETS lorry was parked inside, its back doors open, revealing stacked-up sacks of pellets. The limousine drew up alongside the lorry and Green Boiler Suit came round to open my door, her face eerie in the yellow-white fluorescent light.

'Out!' she barked.

I climbed out, and she and Blue Boiler Suit marched me through the loading bay into the factory itself. Under the fluorescent lights and with no windows, it could be any time of day or night. Conveyor belts slid like silent snakes across the factory floor, supervised by workers in white boiler suits. I strained to see Ma, but there was no sign of her. Each conveyor belt carried a different load. One had hundreds of plastic coffee cups; another, plastic flowers just like the ones in Merry's garden; on a third were plastic stools, all exactly the same; and on a fourth, row after row of plastic water bottles. Robotic arms hovered above the conveyor belts, swooping down to pick out any cup or flower, stool or bottle which wasn't exactly the same as all the others, and depositing it in a large bin. A woman in a white boiler suit grabbed the bin as it was filled and pushed it across the factory floor towards a metal door marked:

DANGER!!!
INCINERATOR

'Hurry!' Blue Boiler Suit pushed me forward.

We marched over to a lift. Blue Boiler Suit pressed a button and the door hissed open. We stepped inside, the door closed and the lift began to climb.

'What—what's going to happen at the Ceremony?' I asked.

But the two Boiler Suits just stared at the walls of the lift, as if I hadn't spoken. The lift juddered to a halt and the door opened. We were in a long, empty white corridor. At the far end was a steel door set into a wall, with another keypad on it. Green Boiler suit punched in the same numbers and the door slid open. Then we were in another corridor, its walls so white and glaring that I had to blink.

The Boiler Suits marched me down the corridor towards a white door marked:

LABORATORY
ENTRY BY PERMISSION ONLY

—and pushed me through the door.

The room, like the corridor, was glaring white. A single conveyor belt ran across it, disappearing into a circular black hole in the far wall. There were four handles on the conveyor belt, with straps dangling from them. In one corner of the room was a cubicle with a white curtain. Set into one wall was a huge computer screen and a control panel with hundreds of buttons. A small figure in a long white coat stood with its back to me, tapping at the buttons. The Boiler Suits shoved me to stand in the middle of the cold white floor, and the figure slowly turned to face me.

Professor Potkettle's ice-blue eyes gleamed behind his red plastic spectacles.

'Miss Ophelia Bottom, yes indeedy!' he said, in his high-pitched voice. 'Welcome to your Ceremony.'

PERFECT:

accurate, exact or correct in every detail

'So...' Professor Potkettle's white teeth smiled, but his eyes didn't. 'You decided to be... em... sensible, after all.'

'Yes,' I said. 'I—I want to be a Prefect.'

'A Prefect. Yes, indeedy!' Professor Potkettle nodded, his shock of hair bouncing. Green Boiler Suit pointed at the white cubicle.

'Clothes,' she said.

'Ah, yes,' said Professor Potkettle. 'Step into the cubicle, Miss Bottom. Inside you will find a gown for your Ceremony. Remove your uniform and change into the gown. Then we can... em...'

'Begin,' said Green Boiler Suit.

Inside the cubicle was a white plastic chair and a long white dress on a hanger. I wriggled out of my rucksack. Then I took off my blazer, skirt and shirt and put them on the chair. The white dress was slithery and cold. I pulled it over my head, shivering. I was just about to go back into the room when I remembered. *The phone.* I pulled it out of the rucksack and tucked it inside my knickers. Then I stepped out of the cubicle.

'Shoes,' said Blue Boiler Suit.

I pulled off my trainers. The floor was cold under my bare feet.

'What—what do you I have to do now?' The sooner we got this Ceremony over with, the sooner I could find out where Ma was.

'Do?' Professor Potkettle pushed up his red plastic spectacles. 'Why, nothing! No indeedy! Everything is... em...'

'Arranged,' said Blue Boiler Suit.

'You will simply go through the stages of the... em... Ceremony. That is all.'

'And then I go back to school as a Prefect?'

There was a silence, then Professor Potkettle giggled.

'Not... em... not exactly.'

Suddenly, I felt even colder. 'Wh-what do you mean?'

Professor Potkettle turned to the Boiler Suits. 'Shall we tell her? Shall we?'

The Boiler Suits nodded together.

'Yes, indeedy!' Professor Potkettle glanced at the yellow plastic watch on his wrist. 'But time is of the essence. We shall proceed with the Ceremony, and as we do so, I shall explain... em... everything. There is nothing more *delicious* than sharing the truth about my Experiment.'

My mind span. What Experiment? And what did he mean when he said I *wouldn't exactly* be going back to school? Had the Professor somehow found out about our plans? But he couldn't have. No one knew except us.

I found my voice. 'What have you done with Ma?'

Professor Potkettle's white teeth flashed. 'Your mother is perfectly... em...'

'Safe,' said Green Boiler Suit.

'I want to talk to her! Where is she?'

'You shall talk to her,' said Professor Potkettle. 'Yes indeedy. All in good... em...'

'Time,' said Blue Boiler Suit.

'Why have you kidnapped her?' I tried to sound calm, but my knees shook. 'Why didn't she come home?'

'*Home?*' said Professor Potkettle. 'You mean that broken-down old van in the... em...'

'Woods,' said Green Boiler Suit.

'It wasn't broken down, until you attacked it!'

Professor Potkettle ignored this. 'You asked a... em... question, Miss Bottom. Why didn't your mother come home? The answer is very simple. Because we discovered that she is a... em...'

'Different,' said Blue Boiler Suit.

'A Different. Yes, indeedy.'

'Wh-what do you mean, a Different?'

'*Diversus periculosus est...* different is... em...'

'Dangerous,' said Green Boiler Suit.

Professor Potkettle stared at me, his blue eyes sad. 'Why, oh why are you Bottoms so stubborn? Why did you insist on remaining in Stopford? Even after we did our very best to... em... persuade you to leave?'

'We *couldn't* leave! And if you don't want us in Stopford, why do you pay us to perform here every year?'

'Differents are for Entertainment only. I pay for your... em... ridiculous show to remind the people of Stopford that Differents are dangerous. To remind them that it is better, far better, to be the... em...'

'Same,' said Blue Boiler Suit.

'Differents must know their place,' said Professor Potkettle. 'Which is in a tent on the Common, for three days only. Not in our town... or in our... em... school. I could not have Differents as *fixtures* here in Stopford, living among us, *contaminating* our town, causing disruption to my little Perfects.'

'Your... what?'

'Enough!' Professor Potkettle's voice was suddenly as cold and sharp as his eyes. He strode across the room to the control panel and began pressing buttons.

'Escort Miss Bottom to the production line.'

The Boiler Suits grabbed me by my elbows and lifted me high into the air, just the way they did when they lifted the Professor at the Potkettle Institute.

'LET—ME—GO!' I shouted, wriggling and kicking. But they carried me over to the white conveyor belt. They fastened my arms to the handles with the straps. Then they did the same with my legs. Professor Potkettle left the control panel and came to stand beside me.

'You should be grateful, Miss Bottom,' he whispered, his breath smelling of peppermint. 'It is a great honour to be chosen for my Experiment.'

I swallowed. 'You won't get away with this! I'll—'

'Won't I?' He leant over me, his mouth a thin, grim line.

'I am doing this for the good of our community. For the good of Stopford.'

He hurried over to the control panel and began pressing buttons.

'And now, let the Ceremony begin!'

The conveyor belt started to move, gliding silently towards the black hole in the wall. My heart thundered in my chest. I opened my mouth to scream, but it was like I was in one of those nightmares where no sound came out.

As the conveyor belt carried me into the black hole, I clamped my eyes tightly shut...

FACSIMILE:

an exact copy

The conveyor belt stopped moving. I opened my eyes. I lay in a dark room. A movement above my head made me jump. A white robotic arm hovered above the conveyor belt, a long metal ruler clasped in its grip.

Professor Potkettle's voice echoed from a loudspeaker on the wall.

'Lie still, Miss Bottom,' he said, 'while you are measured.'

I wriggled, but my arms and legs were held fast. The robotic arm glided over me, its ruler clicking and flashing. Out of the loudspeaker, Professor Potkettle's voice muttered.

'Body length... one hundred and fifty centimetres... elbow to wrist... twenty-two centimetres... breadth of foot... seven and a half centimetres... breadth of hand... six and a half centimetres...'

'Why are you doing this?' I whispered.

Professor Potkettle giggled over the loudspeaker.

'Why? For my Experiment, of course.'

'What—what Experiment?'

'I will tell you, Miss Bottom. But let us begin at the... em...'

'Beginning,' said the voice of Blue Boiler Suit.

'Yes, indeedy. From the very start of my career as a scientist, I knew that plastic was the future. First, I built the factory. Then, I built the town of Stopford for the workers. I paid the people handsomely to work in the factory—and they used the money they earned to buy my plastic goods. A win-win situation!' He giggled. 'Everything ran like... em...'

'Clockwork,' said the voice of Green Boiler Suit.

'Of course,' the Professor said, 'there were the occasional... em... *hiccups...*'

'Like what?'

'The Differents who broke into the factory. Calling themselves *ecologists*—'

Seal's mum and dad.

'—and preaching about the so-called dangers of plastic and how it harms their precious... em... planet. Fortunately, they were rash as well as misguided... just like you.'

'Wh-what did you do to them?'

'It was my duty to remove them. As I said, I cannot have Differents interfering with my Experiment.'

'Where are they? Are they... alive?'

Professor Potkettle's giggle echoed round the room. The robotic arm swung away and the conveyor belt began to move forward again. *What now?* I clenched my fists and closed my eyes.

When I opened them, another robotic arm was gliding over me. This one didn't have a ruler. It had a camera.

'Smile, Miss Bottom,' Professor Potkettle whispered. 'Smile for the camera.'

I grimaced, wriggling my wrists and ankles. But they were held fast. The robotic arm hovered over me and a sudden silver flash, right in my face, blinded me.

Flash!... Flash!... Flash!...

'To continue with my story,' said the Professor. 'Once the... em... *problems* were removed, everything went on *brilliantly*. The factory turned out thousands of perfect, plastic products. But the more I thought about how fantastic plastic was, and how indestructible and long-lasting, the more I began to... em... wonder...'

The robotic arm twisted and changed position, taking pictures of every bit of me, from my head to my toes. All I could see were the flashes, burning into my eyes.

I jerked my head from one side to the other to get away from the flashes, but the arm followed my every movement. Just when I thought I couldn't stand it any longer, the room went dark and the robotic arm swung away.

'Perfect,' whispered Professor Potkettle.

The robotic arm returned, this time gripping a screen. There were words on the screen—hundreds of words, all beginning with A.

A white plastic microphone dropped down above my mouth.

'Read the words aloud, Miss Bottom.'

I clamped my mouth shut.

'I *said*, read the words aloud.'

I shook my head. 'No way! Not until you tell me why!'

'If you want to see your... em...'

'Mother,' said Blue Boiler Suit.

'...then you would be wise to begin.'

I swallowed and began to read.

'A... Aah... Aardvark... Abandon... Ability...'

After what felt like hours, there were words beginning with B.

'Baby... Bachelor... Back... Backward... Bad...'

By the time I reached the Zs, my throat was sore and the words on the screen seemed to blur.

'...Zero... Zone... Zoo... Zz...'

The screen went blank. The robotic arm carried it away.

'Very good, Miss Bottom,' said Professor Potkettle. 'As a reward, I shall continue with my story. Now, where had I... em... got to?'

'Experiment,' said Green Boiler Suit.

'Yes, indeedy! I began with the... em...'

'Baby,' said Blue Boiler Suit.

'Remember the baby, Miss Bottom? The little plastic baby I showed you during your visit to the Potkettle Institute?'

I nodded, my throat burning.

'A much more difficult thing to create than, say, a plastic... em... bottle. Yes indeedy! I had to make plastic skin, plastic bones, plastic fingernails and toenails. Not to mention plastic lungs, a plastic stomach, a plastic heart. And I did it! A perfect facsimile!' The Professor's giggle became a triumphant crow. 'Proving that I, Petrus Potkettle, am a... em...'

'Genius,' said Green Boiler Suit.

'But the baby was easy-peasy lemon-squeezy, compared with...'

There was a whispering over the loudspeaker.

'I am reminded that time is passing,' Professor Potkettle said. 'And there remains one more stage of the... em... Ceremony to complete.'

What now?

Behind me, a door opened and heavy footsteps marched towards the conveyor belt. Blue Boiler Suit appeared, carrying a mass of wires, with little discs attached.

'What's that? What are you going to do?' I wriggled and squirmed, but the plastic chains held my arms and legs fast.

'Fear not, Miss Bottom,' Professor Potkettle's voice crackled over the loudspeaker. 'You won't be... em... harmed.'

Blue Boiler Suit was doing something to my head. Cold little points made my scalp tingle.

'What are you doing?'

'This, Miss Bottom,' said the voice of the Professor, 'is an electroencephalogram.'

'A—a what?'

'A machine for tracking the activity of your... em...

'Brain,' said Blue Boiler Suit.

'Only this is no ordinary machine. I have... em... modified it so that it can do more—far more.'

'Wh-what will it do?'

Professor Potkettle giggled. 'It will copy your every thought, your every... em...'

'Memory,' said Blue Boiler Suit, attaching more cold little discs to my scalp.

I twisted my neck back and forth, trying to shake off the discs.

'Stay *still*,' snapped Professor Potkettle. 'Or your mother will... em...'

'Suffer,' said Blue Boiler Suit, leaving the room.

I lay in the dark, shivering. What would happen next?

The discs on my scalp began to buzz. My head tingled. This was crazy. No one—not even a scientific genius—could copy someone's thoughts and memories.

'Wrong!' Professor Potkettle's squeaky laugh echoed from the loudspeaker. 'But yes, indeedy—I *am* a scientific genius!'

My mouth fell open. Could this machine—this electro-thingy—actually see my thoughts? I went cold. Could it see my plans for Operation Trojan Horse? I screwed up my eyes and tried to make my mind go blank. It wouldn't.

'I—I want to know more about your Experiment,' I said. If Professor Potkettle was listening to *me*, he wouldn't see my thoughts. 'What happened after you made the baby?'

'Why, *then*,' whispered the Professor, 'I got to wondering. Might it be possible to create a walking, talking, thinking *person*—so accurate and... em...'

'Perfect,' said Green Boiler Suit.

'... that no one would ever spot the difference?'

Suddenly, a siren wailed around the factory.

It must be midnight, and the end of the shift. The workers would soon be gone, and I'd be all alone in the factory with the Professor and the Boilers.

There was a bleeping noise and the buzzing and tingling stopped. Behind me, the door opened and both Boiler Suits

245

came in. Blue Boiler Suit removed the discs from my scalp, while Green Boiler suit untied my hands and feet. I sat up, dizzy and trembling.

'Come,' said Green Boiler Suit.

Between them, I walked out of the dark room, back into the white one. Professor Potkettle stood in front of the control panel, flicking switches and pressing buttons.

'When can I see Ma—my mother?'

Professor Potkettle smiled. 'Soon, Miss Bottom. Very soon.'

He pressed a button. Red lights flashed on and off like a warning. A single word appeared on the screen:

FACSIMILE

—and lights danced across the control panel in patterns.

'The Ceremony is complete,' he said. 'And now, you will see the product of my Experiment with your own... em...'

'Eyes,' said Blue Boiler Suit.

Professor Potkettle jerked his head at the Boiler Suits. 'Take her down to the factory floor.'

It was eerie in the empty building, the conveyor belts still and the workers all gone. I shivered in the thin white dress, my bare feet numb on the concrete floor. Professor Potkettle led us to stand beside one of the conveyor belts.

'Yes, indeedy,' said Professor Potkettle. 'The baby, you see, was the first... em... human I ever made.'

'The—first?'

The conveyor belt whirred. With a low rumble, it began to move.

Then my mouth fell open, and I forgot everything—the Professor, the Boiler Suits, my icy feet and even Ma. Because, gliding slowly towards us on the conveyor belt was a girl.

The conveyor belt stopped moving. I stared at the girl lying in front of me—with neat red plaits, bony wrists and freckles, wearing a blazer and skirt and trainers. Pinned to her blazer pocket was a badge, saying:

PREFECT

'Allow me to introduce you,' whispered Professor Potkettle, 'to Ophelia... Cleopatra... Cressida... Cordelia... Goneril... Hippolyta... Portia... Perdita... Juliet... Bottom.'

ACTIVATION:

to make something start

My legs trembling with shock, I walked over to the conveyor belt. The girl lying there, her eyes closed, looked exactly like me. I moved closer. Her chest rose and fell. I held a shaking hand above her mouth. Her breath warmed my palm.

'Yes, Miss Bottom,' Professor Potkettle's voice was triumphant. 'She breathes. Why don't you feel her... em...'

'Pulse,' said Blue Boiler Suit.

I reached out and took the girl's wrist. It throbbed gently.

'Her heart beats, just like yours. Yes, indeedy! Isn't she the most *brilliant* miracle?'

I felt sick. 'Why—why have you done this?'

Professor Potkettle laughed. 'To kill two birds with one... em...'

'Stone,' said Green Boiler Suit.

'Not only do I get rid of an interfering little Different, but I send another Perfect back into Stopford to carry out my... em... mission.'

'A-another?' Suddenly, it all made sense. *That* was why Merry changed—that was why she stopped being friends with me and started hanging around with Chloe and Zoe—that was why she turned against me.

Because it wasn't Merry at all.

'You—you did this to Merry, too—'

'Yes, indeedy!' Professor Potkettle's blue eyes danced with glee. 'And the others.'

'Chloe, and Zoe...'

The Professor smiled. 'How do you think I found out that your family hadn't left Stopford, after my guards ordered them to go—and discovered that you'd moved your van into the woods?'

'From Merry... I told her all about it.'

'Yes, indeedy!' Professor Potkettle chuckled. 'I captured her thoughts and memories perfectly. And my Plastic Mary Jones told me all I needed to know.' He gazed down at the girl on the conveyor belt.

'Three so far. And this will be the fourth. Perfect, plastic children, doing exactly what I make them do. Children who will live for up to a thousand years. And soon, very soon, my mission will be complete.'

'What mission?'

Professor Potkettle's eyes gleamed behind his red spectacles. 'To gradually substitute all the children at Stopford School for plastic ones, of course! They will return to their families, ready to obey the laws of Stopford and, eventually, to work in my factory—such perfect copies that their parents will never notice the difference. One day soon, all of Stopford will be populated by my Perfects. Next step: the world!'

'But what about the... the real people? What will you do with them?'

A shadow passed over the Professor's face.

'For now, they are safely locked up, along with the interfering Differents.'

'Wh-what do you mean—for now?'

'Soon, as I duplicate more and more humans for Perfects, I shall have to find some way of... em... disposing of them.'

I swallowed. 'H-how?'

'Oh, details... details...' The Professor waved his hand in the air. 'The same way we dispose of plastic, I suppose. They can be sent to the incinerator and... em...'

'Burned,' said Blue Boiler Suit.

'But that's—that's *murder*!'

Professor Potkettle giggled. 'This is the... em... problem with you Differents,' he said. 'You all get so *upset* about unimportant things.'

'You'll never get away with it!'

'Who's going to stop me?' Professor Potkettle glanced at his yellow watch. 'But I must return to the laboratory and begin the Activation.'

'What's that?'

'The Activation?' Professor Potkettle glanced at the girl on the conveyor belt. 'It's the moment when we wake Ophelia Bottom up, ready to return to Stopford School as a Prefect.'

He set off towards the lift.

'Wh-what about me?' I called.

Professor Potkettle stepped into the lift.

'Oh, I have no further use for *you*.' He nodded his head at the Boiler Suits. 'Take her down to the cells.'

The lift door hissed closed and the Boiler Suits marched towards me. I hoisted up the white dress and ran, my bare feet slipping and sliding over the floor. Heavy footsteps pounded behind me as I raced towards the loading bay.

I skidded to a halt at the huge entrance door. The limousine was parked beside it, ready to take the plastic Ophelia Bottom back to school. I reached the keypad on the wall beside the door, screwed up my eyes and concentrated. The sequence of numbers appeared like a photograph in my mind. I stabbed at the buttons.

16... 12... 1...

A shadow fell over me, heavy breathing warmed the back of my neck and a large chubby finger punched CANCEL. Someone grabbed my arms. I kicked out as hard as I could at Green Boiler Suit's ankles. She gasped and swore and let go of my arms. I raced back on to the factory floor—past the girl lying on the conveyor belt, past the entrance to the incinerator. *Where to hide?* I stared wildly around the space.

But the Boiler Suits were almost on me.

The lift. I ran, flat out, towards it and pressed the button. The door hissed open. I stepped inside, stabbing at the CLOSE button and frantically pressed a button—any button. The Boiler Suits threw themselves at the door, but it was already shutting.

'Stairs!' Green Boiler Suit's voice shouted, as the lift began to go down to the basement. As soon as it arrived,

I punched the button to take me back up to the factory floor. Once there, I jumped out and pressed the button for the basement yet again. That should keep the Boilers busy for a few minutes.

A loudspeaker crackled into life somewhere above my head:

'*Countdown to Activation! Activation will commence in three minutes...*'

Activation. Professor Potkettle was bringing the plastic Ophelia to life.

Where to hide? I raced across the empty factory floor, my ears peeled for voices and footsteps. The girl—Plastic Ophelia—lay unmoving on the conveyor belt. Could I hide underneath it? *No good. They'd spot me straight away.* Ideas whirled in my head, but they were all impossible.

Unless...

...but it would never work.

Would it?

'*Countdown to Activation! Activation will commence in two minutes...*'

I bent down to Plastic Ophelia lying on the conveyor belt and grabbed hold of her blazer. She didn't move. She was heavy and solid and warm—exactly like a real, human girl—and also floppy as a puppet. Gritting my teeth, I tugged and pulled, and somehow managed to get the blazer off. My fingers fumbled to unknot the tie and undo the buttons on the white shirt and grey skirt. Then I pulled the trainers from her feet. I wriggled out of the white dress and threw on the uniform and trainers. Any moment, the Boilers would be back.

'*Countdown to Activation! Activation will commence in one minute...*'

I lifted Plastic Ophelia's head. *So heavy.* Somehow, I managed to drag the white dress down over her body. *Now for the hardest part.* I grabbed her by the arms and tugged as hard as I could. She was a dead weight. I tugged again. She rose up from the conveyor belt, then flopped back down, her head crashing on the surface. I couldn't help wincing. *Stoppit, Fee. She's made of plastic.* I grasped her shoulders and, with all my strength, pushed her until she rolled towards the edge of the conveyor belt.

'*Countdown to Activation! Activation will commence in thirty seconds...*'

I took a deep breath, placed both hands in the small of her back and gave an enormous shove.

As if in slow motion, Plastic Ophelia teetered over the edge of the conveyor belt and fell, landing with a heavy thud on the factory floor. Then I pushed her, centimetre by slow centimetre, until she was lying half hidden under the conveyor belt.

Voices. And the sound of heavy boots clattering up the stairs.

I leapt up on to the conveyor belt and lay down, just the way Plastic Ophelia did, eyes closed and body still.

'*Countdown to Activation! Activation will commence in ten seconds... nine... eight...*'

The voices came closer.

'*...seven... six...*'

It took every ounce of willpower to stay still.

'...*five... four...*'

Would the Boiler Suits grab me? Or...

'...*three... two... one... ACTIVATION!*'

I couldn't breathe. My heart pumped so hard it felt like it'd leap out of my chest at any moment.

'Let—me—GO!!!'

The voice was mine, but it didn't come from my mouth. It came from underneath the conveyor belt.

'GOTCHA!' panted the voice of Blue Boiler Suit.

'Let—me—' The voice was suddenly muffled as if someone had put a hand over Plastic Ophelia's mouth, and there was the sound of struggling, and heavy boots marching away towards the stairs. The sounds died away. I lay still, trembling and waiting and listening.

The lift door hissed open. Footsteps approached.

But these weren't the footsteps of the Boiler Suits. These were much lighter and softer. Closer and closer they came, until someone breathed peppermint right above me.

'So, my Perfect,' whispered the voice of Professor Potkettle. 'It is time to... em... wake up. Open your eyes.'

IMPRISONED:

locked up or kept captive somewhere

Slowly, I opened my eyes, keeping my face as still and blank as I could—just like Merry's face had been, when she came back from her Ceremony. I stared up into Professor Potkettle's cold blue eyes.

'Get up, my Perfect,' he whispered.

I sat up on the conveyor belt and swung my legs over the edge.

'Genius!' The Professor giggled, running his hand through his shock of hair. 'Another Perfect created—and out of such... em... *dangerous* raw material.' He clicked his fingers at me. 'Stand.'

I jumped down from the conveyor belt and stood very still. The Professor walked around me, muttering.

'Yes, indeedy,' he whispered. 'Perfect in every way.' Then he stopped. 'Tell me who you are.'

I swallowed. 'My name is Ophelia Bottom,' I said, in as steady a voice as I could.

'And how old are you, Ophelia?'

'I am eleven years old.'

'And when was your... em... birthday?'

'Yesterday. June the fifteenth.'

'Yes, indeedy! Now, tell me the motto of Stopford School.'

'*Plasticus stupendus est*,' I said, clasping my hands together. '*Diversus periculosus est.*'

'Perfect! Perfect! Now—follow me!'

He set off towards the loading bay. When he reached the limousine, he opened the door.

'Step inside, my Perfect, and wait here until it is time to return to school.'

I did as he said, sitting up straight on the seat.

'It's been a long night.' Professor Potkettle glanced at his watch and yawned. 'I'll catch some... em... shut-eye before we say goodbye.'

He pushed the door of the limousine shut and set off across the factory floor to the lift.

What should I do now? The sensible thing would be to stick with my original plan and go back to school in the limousine. But I hadn't found out where Ma was—or Seal's mum and dad. I pulled out the phone and scrolled down until I found Ar's number.

Please, Ar, be awake.

The phone rang and rang.

Just as I was about to give up, the ringing stopped and a voice roared into my ear.

'OPHELIA!'

'Ar!' I whispered. 'Thank goodness!'

'Where are you? What's OCCURRING?'

'Have you found them?' Seal must have grabbed the phone.

'Not—not exactly.'

'What d'you mean, *not exactly*?'

'Ma's here, for sure, Professor Potkettle said—'

'Is your mother SAFE?' roared Ar.

'Yes—yes, I think so.'

'And my mum and dad?' said Seal.

'They must be here too. Only I'm in the limousine in the loading bay, ready to come back—'

'STAY PUT, Ophelia! We shall embark on Operation Trojan Horse NOW!'

'Wait, Ar! Wouldn't it be better to—'

'Did you get the PASS CODE?'

I hesitated. Professor Potkettle was dangerous, and deadly. At any moment, he could do something terrible to Ma and the others. I made up my mind. We'd go ahead with Operation Trojan Horse. We'd find Ma and the others and sneak them out of the factory in the back of the Pantechnicon, before the Professor woke up and the morning shift began.

'Yes, I have,' I said. 'Got a pen and paper?'

There was a distant rustling. 'PROCEED.'

I told him the sequence of numbers.

'Got it. Now SIT TIGHT, Ophelia. We know what to do. And once we're in, we'll find YOUR MOTHER!'

'And my mum and dad!' hissed Seal.

'To the PANTECHNICON!' rumbled Ar. Doors banged and there was lots of shuffling, as the engine started.

'Don't forget, Ar—' I hissed, 'you're a lorry driver now!'

'Arfur Green AT YER SERVICE, miss!' Ar sounded like he'd got something stuck up his nose.

'Right—only... don't overdo it.'

Seal's voice, sounding muffled down by Ar's feet, muttered: 'Get off the phone, Mr Bottom! We need to concentrate.'

'Good luck, both of you!' I whispered.

'FORTUNE FAVOURS THE BRAVE!' Ar ended the call.

I switched the phone to vibrate rather than ring, just in case. How long would it be until the Professor woke up? Crossing my fingers, I sat back and waited.

It seemed about a hundred years, but was probably only fifteen minutes, when blue lights flashed above the doors of the loading bay, and the sound of heavy boots approached. The Boiler Suits. They must have locked Plastic Ophelia up somewhere—maybe in the same place they'd locked up Ma and the others. I sat very straight and still in the limousine, my eyes staring straight ahead.

'Delivery,' said Blue Boiler Suit.

The doors to the loading bay hissed open. With a grinding of gears, the Pantechnicon lurched in and shuddered to a halt beside the limousine, the sign on its side—PRATT'S PLASTIC PELLETS—gleaming in the fluorescent lighting. I glanced up at the driver's cab. There was Ar, grinning down at me, with Seal beside him. I frowned and shook my head, and Ar pulled his cap down over his eyes. Just in time—Green Boiler Suit marched up to the driver's cab.

'Unload,' she said, jerking her head at the back doors of the Pantechnicon.

'Yus, missus,' Ar said. 'Me assistant will open up.'

Seal leapt out of the cab and hurried to the back of the Pantechnicon. With a familiar squeak and rattle, the doors were thrown open. Cautiously, I turned round, just in time to see the two Boiler Suits climbing into the back of the Pantechnicon.

Operation Trojan Horse was going according to plan.

As quietly as I could, I leant over and pushed open the door of the limousine. Then I swung my legs to the ground and jumped out. Up in the driver's cab, Ar gave me a silent thumbs-up. The Pantechnicon shuddered as the Boiler Suits marched towards the rows of sacks inside, ready to begin unloading them.

I tiptoed round to the back. Seal stood waiting beside one of the doors. I grabbed the other, and whispered:

'*Now!!!*'

—and we each slammed the doors as hard as we could. They crashed shut, the sound echoing around the loading bay. Seal turned the key in the lock. For a moment, there was complete silence. Then, the sound of boots stomping in the Pantechnicon, and fists hammering on the doors, and cursing voices.

'*Got 'em!*' Seal's eyes were alight with triumph. We high-fived, as Ar climbed down from the driver's cab and limped towards us.

'MISSION ACCOMPLISHED!' he beamed. 'The RUFFIANS are IMPRISONED!'

But Seal was hopping from foot to foot, his eyes darting round the factory floor. 'We've got to find my mum and dad!'

I nodded. 'Professor Potkettle's sleeping, but he could wake up any minute!'

'Come *on*, then!' Seal set off across the factory floor at a run, Ar limping behind. The sound of roaring and cursing echoed from the back of the Pantechnicon, as heavy fists beat on the doors. I turned back to Ar.

'Stay here, Ar. You can't keep up with us, not with your leg. Stand guard at the Pantechnicon and make sure the Boiler Suits don't get out. Keep your phone on in case I need to call you. But don't call me unless you have to. And be ready to do a quick getaway when we come back with Ma and the others!'

Ar nodded reluctantly and limped back towards the Pantechnicon.

'Hurry *up*!' Seal hissed. 'Where shall we search?'

'Professor Potkettle said something about taking Plastic Ophelia down to the cells, so—'

'Plastic Ophelia? What are you on about?'

'Professor Potkettle's made a...'

A sound from inside the Pantechnicon made me stop.

'What now?' whispered Seal.

I shook my head and put my finger to my lips. 'Listen!'

The sound wasn't the voices of the Boiler Suits. And it wasn't their fists, hammering on the doors.

It was a hissing, crackling sound, and it made my blood run cold.

CURMUDGEONS:

bad-tempered people

'The walkie-talkies!' I gasped.

'So what?' said Seal.

'If Professor Potkettle's got a walkie-talkie, the Boilers will wake him up and tell him what we've done, and that'll be the end of Operation Trojan Horse! We've got to find Ma and the others and get them out, fast!'

I set off at a run for the lift, Seal right behind me, and stabbed at the call button. The door slid open and Seal and I leapt inside. It seemed to take forever for the door to close again. Beside me, Seal clasped and unclasped his fists, his knuckles pale.

Down, down, down… At last the lift shuddered to a halt, the door opened and we jumped out.

We were in a dark corridor. No white walls here—just old, cold stone. The air smelt damp and musty, and the only light came from dim bare bulbs hanging from the ceiling. At the far end of the corridor was a row of five identical doors, each with a thick glass window set high above it and a keypad below.

'Where are we?' muttered Seal. 'Some kind of cellar?'

I shook my head. 'I think—it might be a prison.'

'You mean—this is where...?'

'Let's find out.' I grabbed his arm and we moved silently down the corridor to the first door. The window was twice the height of us. I pressed my ear to the door and listened. Nothing.

'Bend down,' I whispered.

'What?'

'So I can get up on your back.'

'*You* bend down,' muttered Seal. 'I've been scrunched up in the Pantechnicon for ages and—'

'*Shhhhh!*' I bent down and grabbed my knees. Lucky Seal was smaller than me, and thin and wiry, or I'd never be able to hold him up. He scrambled on to my back, still muttering.

'What can you see?' I whispered.

'Give me a chance!' he hissed back. 'I'm trying to stand up.'

'Hurry! Professor Potkettle—'

'All right, all right!'

My back felt like it was going to break. My knees wobbled.

'Stay *still*, can't you?'

I gritted my teeth. Seal's feet pressed down unbearably. I hardly dared breathe.

There was a gasp from above me.

'What? What is it?'

'Someone's in there. Sleeping.'

'Who? Is it Ma?'

'Dunno. They're lying on a bunk with a blanket pulled up over their head. What'll I do?'

262

My brain jumped around. 'It might be Ma—or your mum and dad. But what if it's Professor Potkettle?'

The phone vibrated in my blazer pocket. What was Ar doing, phoning me?

'Get down!' I hissed at Seal. He leapt off my back and, trying not to groan out loud, I straightened up painfully and grabbed the phone.

'OPHELIA—!' In the background I could hear the Boiler Suits' fists thumping inside the Pantechnicon.

'Ar!' I hissed. 'I *told* you not to ring me!'

'This is an EMERGENCY!'

A high-pitched, all-too-familiar voice was shouting above the thumping and banging. My heart thudded into my trainers.

'What's going on?' Seal's breath warmed my face as he tried to listen in.

'The two CURMUDGEONS in the back called their PINT-SIZED BOSS!' panted Ar.

'Professor Potkettle? Where is he?'

'I've GOT HIM SAFE—for now!'

'What do you mean?'

'He was NO MATCH for me!' rumbled Ar. 'I APPRE-HENDED him and tied him up in my BRACES. He's struggling like a good 'un!'

'Can you keep him there till we get back?'

'WILCO! But MAKE HASTE—his SIDEKICKS are beating down the doors of the Pantechnicon! It's only a matter of time before they BREAK OUT!'

And the phone went dead.

Seal and I looked at one another.

'Are you thinking what I'm thinking?' muttered Seal.

I glanced at the door with the thick glass window, and nodded.

'If Ar's got hold of Professor Potkettle, then...'

'...whoever's sleeping in there *isn't* Professor Potkettle. Which means...'

'Ma!' I whispered, banging on the door. 'Wake up! Are you in there?'

There was no answer. But from the second door along came a shuffling sound, as if someone on the other side was moving towards it.

'Ophelia?'

It was Ma's voice.

'Ma!' Suddenly, my heart felt all warm and happy. 'Are you all right?'

'How did you *get out*?' Ma didn't seem especially surprised to hear my voice.

'Get out?' I looked at Seal. What was Ma talking about? Seal shook his head.

'We've come to rescue you!' I called.

'*We*? Is Arthur with you?' Ma's voice sounded anxious.

'Ar's waiting for us with the Pantechnicon. He's been a real hero, Ma—he's captured Professor Potkettle!'

'That *odious little man*,' said Ma. 'About time!'

Beside me, Seal jumped up and down.

'Ask her about my mum and dad,' he hissed.

'Ma—do you know who's in the other cells?'

'Only *by sound*,' said Ma. 'There are *children* next door...'

264

'Children?' I ran to the third door and banged on it. 'Who's in there?'

'Fee!' shouted a voice.

Merry. I couldn't help grinning. I never thought I'd hear her call me Fee again.

'Merry! I'm so glad—I mean, that it's you and that it wasn't you that—'

But before I could finish, other voices joined in. Voices I'd heard before.

'Help us!'

'Get us out of here!'

'Who's in there with you, Merry?'

'It's Chloe, and Zoe!'

Of course. Professor Potkettle made Plastics of Chloe and Zoe too.

Seal pushed past me to the fourth cell and thew himself against the door like an excited puppy.

'Mum? Dad? Are you in there?'

A man's voice, deep and sweet as honey, called out.

'*Seal?*'

—and a gentle woman's voice said: 'Seal—my dearest boy... my son!'

'We've—we've come to get you out!' Seal's voice came out all crackly and hoarse. He blinked hard and wiped at his eyes with the back of his hand.

Suddenly, everyone was shouting at once, voices echoing down the corridor.

'*Ophelia—get your father!*'

'*Dad—Mum—I've missed you so—*'

'Seal, child—I can't believe...'

'Get us out, Fee!'

'Son—how did you—?'

'QUIET, EVERYBODY!' I yelled, and they all stopped shouting. 'Ma—Mr and Mrs... er... Seal. Do you know the pass code? To open the doors?'

'No,' said Ma.

'They never open the doors,' said Merry's voice.

'They just drop food and water through the window twice a day,' said Seal's dad.

I looked at Seal. His mum and dad had been kept in that cell for nine whole months. Seal gave a huge sniff and wiped his nose on his sweatshirt. 'We've got to get them out, Fee—now!'

I ran to the fifth cell and banged on the door.

'Is anyone in there?'

Something shuffled, then silence. *Someone* was inside, but who? I was about to bang again when the phone rang. *Ar's number.* Quickly, I answered.

'Ar—we've found Ma, and Seal's parents! And Merry, and Chloe and Zoe! They're all locked in cells in the basement—'

A high-pitched giggle echoed from the phone.

'Ar? Is that you? What're you—'

'Miss Bottom, I presume,' said the voice of Professor Potkettle.

GENIUS:

a highly talented or intelligent person

'Wh-what have you done with Ar?' I whispered. Seal leant to listen in. 'Where is he?'

'Your father is right here beside me,' said Professor Potkettle. 'My security guards are... em... looking after him.'

'How—how did they get out of the Pantechnicon?'

'Easy-peasy, lemon-squeezy!' giggled the Professor. 'If you're silly enough to lock up two strong people in the back of a van, make sure you don't leave, em...'

'Weapons,' said the voice of Blue Boiler Suit.

'Weapons, yes, indeedy!'

The spears from Julius Caesar. The Boilers must have broken out, just as Ar warned. And Ar couldn't run away, because of his leg being in plaster.

'You'd better not have hurt him!'

The Professor giggled again. 'Never fear, Miss Bottom. Your father is fine for... em... now.'

Seal grabbed the phone. 'Evil—that's what you are! Kidnapping my mum and dad—locking up anyone who's—who's different! Poisoning the sea with your plastic muck!'

'And who, may I ask, are you?' The Professor's voice was icy cold.

'Never you mind!' shouted Seal. 'You won't get away with this—you—you—'

'Genius?' Professor Potkettle interrupted. 'Is that the... em... word you're looking for?'

I grabbed the phone back and shoved my hand over Seal's mouth. 'What do you mean, Ar's fine *for now*?'

'Listen to me very carefully, Miss Bottom,' said Professor Potkettle. 'Unless you and your young friend return to the loading bay *immediately*, I shall assume that your father is... em...'

'Unwanted,' said the voice of Green Boiler Suit.

'And you know what we do with unwanted things...'

'Wh-what do you mean?' I clutched the phone. I longed to throw it away, to smash it against the wall, but I had to listen to what the Professor said.

'Come now, Miss Bottom. For all your failings, I know that your... em... memory never falters.'

'I don't understand...'

'Then I suggest you cast your mind back to your school visit to the Potkettle Institute. You asked me a... em... question there—a very foolish question in my opinion. You asked what happened to the plastic that no one wanted. And what did I tell you?'

'You—you said you could bury it, or... or...'

'Well, Miss Bottom?'

'Or burn it,' I muttered.

'Burn it, yes indeedy! And I told you that here in the factory we have a simply brilliant, em...'

'Incinerator,' said Green Boiler Suit.

'I'm sure you wouldn't want your father to have a terrible... em... *accident*, would you?'

A river of ice seemed to seep through my body. He *couldn't* do that to Ar... could he? I opened my mouth to reply but nothing came out.

'Cat got your tongue, Miss Bottom? Then I will make it very... em... simple for you. Unless you and your little friend return to the loading bay in three minutes, I shall have no option but to deal with your father just as we deal with our unwanted plastic.'

'But—that's murder! You wouldn't dare!'

'Watch me, Miss Bo—' His voice faded and disappeared.

I stared at the phone, shook it. The battery must have died. My shoulders slumped. 'We'll have to go back.'

Seal stared wildly at the row of closed doors.

'We can't! Not now we've found them...'

'We have to! If we don't, he'll, he'll—'

Seal turned to me, desperation in his eyes. 'Fee—we've got to get them out! *Please.* Remember Operation Trojan Horse! It's our last—our only—chance!'

Above our heads, a loudspeaker crackled into life.

'*Countdown to incineration! Incineration will commence in three minutes...*'

My brain felt like it was about to explode. 'If we don't go back right now, the Professor will—will—'

Seal gave a howl of frustration and hammered on the cell door.

'What's going on, Ophelia?' Ma's voice called. 'Who's talking about *incineration*?'

I swallowed. 'It's Professor Potkettle, Ma. He's got Ar, and he says if me and Seal don't go back now—he'll—he'll send Ar to the incinerator.'

'Don't let them hurt Arthur.' Ma's voice sounded thin and scared. 'Go back, Ophelia—*go now*!!!'

'She's right,' shouted Merry's voice. 'Professor Potkettle's mad—and dangerous. He'll do what he threatens. Go back, Fee!'

The voices of Seal's parents joined in. 'Seal, go back. No one must lose their precious life to save us.'

Tears rolled down Seal's cheeks.

'We'll find a way,' I whispered. 'We'll get them out somehow.'

'*How?*' snarled Seal. 'If we go back to the loading bay, the Professor will take *us* prisoner.'

'I *know*,' I muttered. 'But it's the only thing to do. C'mon.'

I grabbed his arm. Seal gulped and wiped his eyes. My legs and feet were so heavy it was like they were rooted to the floor, but I forced them to move. Dragging Seal with me, I stumbled towards the lift. Every step away from Ma and the others felt like torture. But we *had* to go back. We didn't have any other choice.

We were almost at the lift when I stopped. Seal bashed into me.

'What're you doing?'

270

I turned, slowly, and stared at the door of the first cell.

'Plastic Ophelia,' I whispered.

'What?'

'Remember what Ma said, when we found her? She asked how I got out. She must've thought I was in the cell next door. But I wasn't, of course—it was Plastic Ophelia.'

'Who *is* this Plastic Ophelia?'

'She's me—a plastic me. The Professor built her.'

Seal opened his mouth to speak.

'Shhhh!' I whispered. 'I think... I think I know what to do.'

'Well?' Seal stared at me, his eyes full of hope.

'The Professor's expecting you and me to return to the loading bay, right?'

Seal nodded.

'If we do, he won't incinerate Ar.'

'I *know* that...' hissed Seal.

'But what if... what if it's not *me* you take back with you?'

'What?'

I pointed to the first cell, keeping my voice to a whisper. 'In there, there's a girl who looks exactly like me. If I can get her out, you two can return to the loading bay and the Professor will think she's me...'

'Yeah, but how are you going to get everyone out by yourself? And anyhow, I'm not going back there with a—'

'Shut up and listen!' I took a deep breath and whispered in his ear. 'There's a chance—a small chance—that the pass code to the cells is the same one as the one that got us into the factory. But we only have seconds, and I need to concentrate.'

Seal grabbed my arm. 'If you know the pass code, get my mum and dad out first! And then your mum, and the others! Then we can all—'

'*Countdown to incineration! Incineration will commence in two minutes...*'

I shook my arm free. 'There's no time to get everyone out, Seal—but if I can get Plastic Ophelia out in the next thirty seconds, and if you take her with you to the Professor, he'll think she's me—and that'll buy me enough time to use the pass code to free everyone else. Then we can all sneak to the loading bay and take Professor Potkettle and the Boilers by surprise.'

Seal glared at me.

'You've got to trust me, Seal!' I ran to the first cell door and stared at the keypad. The sequence of numbers was safe in my memory. With shaking fingers, I tapped in each number, Seal's impatient breath tickling the back of my neck.

I pressed ENTER.

For a moment, nothing happened.

Then, very slowly and with a rusty squeak, the cell door swung open. Sitting on a narrow bunk in her white dress was Plastic Ophelia. Seal stared at her, then at me, then back at her again.

'She—she's... *you!*'

Plastic Ophelia stood up. 'Who're *you?*'

I ran over to her and grabbed her arm.

'Let go of me!' she said, in my voice, and tried to shake her arm free.

'Listen to me, Ophelia,' I whispered. 'Professor Potkettle wants to see you. *Immediately.*'

'Professor Potkettle?' said Plastic Ophelia.

'Yes. You've got to go—straight away. He's waiting for you.' I nodded at Seal. 'You remember Seal, don't you? He's going to take you.'

Plastic Ophelia stared at Seal for a moment, then turned back to me. 'Why should I trust what you say? Who *are* you, anyway? And why do you look and sound like *me?*'

'*Countdown to incineration! Incineration will commence in one minute...*'

If Plastic Ophelia didn't go with Seal *now*, I'd have to go back with him. I tried to keep my voice even, though my heart felt like it was trying to break out of my chest.

'Professor Potkettle will be furious if you don't go *right now!*'

I made a face at Seal. He grabbed Plastic Ophelia's hand. 'C'mon. We'd better hurry.'

Plastic Ophelia frowned at him. 'All right. But let go of my hand.'

Seal dropped it and pushed her down the corridor. As they headed towards the lift, he looked back over his shoulder at me.

'Good luck,' he mouthed.

'You too,' I whispered back. Then the lift door hissed open and they were gone.

PASS CODE:

a system of words, letters, figures or symbols used as a password

As the lift door hissed shut, I turned back to the cells.

'Listen, everybody—I've got the pass code! I'm going to get you all out, one by one. Ma first.'

'Don't even *think of it*, Ophelia!' shouted Ma. 'Get back to Professor Potkettle. Otherwise he'll send your father to the—'

'It's all right,' I called back. 'Ar will be safe. Seal's gone back to the Professor with—'

'Seal's gone back without you?' Seal's mum sounded panicky.

'It's OK,' I said. 'We—I mean, I—thought of a plan. To give me time to free you all. And when you're out, we can all sneak into the loading bay and ambush the Professor and his guards, and rescue Ar and Seal...'

'You say you have the pass code?' called Seal's dad.

'Yes. It's the same one that got us into the factory.'

Then, everyone was shouting at me.

Use the pass code!

Quickly—quickly. Or Seal will—'

Get us out, Ophelia!

'Go, Fee!' shouted Merry from her cell and I couldn't help grinning. No more O-*failure*. Having Merry back as my friend made all the difference. I tapped the numbers into the keypad on Ma's cell door and pressed ENTER.

Nothing happened. I stared at the keypad.

'Well?' called Ma.

'It—it didn't work.' *Why not? It worked on Plastic Ophelia's cell.*

'You must have got it wrong!' Zoe's voice.

'Do it again!' That was Chloe.

I shook my head. My sticky memory didn't get things wrong. But I tapped the numbers in once more, just to be certain.

Nothing.

'*Now* what?' called Ma.

'It must be a different pass code for each cell,' I muttered. But what? And how could I possibly work each code out? I'd been so sure I had the pass code—so certain of it that I'd sent Seal back to Professor Potkettle on his own. I'd told him to trust me, and now it turned out I had no answers after all. Any moment, the Professor could find out that the girl with Seal wasn't me, and... a sob wrenched out of my chest.

Then someone called my name.

'Ophelia!!!!'

The voice wasn't Ma's, or Seal's mum's or dad's. And it certainly wasn't Merry's voice—or Chloe's, or Zoe's.

'Ophelia—are you there?'

I pulled the phone out of my pocket and stared at the blank screen. Still no battery. But the voice went on speaking.

'Listen to me, Ophelia. Time is of the... em... essence!'

It was the voice of Professor Potkettle. And it wasn't coming from the phone.

It was coming from the fifth cell.

I stared at the cell door. How could Professor Potkettle be in the loading bay with Ar and Seal and the Boilers—and inside this cell, both at the same time? It had to be some kind of a trick. Maybe Professor Potkettle had put a loudspeaker inside the cell. Maybe he was giggling with the Boilers about his latest jape.

'There's only one way to save your father and your friends, Ophelia, and that's by... em... listening to me.'

'No way!' I wiped the tears from my cheeks. 'You're not tricking me.'

'This is no... em... trick, I swear!' whispered the voice. *'Like your friends, I am a prisoner—a prisoner of Professor Potkettle.'*

'But... but you sound exactly like Professor Potkettle.'

There was a silence. Then the voice whispered:

'Yes, indeedy! That is because I am Professor Potkettle... the first Petrus Potkettle.'

'The first?' What was he talking about?

'I can stop your father being sent to the... em... incinerator. And I can stop the Professor's evil doings forever. Give me but one minute of your time!'

My mind boggled, thoughts jumping everywhere. What if it *was* all a trick? Yet something deep inside me seemed to tell me to listen, to find out what this person had to say to me. I made up my mind.

I ran to stand outside the fifth cell.

'Well?' I whispered. 'What is it you want to tell me?'

'*I will be... em... brief,*' the high voice whispered back. '*I am the real Professor Petrus Potkettle. It was I who founded this factory and who built the town of Stopford. It was I who discovered how to create a person made of plastic: a person so perfect that no one could tell the... em... difference.*'

'I know all that!' I said. 'You made a plastic Merry, and Chloe and Zoe. And—and you made a plastic me.'

'*No indeedy,*' whispered the voice. '*I made none of them.*'

My mind spun. What did he mean? But he was still speaking.

'*I made a copy of only one person, Ophelia,*' whispered the voice. '*And that person was... myself.*'

DEACTIVATE:

*to make something inactive by
disconnecting or destroying it*

'I don't understand...' I whispered.

'*I am a genius, yes indeedy!*' whispered Professor Potkettle's voice. '*But even geniuses make... em... mistakes. And I made the greatest mistake of my life in creating a plastic version of myself.*'

'You mean... Professor Potkettle—the one in the loading bay—is a fake—made of plastic?'

'*Yes, indeedy! I was so proud of what I'd created: someone who looked and sounded exactly like myself. Who even* <u>thought</u> *like me. Only I didn't bargain for what he'd do. No sooner had I... em... activated him, than he turned on me—convinced my security guards that* <u>he</u> *was the real Professor Potkettle—ordered them to lock me up in this cell. That was twelve long months ago.*'

'And then,' I said slowly, 'he began his mission to take over Stopford...'

'*Yes, indeedy. I knew nothing, of course, of what he was up to. Not until he began locking up others. First, the two who tried to... em... stop him...*'

'Seal's mum and dad—'

'I heard everything through the wall. How the Plastic Professor had convinced everyone in Stopford that plastic was fantastic—that different was... em... dangerous. How he disposed of his unwanted plastic in the incinerator, and when that was full, by dumping it in the... em... river. How he locked up anyone who disagreed with what he was doing, anyone who threatened his mission—anyone who was... em... different. And then he locked up the children.'

'Merry—my friend. And Chloe and Zoe...'

'And I knew that the Plastic Professor had moved into an even more terrible and dangerous phase of his mission: using innocent children as his... em... guinea pigs.'

'But why—why didn't you speak up? Why didn't you tell them who you were?'

The voice went very quiet, so I could hardly hear it.

'I was... em... ashamed. Ashamed at what I'd started. Ashamed at the terrible mistake I had made.'

'Why now, then? Why are you telling *me* all this?'

'Because now he has, em... gone too far. Locking people up is one thing. Killing them is another. I cannot stand by and watch that happen.'

His words jerked me back to the present.

'The Professor could find out any minute that I've tricked him! And if he does, he'll send Ar and Seal to the incinerator!'

'We have time—with luck—to stop all this.'

'How?'

'You must go to the laboratory,' whispered the voice, *'and deactivate the Plastic Professor.'*

279

'But—but I don't know what to do!'

'*I will tell you the sequence of... em... instructions. They are complex. Can you record them on your phone?*'

I shook my head. 'No. The battery's died. But I've got a sticky memory. Just tell me them.'

'*Then listen very... em... carefully.*'

I pressed my ear to the door of the cell, and the Professor told me what to do.

The laboratory was empty and silent. Lights gleamed on the control panel and the conveyor belt lay empty. I shuddered, remembering being tied there, helpless, while the Professor—the Plastic Professor—measured me and recorded my voice and copied my thoughts. Just as he must have done with Merry, and Chloe, and Zoe. Just as he would do with all the children at Stopford School, unless I stopped him. I ran to the giant computer screen and stood in front of the control panel with its hundreds of buttons.

Professor Potkettle—the real Professor—was right. The instructions were complicated. Much more complicated than the pass code that got us into the factory, and which opened the door to Plastic Ophelia's cell. More complicated, even, than remembering a whole Shakespeare play. My heart thudded, measuring out the seconds. I had to be quick. Even now, Ar and Seal might be... *stoppit, Fee.* Were the Professor's instructions safe in my memory? *Yes.* They were all there, just as clearly as when he'd told me. I reached to the control panel and, with trembling fingers, tapped in the letters and symbols, one by one.

The control panel began to buzz and hum. Combinations of words and numbers appeared on the screen, just as the Professor said they would. I kept tapping in the instructions until the screen was full. A large button on the control panel began to flash. This was the one which would start the deactivation process.

I was just about to press it when I noticed one button lit up.

The loudspeakers.

The Plastic Professor would hear the countdown to his deactivation and would know exactly what I'd been up to. Quickly, I swiped at the button and the light went off.

Then, with trembling fingers, I pressed the deactivation button.

Instantly, the computer screen flashed and the word DEACTIVATION scrolled silently past, again and again.

It's happening.

I ran. Out of the laboratory, down the corridor. At the lift, I stopped. *No, it'll take too long.* I dashed for the stairs and half tumbled down them, my feet getting all mixed up in my rush. Across the empty factory floor I sped, my breath burning my lungs, towards the loading bay.

It was empty. The Pantechnicon's back doors hung off their hinges, the spears from *Julius Caesar* lying on the floor. The limousine was empty too.

The Plastic Professor, the two Boilers, Plastic Ophelia and Ar and Seal were gone.

A chill crept into my heart. He couldn't have... could he?

I ran back across the factory floor to where a red light flashed above a door. The sign on the door said:

DANGER!!!
INCINERATOR

I grabbed the handle and pushed it open.

INCINERATE:

to destroy by burning to ashes

I was in a small room like a viewing gallery. One wall was made of glass. The Plastic Professor stood with his back to me, with Plastic Ophelia by his side, looking through the glass. Blue Boiler Suit sat in a plastic chair set high up near the ceiling, turning some kind of wheel. Green Boiler Suit sat in front of a huge blank computer screen. Beside the screen, a red lever was lit up, with the single word:

INCINERATE

In the centre of the room there was a great round hole in the floor.

Why hadn't the Plastic Professor and Plastic Ophelia deactivated? How long did the process take? Did I forget to do something important? And what were they staring at? I crept up behind them.

Through the glass was a gigantic rubbish tip of plastic junk—plastic furniture, plastic bottles, laptops and televisions. A walkway ran above it, beside a high brick wall. In one corner of the tip was a plastic chute, like a giant playground slide. This must be where the workers tipped the unwanted plastic—down through the hole in the viewing gallery and on to the rubbish tip.

But it was what was beside the chute that made my heart drop down into my tummy.

Lying up to their waists in plastic junk were Ar and Seal. They were blindfolded and their hands were tied. And hovering above them was a giant metal grabbing claw—like the ones in amusement arcades that you use to try to grab a prize. As Blue Boiler Suit turned the wheel, the grabbing claw moved down until it hovered right over Ar's head. Blue Boiler Suit pressed a button and the claw slowly opened, ready to grab.

'*Stop!!!*' I screamed.

The Plastic Professor swivelled round. A horrible smile crept across his face. His teeth gleamed, whiter-than-white.

'So, Miss Bottom. Interfering again?' He gave his high-pitched giggle. 'Thought yourself clever, did you? Cleverer than me? Did you really believe that a genius like myself could be... em... duped into believing my Perfect was *you*?' The Plastic Professor shook his head, his shock of hair bouncing. 'If so, you were sadly... em...'

'Mistaken,' said Green Boiler Suit.

The Plastic Professor jerked his head at Blue Boiler Suit, who leapt from his seat and grabbed me by the arms. I tried to wrench free, but he was far stronger.

'Now I have all three of you,' said the Plastic Professor. 'And this will be the last of your... em... interference in my mission. Because of your foolishness and stubbornness, Miss Bottom, you have sentenced your father and your friend to their... em...'

'Deaths,' said Blue Boiler Suit.

I swallowed hard. I'd got to trust that I'd remembered the sequence of instructions right. I'd got to trust that any minute, the Plastic Professor would be deactivated. Otherwise... I tried not to think about it. I must stall him, keep him talking. I took a deep breath and tried to sound calm.

'Wh-what are you going to do?'

'Easy-peasy lemon-squeezy!' giggled the Plastic Professor, pushing his red spectacles up his nose. 'I told you, did I not, what we do with our unwanted plastic? Perhaps it's time to... em... *show* you, instead.' He nodded at Green Boiler Suit. 'Take a look at my *marvellous* incinerator.'

Green Boiler Suit pressed some buttons and the screen lit up to show an empty brick room with blackened walls. Then, she pushed the lever marked **INCINERATE**. A great wall of fire reared up on the screen, blinding me so that for a moment all I could see was yellow and black and red.

'Seven hundred and fifty degrees Celsius,' whispered the Plastic Professor. 'Hotter than anything you've ever known, Miss Bottom. Hotter than... em...'

'Hell,' leered Green Boiler Suit, pulling the lever again. The flames died down, leaving only blackness.

'Yes, indeedy. In a matter of seconds, after your father and your friend have been hoisted over the wall and dropped down into my incinerator, they will be reduced to... em...'

'Ashes,' said Blue Boiler Suit.

'And then my mission will proceed, uninterrupted,' said the Plastic Professor.

My eyes were still half blinded from the flames. I took a deep breath.

'I know all about your mission. And I know what you really are. I know exactly what you did to the real Professor Potkettle.'

'The *real* Professor Potkettle?' The Plastic Professor narrowed his eyes. 'There is only one *real* Professor. Yes indeedy! And that is... em... *me.*' He puffed out his little chest.

I had to get the Boiler Suits on my side.

'He's lying,' I said. 'You've been fooled. This so-called Professor is a fake—as plastic as the plastic he makes in his factory. He fooled you into locking up the real Professor in a cell for a whole year.'

The Boiler Suits looked at one another, then at the Plastic Professor.

'And *this* is why Differents are so dangerous!' hissed the Plastic Professor. 'They spread lies to confuse and mislead loyal people like... em... yourselves.'

'*He's* lying!' I shouted again. 'I'm telling the truth—'

Before I could go on, the Plastic Professor stepped towards us.

'Take her to the chute,' he said.

Blue Boiler Suit dragged me to the hole in the centre of the room. I dug my heels into the floor and squirmed like a worm, but Blue Boiler Suit kept dragging me until I stood at the very edge of the hole. Below, there was only darkness.

I turned and stared into Blue Boiler Suit's eyes.

'Please listen to me,' I whispered. 'He's fake. Your real boss is locked up in the cells.'

'Quiet!' Blue Boiler Suit obviously didn't believe me. I kept whispering.

'He's fake—made of plastic, just like *her.*' I nodded at Plastic Ophelia. 'I'm deactivating them. If they stop working, you'll *know* I'm telling you the truth...'

Blue Boiler Suit hesitated and glanced over at the Plastic Professor and Plastic Ophelia. Then he tightened his grip on my arms.

'You won't get away with this!' I shouted at the Plastic Professor.

He giggled. 'Goodbye, Miss Bottom.' His white teeth gleamed in the dim light. 'And good riddance.'

He turned to Blue Boiler Suit.

'Send her down.'

And Blue Boiler Suit pushed me into the darkness.

CLAW:

mechanical device used for gripping or lifting

Down, down, down I fell, banging my elbows and my knees on the sides of the chute as I tumbled through the darkness.

Then I shot out into the light. For a moment I lay still, battered and bashed by my fall. A plastic carrier bag twined about one of my arms and I was up to my neck in an ocean of plastic junk: it was like being in a toddlers' ball pit, only this one wasn't going to be any fun at all. A few metres away, Ar and Seal lay blindfolded among the junk, their hands tied.

'Ar!' I shouted. 'Seal!'

Ar's head twisted towards me. 'OPHELIA? Is THAT YOU?'

'Yes,' I shouted back. 'I'm coming over.'

Frantically, I pushed at the junk around me, trying to get to him. It was like trying to swim through treacle.

'Where's your MOTHER?' Is she UNHARMED?'

'She's—she's still locked up.'

Seal shouted: 'What about my mum and dad?'

'Same,' I called back. 'I'm so sorry, Seal. I thought I was doing the right thing—'

'Never mind that! We've got to get out of here and rescue them!' Seal thrashed about in the junk with his tied hands.

'Have they TIED YOUR HANDS too, Fee?' shouted Ar. 'Have they BLINDFOLDED YOU?'

'No.'

'Then please DISCLOSE where we are.'

'It's a sort of giant rubbish tip,' I said. 'Full of plastic junk.'

'How do we get out?' shouted Seal. 'Is there a door?'

I glanced up at the metal claw hanging above Ar's head, and the black brick wall rising above us. Over that wall was the incinerator. Should I tell them that we were all in mortal danger? But what good would it do?

'No,' I said. 'There's no door. There's no way out.'

'COME HERE and UNFETTER US!' shouted Ar.

'I'll try,' I called back. 'But it's hard to move.'

I pushed, as hard as I could, at the mass of plastic junk hemming me in. It shifted a tiny bit. I scrabbled and kicked my feet and managed to move a few centimetres forward. If I kept going, I'd reach Ar. But would there be time? I looked up. Behind the glass window, the Plastic Professor grinned down at us. Beside him, Plastic Ophelia stared too, her face blank. The Plastic Professor turned to Blue Boiler Suit and said something to him. Blue Boiler Suit nodded and climbed back into his chair. Then he grabbed the wheel and twisted it.

The metal claw lowered until it hovered right over Ar's head.

'*Get out of the way, Ar!!!*' I screamed.

Ar looked puzzled. 'What do you MEAN, OPHELIA?'

'They're trying to grab you, Ar! Move about as much as you can!'

Ar wriggled his shoulders in the sea of plastic. But he was too big and heavy to move much, and his plaster weighed him down. The claw came down, closer and closer...

I shoved and pushed at the plastic, kicking my legs like I was swimming. Above Ar's head, the claw opened. I reached him just as it began to close. With every bit of strength I had, I shoved Ar out of the way. He only moved a tiny bit, but it was enough. The claw closed on empty air. But immediately it swung round, until once again it was right above us. I watched it coming down.

I won't let them hurt Ar.

I reached up and grabbed the claw and held on tight. My body swung in mid-air as it hoisted me up, up, up—until I was hanging right in front of the glass window. The Plastic Professor clutched his sides in silent laughter.

'OPHELIA?' called Ar's voice from below. 'WHERE ARE YOU?'

'It's—it's OK, Ar.' My voice sounded thin and scared. 'Keep moving about!'

Behind the glass wall, the Plastic Professor stared at me, his blue eyes as cold as chips of ice. Then he raised his hand to his neck and pulled his finger across his throat. Blue Boiler Suit twisted the wheel, sending me lurching towards the brick wall of the incinerator. I tried to let go of the claw, but the sleeve of my blazer was caught in it. I wriggled frantically to free myself from the blazer.

But it was too late.

The claw swept me over the brick wall and down into darkness. Above me, a great chimney reared up. And below me was what I'd seen on the computer screen: brick walls stained black with soot, and a mass of grey ash.

The incinerator.

It was suddenly hard to breathe. The air was hot and heavy with fumes. My eyes burned and tingled. Tears snaked down my cheeks. All I could see in my mind was that big red lever and the flashing **INCINERATE** sign. Any second, the Plastic Professor would order Green Boiler Suit to pull that lever. Any second, I'd be roasted alive like a chicken on a spit. The red fire would bellow and belch over me, 750 degrees of heat, hotter than hell.

This is the end.

I screwed my eyes tight shut and waited to die.

DOPPELGÄNGER:

a lookalike, or double

I seemed to hang in mid-air for centuries. Sweat dripped down my neck and my heart felt like it was hammering its way out of my chest. The Plastic Professor must be giggling and rubbing his hands with glee, stringing out the time to make me suffer as much as possible.

Then the grabber began to move again.

What now? I was almost too scared to look. But I forced my eyes open.

The grabber was rising—high above the incinerator. Now it was hoisting me back over the brick wall. Below me, Ar and Seal still lay among the plastic junk. What was going on? Why hadn't I been incinerated?

The grabbing claw swung me in front of the glass wall.

Green Boiler Suit was on her knees, her face pale, staring down at something on the floor beside her. As the claw swung me closer to the glass, I saw what it was.

The Plastic Professor lay still, his long white coat spread about him. And beside him lay Plastic Ophelia.

The Deactivation had happened.

Green Boiler Suit shook the Plastic Professor's shoulder. He didn't move. Then she looked up as Blue Boiler Suit said something. As he spoke, her face changed. She slowly got to her feet and backed away from the Plastic Professor and Plastic Ophelia. Then she looked through the glass window, at me.

I stared back. Green Boiler Suit started talking to Blue Boiler Suit and waving her arms. Blue Boiler Suit twisted the wheel again, and the grabber swung me over to the walkway, and very gently lowered me on to it. It took a while for me to free my trapped blazer, but at last I managed it. I pointed down at Ar and Seal.

Blue Boiler Suit nodded and sent the grabber down towards them.

With shaking hands, I untied Ar's wrists, then Seal's. The two Boilers cowered with their backs against the glass, looking scared and ashamed. Ar wrenched off his blindfold. His face went a sickly shade of white when he saw Plastic Ophelia and the fake Professor lying on the floor. Then he looked up and saw me. His mouth opened like a fish, and he gawped from me to her, and back again.

'She's fake,' I said. 'Made of plastic.'

'You mean—you have a DOPPELGÄNGER?'

Seal pulled off his blindfold.

'Is he—is he d-dead?' he whispered, stepping back from the fake Professor.

'Not dead,' I said quietly. 'Deactivated. Professor Potkettle's evil mission is finished.'

'You mean—it's safe to get my mum and dad out?'

I hesitated. 'Safe, yes. Only—'

'Only *what?*' Seal bounced up and down with impatience.

'I don't have the pass code.'

'But you *did!*' Seal hissed. 'You got *her*—that plastic girl—out!'

'I tried those numbers on Ma's cell, and they didn't work.'

'But *somebody* must know the pass code, apart from *him.*' Seal jerked his head at the fake Professor on the floor.

Of course. The Boilers. I glanced over at the glass window. But the Boilers were gone.

I ran to the door and threw it open. The factory floor was deserted. Then, the hiss of doors made me race across the floor to the loading bay. The two Boilers leapt into their truck. Green Boiler Suit switched on the engine and it began to inch towards the opening doors.

'*WAIT!!!!!!*' I screamed and launched myself at the moving truck. Blue Boiler Suit's window was open and I grabbed it.

'*Tell me the pass code!*'

Blue Boiler Suit tried to push me off, but I held tight.

'D'you want innocent people to stay locked up forever?' I shouted. 'D'you want your real boss to know you ran away and left him?'

The truck was almost through the doors. Blue Boiler suit prised my fingers from the window. As the truck accelerated, he hissed:

'*Periculosus!*'

And the car shot through the doors and out of the factory.

'Did you get the code?' Seal ran to join me.

I shook my head. 'He just said *periculosus*. Calling me dangerous—again.'

Seal's face fell. Then he looked up. 'What if—what if the pass code is *periculosus*?'

'It can't be,' I said. 'The pass code isn't a word. It's a series of numbers.'

Seal's shoulders slumped. Suddenly, everything that had happened hit me: the Ceremony, Plastic Ophelia, the chase through the factory, Ar and Seal being taken prisoner, the Deactivation, being hoisted into the incinerator. My knees wobbled and tears leaked out of my eyes. I sniffed hard and wiped at my cheeks with the sleeve of my blazer.

And that was when I saw it. On the pocket of my blazer. The Stopford motto.

Plasticus stupendus est, diversus periculosus est.

The answer was right in front of me.

'*Periculosus*,' I muttered. 'P is 16. E is 5...'

'What?' whispered Seal.

'Twenty-six numbers on the keypads—twenty-six letters of the alphabet. Each number stands for a letter. *Plasticus* was the pass code to get into the plastic factory—and the code to release Plastic Ophelia. But *periculosus* is the pass code for everyone else. Because they were the most dangerous threats to the Plastic Professor's plans. If they were discovered, his whole evil mission would've been over.'

'Brilliant, Fee!' Seal grabbed my arm and pulled me towards the lift. 'Now, let's get them out!'

REUNITE:

to bring people together again
after a time of separation

I didn't need my sticky memory to remember what happened after that:

How I used the pass code to open the cells, one by one.

How Ma folded me in the hugest bear hug—and how she stared down the corridor as if she could somehow magic up Ar.

How Merry shot out of her cell, followed by Chloe and Zoe. How she grabbed my hands and danced me round and round, her green eyes shining.

How the next cell door opened to reveal two people—a man with kind brown eyes and a woman with a thin, gentle face. How Seal cannonballed into their arms. How the only sounds after that were Seal's mum sobbing, and Seal's dad repeating over and over: '*My son... my son...*'

How the lift pinged and Ar limped out. And how Ma ran straight into his open arms.

'Looks like your mum and dad are reunited!' Merry whispered.

'*Everyone's* reunited,' I grinned.

A high voice called from the fifth cell.

'*Hello? Don't... em... forget me! I'm still here, yes indeedy!*'

Everyone stared at the door of the cell.

'That's—that's *him*!' whispered Ma, grabbing Ar's hand. 'That *odious little man*.'

I hurried over to the fifth cell and tapped in the code.

'What are you *thinking of*, Ophelia?' shrieked Ma. 'That man is *dangerous*!'

The cell door swung open.

Everyone stared at the small figure standing in front of us. He looked exactly like Professor Potkettle, with his long white coat and red plastic spectacles. But the Plastic Professor had been jaunty and full of himself. This Professor stared down at his shoes, as if he dared not look into our eyes.

Ar stepped forward and lifted the Professor up by the lapels of his coat.

'EXPLAIN YOURSELF, MISCREANT!' he roared.

I grabbed his arm. 'Hush, Ar! There'll be plenty of time for explanations. But first, we've got to get back to the factory floor. The workers will be arriving for the morning shift. We've got to tell them that the factory is shut.'

'No more plastic?' said Seal, his eyes full of hope.

'No more plastic.' I stared at the Professor.

'No, indeed.' Professor Potkettle turned to Seal's mum and dad. 'I listened to you, you see. Through the wall. Talking about the earth, and the air, and the sea and how they were being... em... poisoned. And I decided that if I ever got out, I'd begin a new mission...'

'A mission?' Seal's dad frowned.

'My mission will be to set right what I did wrong.' The Professor lifted his chin. 'I shall make many... em... changes. Yes indeedy!'

'Such as?' I said.

The Professor smiled at Seal's mum and dad. 'I shall hand over the running of the factory to *you*,' he said. 'It will be dedicated to recycling waste, rather than... em... creating it.'

Seal and his mum and dad stared, open-mouthed. A huge grin spread across Seal's face.

The Professor turned to Ma and Ar. 'And who are you— apart from being Ophelia's parents, that is?'

Ar puffed out his chest. 'We are ACTORS!'

The Professor thought for a moment. 'Then perhaps,' he said, 'you'd care to take on the Potkettle Institute? It will be perfect, I believe, as a... em... theatre.'

'You mean,' I breathed, 'we'll stop travelling? We can stay in one place and still be *Bottom's Theatre*?'

Ar smiled down at Ma.

'Perhaps,' he rumbled. 'it is time to COMPROMISE. If you will agree to CARRY ON ACTING, Marina, I will give up the TRAVELLING.'

Ma nodded and kissed his cheek.

'We can still keep the Pantechnicon,' she murmured. 'And *tour* from time to time.'

'*Yes!*' Merry grabbed my hand and jumped me up and down. 'You're staying!' Then she looked up at Ar and Ma. 'Do you think you might, er, teach *me* about acting?'

Ar looked at Ma, and they grinned. 'I think, young lady, that that would be ENTIRELY POSSIBLE!' said Ar.

Merry squeaked with excitement.

I got up on tiptoes to whisper in Ma's ear. 'Ma—what made you change your mind about Ar?'

Ma whispered back: 'It was sitting *alone* in that cell. Thinking I might never see him again. It was so... *quiet*, and, well... *boring* without him.'

'Maybe,' I said slowly, 'it's time Stopford had a new motto.'

Professor Potkettle nodded his head hard, and his curls shivered. 'No more *plastic is fantastic, different is dangerous!* No, indeedy!'

Everyone thought.

'*Plastic is perilous?*' suggested Seal.

'*Different is delicious?*' said Merry, looking around at everyone. 'Because it really, really is!'

'They're good,' I said. 'But I have another one.'

'What?' everyone chorused.

I smiled up at Ar and Ma.

'*Love all...*' I said.

Then I grabbed Merry's hand, and Seal's, and squeezed them tight.

'*Trust a few...*'

Finally, I looked at Professor Potkettle.

'*Do wrong to none.*'

Professor Potkettle blushed and nodded a lot. 'Do wrong to none, no indeedy! Never again!'

'An excellent motto,' smiled Seal's dad.

'How did you think it up?' asked Seal.

'I didn't,' I said. 'I remembered it.'

Ar winked. ''Twas written by my ANCESTOR, THE BARD.'

'Tell them the title of the play, Ophelia,' said Ma, taking Ar's huge hand.

I looked around. At Ar and Ma, holding hands and gazing into each others' eyes, gooey as a couple of lovesick teenagers. At Professor Potkettle, in a huddle with Seal's mum and dad, discussing recycling. And at Merry and Seal, my friends.

'It's called *All's Well That Ends Well*,' I said.

And it did.

ACKNOWLEDGEMENTS

Bottom's Travelling Theatre would grind to a halt if it wasn't for Ophelia's talent for organization and support behind-the-scenes. And I've been lucky enough to have a group of 'Ophelias' who have helped to bring this book into being:

My agent, Silvia Molteni: thank you for continuing to believe in me and my writing and for working so hard on its behalf.

All at Pushkin Press: thank you to my amazing editor Sarah Odedina for your wise comments and suggestions, and for helping me to become a better writer; to Poppy Luckett for all your publicity support; to India Edwards and Rory Williamson who quietly and efficiently organize everything backstage; to Sarah Taylor-Fergusson for your thoughtful and sensitive copy-editing; to Robert Snuggs and Bounce Marketing whose enthusiasm propels my books into the world; and to Thy Bui for your extraordinary, exciting and always-beautiful cover designs.

Thank you to now>press>play, who bring kinetic learning to hundreds of schools – the first ideas for Ophelia came whilst I was developing an audio script about plastic waste for them.

A special mention for K C Chamberlain, who has been a one-woman cheerleader for Pushkin Children's Books.

And finally, thank you to all the booksellers, librarians, teachers, reviewers and book bloggers who have tirelessly supported my books and put them into the hands of readers.